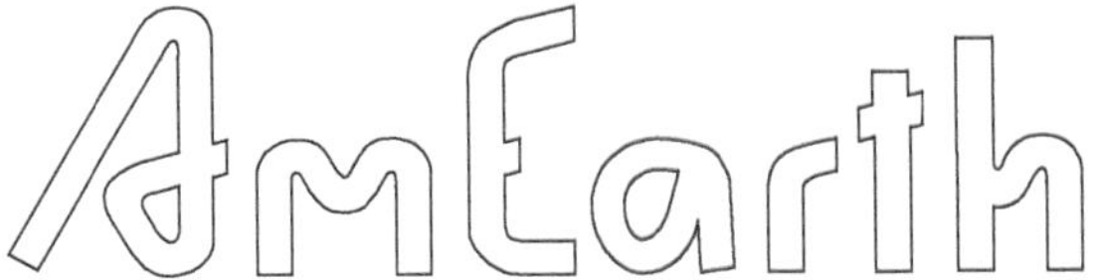

A.A. Dober

ISBN: 0-9965491-0-3
ISBN-13: 978-0-9965491-0-3
LCCN: 2015910915

TO LORRAINE

My true love.

CONTENTS

ACKNOWLEDGMENTS

Many, many thanks to my wife for her patience with my focus on writing and her love. To my son which his input became integral to the creation of this book. To my daughter for her personality which so inspires. To my friend Brendan Myers for his listening skills and support, and to my editors.

ONE

(Tuesday, March 25, 2045)

"Mommy, I'm scared."

"Yes, darling…we all are."

"But Mommy! I can't fall asleep."

"Just try, darling. I'll be awake, watching you."

"You can't sleep, either?"

"It is best to just sleep, sweet pea. Try to close your eyes and forget about everything."

"But they're terrible! They're monsters!"

"I know, but they are far, far away. They can't hurt us."

Barbara Johansen was a slim, beautiful woman of forty who was trying to put her daughter to sleep in a new world full of innovation and promise. This was also a united world with a new system of government that had arisen peacefully and had benefitted most of the world's population by elevating them out of poverty. This new world was governed by a central authority called AmEarth, based in New York City. It boasted massive supercomputers that optimized the world's resources for "the greater good." It relied heavily on the private sector, as its system was a derivative of the American structure and was based loosely on that country's constitution. The trade-off for all of this apparent value was an ominous, unexplained fear that all of the citizens on the planet experienced from time to time. Barbara Johansen could no longer sleep for more than a few hours at a time, and her deep fears had slowly transferred to her precious twelve-year-old, Brianna. They lived in a beautiful Georgian estate in the northeast region of the former United States, only a short hour's commute from New York City. Barbara lived in a seven-bedroom, four-bathroom home with all the gadgets and modern comforts imaginable, even an indoor swimming pool. However, knowing that the Earth was in imminent danger had taken a toll on her, and had begun to affect her child.

After finally getting Brianna to sleep, Barbara left the bedroom and closed the elegant door into its frame with care. She tiptoed down the wide corridor on the Persian rug runner, past the family photos on the wall showing her perpetually photogenic family posing at beaches, ski resorts, and family reunions. Other pictures showed her young husband with former American president Barack Obama and with former president Donald Trump as well as with the former British prime minister David Cameron, among other notable figures. She went into the master bedroom, closed the door behind her, and walked past her fluffy bed, replete with pillows but empty of her husband. She entered the master bathroom and flicked the light switch, which illuminated her image in the mirror.

New, bigger bags under her eyes had compromised her youth, and the sleeplessness also made her skin saggy and pale. She looked at least ten years older than she had only a year earlier. She looked hard at herself and realized that she was still a beautiful woman, but one in a cycle of deterioration that no cream could fix. At this rate, Peter might well leave her for a younger woman before the year was out. Now she could add another fear to the list—abandonment, in addition to the constant threat from beyond the stars.

Her husband, Peter Johansen, was a jovial and happy man, standing a handsome six feet tall, and quite fit for his forty-two years. Barbara's fear of abandonment was unfounded. The last thing Peter contemplated was leaving her. She was his soul mate and true love—something that a few wrinkles wouldn't change. Peter's parents had stayed married throughout his childhood and his upbringing had been ordinary, even boring at times, but his past had instilled strong values of family ties.

Peter's job at the AmEarth Central Authority (known simply as ACA) as a foreign affairs deputy absorbed his intellect and challenged him every day. He approached the job with a level of seriousness that fostered his significant success. The alien civilization that terrified Barbara, along with billions of other people on the planet, was incredibly distant and seemingly friendly, and Peter never seemed particularly worried about the threat. Barbara sensed either denial or bravery in him, and it seemed to fluctuate every day. She had always known Peter on a deep, intimate level, but his attitude toward the aliens kept her guessing about who he really was inside. The last year had been a difficult one for their relationship.

Peter was now in the high ranks of the ACA, which limited his available time with the family.

He would be kept late again. "The Bolivian crisis," as he called it, was coming to a head. Earlier, Barbara had received a call from him and had been upset at how short he had been with her. She didn't care about the why. All she knew was that the news was scaring her. The world, in fact, had become something of a terrifying place. The old types of fear, like the possibility of a crazy person committing a crime, or news of some vicious conflict in another part of the world, had faded and been replaced with a new fear: the threat of otherworldly beings without clear motives. This was a new type of terror altogether.

Peter had explained that there were aliens out there, but that they posed no imminent threat. The World Protection Project had been started specifically to address these fears. *The Earth is very big*, he had calmly explained over and over, and he had promised that things would be easier in a few years once the ACA had its massive infrastructure project in place. Barbara remembered the basic idea of the protection plan, but she desperately needed Peter tonight and he was not there for her. The World Protection Project wouldn't do her any good. His soothing words rang true, but they worked better when he was attached to them. She washed her face and rubbed on some anti-aging cream, even though she knew that it was just creative marketing. Some creams were better than others, but an anti-aging promise was one of the oldest gimmicks in the book.

Barbara left the bathroom and went downstairs to find Scott, her seventeen-year-old son sitting in the den, playing on his computer. He was wearing a special headset and slim glasses that provided him with an immersive 360-degree view of the game map. In that fantasy world, he dueled and fought with his friends. Some of these players were his actual friends from high school, where he was a senior, but he also had some online "friends" who lived in distant corners of the world. These "friends" were yet another of Barbara's fears. Who knew what ideas could come into her son's ears through strangers posing as teenagers?

She touched him on the shoulder and motioned for him to stop and talk to her. He gestured with a flash of five fingers, meaning minutes, she assumed, and began typing furiously, explaining to his buddies that he was needed elsewhere. A few minutes later, he stood up, took off his game gear, and sat down next to his mother at the granite counter attached to the cooking area. She still found it hard to believe that this strong, young, six-foot-tall man had come out of her. She was sipping on a cup of tea as he slumped down into the seat and turned to her.

"What's up?" Scott asked.

"I'm worried," she replied, setting her cup down.

She knew from the look on Scott's face that he could practically feel her apprehension.

"What's eating at you? Still the same things about…what's out there? Dad already told us that we're not in any real danger. Shouldn't we believe him?"

"Yes, but…" She tried to explain, but her voice trailed off.

It was only a feeling.

"It's starting to get to Brianna, too. This whole thing is so unfair to you kids. You've barely had a life yet, and…" She was feeling panicked and her thoughts were coming too quickly.

"Can we stop going to school?" Scott asked with a smirk.

"No."

"Then it's not that serious! You'd take us out of school if you thought the world was ending, right?"

"Yeah, and we'd all go to Hawaii!"

She became a bit more animated and started to snap out of her brief depressive spell.

"Mom?"

"Yes, honey?"

"Do you remember when AmEarth began?"

"Of course. It was the twenty-third anniversary this year. I was working and I think I met your father that year. Why?" she replied, curious to see what her son was getting at.

"The first announcement for uniting the Earth was before that, though, right?"

"Yes, it was announced at a State of the Union address."

"Right, I've seen that over and over, but what were things like before that…you know, years ago? When America was normal, before the threat?"

"They're not teaching you about that in school?" she answered, wondering what he was after.

"Yes, of course, but…what was life like for you…before?"

"Well, it was similar. Countries were different, and to some degree they still are. But back then they were in constant conflict with one another." She heard her "teaching voice" fall into place.

"No, Mom, I understand that. I mean life in general. What was the main difference? What were you afraid of back then?"

"Arabs," she said without hesitation.

"Arabs?"

"Yes. Before the world united, the biggest fear here in America was a nuclear device being stolen and detonated in New York or Chicago or Los Angeles by terrorists. Now, NASA controls all the nuclear weapons, so that fear just…went away," she responded.

"So when the US revealed the true purpose of NASA, it came as a surprise?"

"You have no idea. I remember it like it was yesterday. The entire planet was listening online and on television. It was a massive shock. But looking back, we all should have known!"

"What do you mean?" Scott asked.

"Well, NASA had been around for decades, but they only had one original mission—to get a man to the moon—and they did that back in 1969! Yet, they were still getting appropriations of billions and billions of dollars, but for what? Going up in shuttles into space and coming back a few months later? It was almost incomprehensible that society allowed such massive spending for meaningless missions. Get it?"

"I guess…"

"Think of it like this…before we were told what NASA was really doing, it simply looked like an extremely expensive division of the government throwing money away, but we kept voting for it to go on and on. It was crazy, Scott. The numbers didn't match up, but everyone accepted it. After all, most people aren't rocket scientists. Looking back, it was so obvious, and now we understand. That type of extreme spending drove us into the debt crisis. The US government knew that most of those expenses were going into the World Protection Project. It was one of the biggest secrets in global politics. Now, it all makes perfect sense."

"I guess…to older people like you."

"Thanks a lot, Scott!'

"You know what I mean, Mom," Scott replied with a charming smile.

"It wasn't just politics and spending, though; the alien announcement also caused huge issues within religions across the world."

"How so?"

"Well, people are free to practice any religion in AmEarth, just like how it was in America, and there is still a separation of church and state. However, that separation is much stronger now."

"Why?"

"Basically, the moment that alien life was confirmed, it became difficult for religions to cope. Some tried to embrace this new development, like the Catholic Church, which went on a campaign to baptize the aliens. However, in reality, the situation became untenable and their followers dwindled even further."

"Untenable?"

"If we're 'made in God's image,' then these Keplerians are obviously not. I mean, they are physically different than us, but what does that mean? No religion of the past had made any provisions for aliens!"

"Most people that I know believe in God."

"I believe in a God, too, Scott…sort of. But I can no longer conform to a single religion. I believe in a greater energy—a life force."

"I don't," Scott replied confidently.

"That's fine. People have the right to believe whatever they want. One good thing that AmEarth has managed to do is eliminate most religious extremism. That's no longer such a huge problem as it was in the past. Extremists can try to live in the Dark Ages, but the younger generation is not going back. AmEarth is helping people get a better education and find opportunities; fortunately, that's stopping a lot of that past craziness."

"AmEarth is antireligion?"

"No, no…AmEarth is a secular government that believes in freedom of religion. It believes that all forms of education should be evidence-based, so scientific thought is not compromised. The thing is, when you educate purely through science, most religions fade behind the facts. AmEarth is pro-science. There was a time when evolution was being contested, and even refuted in certain backward areas, but it can no longer be removed from school curriculums."

"That's good to know. It must have been a weird place to grow up," Barbara's son mused.

"It certainly had its strange moments," she admitted.

Barbara continued cooking as her fears gradually diminished throughout the history lesson—one that Scott already knew. She realized that he was merely engaging her and calming her fears through discourse, but she appreciated the effort.

AmEarth had begun with the revelation that an alien society existed and had made contact. To Scott, this was no longer a big deal, since it had happened before he was born. It was normal and he had found a place for it within the greater context of his life. Scott was oblivious to many of the emotions that had gripped people after that initial announcement. The young were always more receptive to reality-shaking revelations, and Scott was particularly hardy. Only very strong emotions could shake him, and these came few and far between.

When the announcement about the Kepler planet and its inhabitants was made, a lot of complex information had to be convincingly conveyed in lay terms. Scott could still remember that first "alien life" speech, not from the day it actually happened, but from videos and recordings seen at school and online.

The speech began with President Donald Trump speaking during his last State of the Union Address. The Senate chamber was full and widespread applause interrupted him every few minutes. The most memorable moment followed a particularly raucous standing ovation, when the president's tone changed. He cleared his throat, put his papers down, and asked Congress to listen quietly and carefully to a difficult truth.

TWO

That same evening, Peter Johansen was at the crisis management center of the AmEarth Central Authority in New York City. It was located in the former United Nations headquarters next to the East River, with its design inspired by famed Swiss architect Le Corbusier. The center of the ACA was a huge room with soaring ceilings; the AmEarth logo was plastered on the wall above the dozens of monitors with live feed images from around the world.

The logo was a colorful rendering of planet Earth covered in a larger honeycomb-patterned sphere a few inches wider, overlaid with the letter A. Dozens of ACA agents worked in the room at all times, giving it the feel of central command for the old Apollo missions—nervous academics with rolled-up sleeves and ties.

Peter felt hungry on that cold Friday evening. Most of the monitors contained images from the streets of Bolivia. In one of the larger monitors, the central square of Bolivia's old capital city, Sucre, held the partially collapsed supreme court building; a massive metal piece of a multi-colored spaceship extended from the caved-in roof. The debris was still smoking. On another monitor was the face of the president of Bolivia, Emilio Saldivar. He looked distraught and tired. Peter was also tired and had removed his coat and tie hours earlier.

"Mr. President," Peter spoke, trying to get a word in edgewise.

"I tell you, the whole world will…" President Saldivar ranted.

"Mr. President! Please, stop. Stop!"

The president of Bolivia finally ran out of steam and began to listen. Peter wasn't in the mood for fighting with a sitting president, and he intended to solve this issue quickly.

"Mr. Saldivar, you are no longer in a position to bargain. If you look at your country, there is mass disinformation being spread. That could potentially get very dangerous, very quickly. You must immediately address your population and tell them what you now know. It is your duty as a leader," Peter argued, walking a fine line between advising and bullying.

"I can't. It is treason for me to join AmEarth. I don't care if Argentina and Chile have done it. We in Bolivia are different," Saldivar shot back angrily.

"Mr. Saldivar, there was an extraterrestrial missile impact on your doorstep. Literally. It is sitting in the middle of Sucre's main square. The population has seen it and your troops can't hide it. This is undeniable proof that the alien civilization exists. Not only that, but they could land in your country as a first step. You don't have a missile-defense program that could withstand an invasion from space. If you do not join AmEarth, how can you protect your people or make them feel secure? Your army?"

Saldivar looked down at his console, acknowledging his country's inadequacy without words.

"The only solution is to prevent them from entering our atmosphere. That is our hope. What if they don't come to invade? What if they instead send a deadly virus or disease? They will pass through your airspace and your beloved Bolivia will be ground zero for the end of life as we know it. You will be the open door that lets them in. Your people will be the first to die." Peter dropped the pitch of his voice for the last statement, and he could practically feel them striking Saldivar.

"I…" Saldivar stammered.

He had always been a strong man, but his knees were knocking under his desk. He didn't even have the strength to stand up.

"Mr. President?" a Bolivian general said as he entered from the right side of the screen. The general bent and spoke into Saldivar's ear.

"What is it?" Peter asked.

"Nothing, nothing," Saldivar said with a dismissive wave.

Peter gestured to Marsha, his assistant, to get him something to eat.

"What is it?" Peter demanded. "Does this have anything to do with the ship landing?"

Saldivar hesitated for a moment before answering. "Yes. The people have entered the ship and are taking pieces with them. They have begun to dismantle it."

"Like a car in a bad neighborhood?" Peter was legitimately shocked. An alien spaceship had landed in the heart of their city and they'd decided to scrap it by hand.

"Yes," Saldivar replied quietly, seemingly ashamed.

"What will your decision be? Do you want to stay in the Dark Ages? Do you want to be the one who let them in? Even North Korea is part of AmEarth!" Peter roared, feeling the president's opposition weaken.

Saldivar hesitated, giving Peter space for one more push.

"Mr. President, you will retain your culture, religion, and assets. This is not about money," Peter said, taking a slightly pleading tone.

"Fine. I'll do it." Saldivar stared dead-eyed into the camera.

Peter smiled. "You're a wise man making a wise choice for your people. Sign the form online. We can be there in four hours."

Saldivar placed his thumbprint on the glass screen of his monitor, prompting an executive order that allowed AmEarth to annex Bolivia—effective immediately. The entire process took less than ten seconds.

"Emilio—" Peter used the president's given name for the first time ever—"you can kiss poverty good-bye and kiss being the pariah of that continent good-bye. You will see an immediate transformation of your society for the better. You will be remembered as the father of Bolivian AmEarthism. Welcome."

From the corner of his eye Peter saw Marsha gesturing to him that his meal was ready. She also flashed him a sign on a piece of paper that said *ETA 30 minutes*.

"One more thing, Emilio. I've just been informed that the four-hour window has been reduced," Peter informed the president.

"Really? When will your men be here?" Saldivar asked, a hint of suspicion creeping into his voice.

"Thirty minutes! I need to go, Mr. President. Thank you for making the right choice."

"Thirty minutes?" The president seemed shocked, as though there was so much to do in so little time.

"It seems that the heads of AmEarth wanted to make you a priority today." Peter disconnected the link.

It was a good day for AmEarth. Bolivia, the thorn in Latin America's side, had at last been removed. Bolivia was now aligned with the new world system. A veritable army of AmEarth consultants, military personnel, alien recovery teams, and government bureaucrats would descend onto that small country in the next few hours. Every piece of the alien craft would be recovered and all unemployed Bolivians would be immediately offered jobs. This AmEarth deployment also carried many advantages. Satellites in the air would immediately turn on wireless Internet capabilities and in a few days the country would essentially be online, entering the twenty-first century and becoming a new entity devoted to the protection of the Earth. The majority of the jobs would be entry-level building jobs dedicated to the construction of the huge honeycomb "roof" that would eventually cover the entire globe.

Bolivia would soon be educated and integrated as a part of the AmEarth community and would have an express ticket into the history of intelligent life in the universe and all the astronomical and physical details necessary to comprehend what was really happening on Earth. AmEarth knew that the main resistance would come from orthodox religious groups claiming their holy books as science, but evidence of life outside their planet had shocked the masses into purging many of their belief systems. If their religion had not foreseen the fact that there were billions of stars in each galaxy and billions of galaxies in the universe, why would they believe the other tenets of the religion?

Many in Bolivia had already seen video footage and newsfeeds showing the deployment of the advanced world protection system. They would also have seen that only the AmEarth Navy was capable of installing the system over the oceans. This navy was largely composed of the former United States Navy, using its famed aircraft carriers. The world was deeply indebted to America and was reminded constantly of what the *Am* in AmEarth stood for. In these images and videos, long wires were stretched between huge ships that stood in pentagon formation. From a very high point, you could see that all five aircraft carriers would launch rockets at exactly the same time, raising a pentagon of cables up into the atmosphere. In space, these pentagons would be attached to other pentagons already "floating" there. Small shuttle ships would join them at the corners, and the remaining parts of the rockets would become antispaceship laser stations. The wiry material of the cables was made rigid with a super-freeze system, and held in that state by the icy chill of space. Videos and images of this system were a large part of the media campaigns that AmEarth continually presented; they were used in schools and universities worldwide, except in those few hesitant countries, like Bolivia. Now, the population in this Latin American holdout would have access to all of that information, as every worker was given a cellular communication wafer, which looked like a thin flexible sheet and offered a free wireless connection to the AmEarth Internet.

Peter went to the executive dining room, where his meal waited for him. Various assistants followed him into the room. They were jubilant and celebrating, but he was merely hungry. Peter had handled himself well during this "engulf," the informal name coined for these situations. The fact that Peter, a deputy for foreign affairs, had dealt with the Bolivian president directly had worked wonders. This strategy had delivered a blow to Saldivar's ego, as he was not even speaking directly with the supreme president. When AmEarth had incorporated the "great" countries of the past, it hadn't been the result of the efforts of the foreign affairs department, but rather due to direct calls and anxious deals made between AmEarth's supreme president, Neil Chen Tyson, and the heads of powerful nations like France, the United Kingdom, Germany, Russia, Japan, and China.

The trajectory that had led Neil Chen from being the frontrunner in the Democratic Party to win the nomination for president of the United States, and finally to his existing position as supreme president, was now legendary, and Peter saw Neil Chen's career as the epitome of success in politics. In the final years of the United States, as it became AmEarth, the process had become less democratic, as country by country fell into the ranks and allowed itself to be absorbed by the new central command. The need for human survival trumped nationalism—and even democracy. The incentive for leaders to integrate with AmEarth was huge, as the new central government ruled over a vast amount of land and resources and its power became immense.

In the final decision-making stages, the former UN building was chosen as the logical point for the AmEarth Parliament. All the different nations, now regions of AmEarth, met in this parliament to enact new laws and keep global peace. The former leaders of these nations had become high-ranking members of parliament, often carrying more power than in their former positions. A president of a country like Italy could now be in charge of transportation for AmEarth and his contracts ranged in the billions of Orbs, making him much more powerful than in his previous post.

Control of any division of AmEarth was planetary and included knowledge about directives that AmEarth's supercomputer was preparing for the survival of the species. Many of these directives would concern the optimal use of Earth's resources, but the subjects it analyzed and advised on were endless. Knowing these global directives ahead of time could make a politician's family very, very wealthy. For example, a directive on the need for manganese for the WPP could earn the owners of said resources somewhere in the trillions of Orbs. The higher-ups in the most developed countries controlled the majority of the important members in Parliament, but this was expected, and not every citizen on the planet was content. The underlying purpose was the survival of the species, the greater good, and then human happiness.

In that order.

THREE

A few hours after the chat with her son, Barbara Johansen received a call on her slim cell phone wafer.

"Bolivia conceded?" Barbara asked.

"Yes! I'm on my way home, honey. This is really going to change things. I did it!" Peter said, overjoyed for the first time in what felt like ages.

"I'm so happy, darling. Come home soon. I can't wait to see you tonight."

"I need you, too."

"That means all of South America is done, right?" Barbara's voice was filled with sincere excitement.

"Yes. They'll announce it tomorrow morning in the news. I got interviewed…they might show me." Peter tried to be professional, but occasionally he got a bit star-struck by it all.

"That's good, honey, that's good, but how long will it be before they close the gap? I mean, in the sky? That's what really worries me."

"Honey, don't worry about that, please. We are completely safe here in Connecticut. The gap is on the other side of the world, my dear. You shouldn't lose any sleep over that."

"Promise?"

"As always, yes. Now go to bed…don't wait up. I'm still a couple of hours out."

"All right, see you soon."

Barbara touched the phone screen off and placed the wafer back onto her robe sleeve, where it adhered like a magnet. Scott had been watching his mother throughout the whole conversation and smiled. She kissed and hugged him, tousling his hair as she leaned over.

"You see, Mom? There's nothing to worry about," Scott spoke quietly.

"I know, I know…You're right."

She looked up into the sky and closed her eyes, as though she were praying. A few minutes later, Scott watched her head back upstairs to sleep. As soon as she turned up the main staircase, he went straight for the back door. From a wall hook in the mudroom he grabbed his down jacket and went out of the back door toward his electric Audi-3, parked directly in front of the garage doors. As he left, he threw the jacket over his shoulders and reveled as puffs of steam burst from his breath in the cold March air.

Driving at fifteen miles per hour brought Scott to Cate's house in less than three minutes. Fortunately, she only lived ten blocks away. In the summer, he usually walked there. Cate Richardson and Scott had been off-and-on best friends, worst enemies, a couple, and everything in between. Their fathers both worked at the ACA. They had attended the same schools since kindergarten and they were both graduating that year. They had also shared the loss of their virginity to one another. He parked a block away from Cate's house, as it was already close to eleven at night and formal visiting hours were over. He walked around the house to the back and climbed up the oak tree that leaned toward the second story. He used the back sunroom roof that met up with Cate's bedroom window. This entry was as normal to him as using the front door. He'd been doing it for years.

"Hey," Scott said as he gracefully dropped through the window frame. He lowered his legs onto Cate's carpeted bedroom floor.

"Hey yourself," Cate replied.

Scott closed the window behind him, sat on Cate's bed and leaned in for a kiss. There was a brief spark of more, but he felt distracted, unable to clear his head. Cate could sense that he wasn't completely there with her, and she pulled away.

"Bolivia fell," Scott said.

"I heard."

"How? My dad was the one who did it. A few minutes ago!"

"I heard my dad talking on the phone. It was a big deal. The American continent is now fully AmEarth."

"Right. News sure does travel fast. Even top-secret news." He laughed.

"He also said that an alien ship crash-landed in Sucre."

"What?"

"That's what he said. I'm sure that's what I heard. Where's Sucre?"

Scott spoke the name into his wafer. The answer appeared on the screen.

"Bolivia," Scott said.

"My dad said that only a few Pacific islands haven't signed, but there's nothing important left. New Zealand, Burma…not sure exactly, but I think it's like ninety-nine percent now. Ninety-nine percent! I heard my dad say that number. Can you believe it?"

"Yeah, it's amazing. It's crazy.." Scott's face fell, suddenly pensive.

"What is it?"

"Well, I don't know…"

"What?"

"Well, something just feels weird about it, you know? I know that millions of people say that, but…I don't know. Maybe you haven't noticed, but everybody seems really scared about this whole alien thing. But not our dads. It seems like everyone that I meet without a connection to the ACA is terrified. Have you noticed that?"

"Our dads are hardly a control group, Scott. Two people who don't rattle easily are not exactly statistically significant."

"Yes, but all the ACA events and parties, you've been to them. Everyone is just so happy and content."

"They're in power, Scott. Most people in control are happier than those being controlled."

"I guess. That's it, then. Global rule by ACA and the World Protection Project."

"Would you prefer the alternative? When we study the past, how much of it was about wars and famine and suffering? I certainly think the world is a better place now."

"I know. You're right." Scott kissed her again. And then a few more times. The next fifteen minutes were a swirl of hands and tongues and tumbling bodies, but at a natural break point, when they were both catching their breath, he looked at his watch and knew that he should get to sleep. He kissed her good-bye and left the same way he'd come in, unbeknownst to her parents.

Scott had been feeling the distance between he and Cate growing as of late. She simply didn't share some of his concerns and thoughts about the world around them. There was something that stopped her, as though she were not willing to argue anything to its natural end. This frustrated him, despite knowing that this was common in many people. She had always been something different, but maybe that was changing. Walking back home, his mind drifted as he yearned for a deeper conversation.

FOUR

Scott Johansen sat on the plush sofa of the den, ignoring his computer, slim goggles, and phone. He was watching the morning news to see how the Bolivia story was being reported. His mom sat next to him and they watched expectantly, hoping to see peter's interview. Upstairs, peter was sleeping off a hard Friday night of work and subsequent celebrations. On the tv, the reporting was brief and it placed little importance on Bolivia, except for a quick explanation of how Bolivia was the final South American country to join AmEarth.

"And now, for a bit more on this story, here is a statement by the foreign affairs deputy, Peter Johansen of ACA," the anchor said.

"President Saldivar was gracious and accepted the invitation to join the AmEarth alliance to improve the quality of life for the Bolivian people.

Bolivians will now contribute to helping AmEarth to achieve the canopy protection system around the entire globe," Peter's recorded image said.

He was standing at a podium with the AmEarth symbol on it, in the gigantic lobby of the ACA office building; he was partially hidden by a large group of microphones in front of his face. The video cut to the next news story after those two sentences; they had used a very short segment of his rather extensive statement.

Scott and Barbara were both proud, but it was clear that they had been expecting more. Barbara was unaware of what Scott knew was missing from the story altogether. A few minutes later, Peter came down and met the two at the marble bar of the open kitchen, where Scott was anxious to talk to him.

"You were wonderful on TV, honey!" Barbara said first, giving him a hug and a peck on the cheek.

"Thanks."

Scott sat silently, looking at his father, who returned the gaze with a questioning expression.

"Oh, right. Congratulations, Dad," Scott said sourly.

"Thanks."

"Dad?"

"Yes?"

"Why did the news ignore the alien rocket that crashed in Sucre?"

"How do you know about that?"

"I asked you first."

"I happen to be your father, so you'll let me know how you obtained that information right now." Peter's voice changed sharply. It was the tone that everyone in the Johansen family understood meant business.

"I…Well…It was Cate's dad. I overheard him talking on the phone last night."

"You went to Cate's?" Barbara said.

"Yes, Mom. I always do," Scott said, although this wasn't exactly news.

"Listen, son, that information is highly sensitive. You cannot tell anyone that you know about the rocket landing in Sucre. No one. Is that clear?" Peter loomed large over his son. There was no mistaking how serious he was.

"Yes sir. I haven't told anyone but you," Scott stumbled to reply.

"Good, let's keep it that way, all right?"

"Okay, but can you at least tell me about it? After all I'm your son!"

"Well, there's not much to tell. Basically, a rocket bearing cultural and technical information from Kepler 3763 crashed in Sucre, Bolivia, last night. This rocket was launched sixty-seven years ago, but having it land there was lucky for us. It totally tipped the popular opinion, as Bolivians could see the truth firsthand."

"So why wasn't it in the news?" Scott asked.

"Because it's not news. Alien ships have been landings for years now. You've been to the museum, seen their technology. Where are you going with this?"

The telephone rang in the kitchen. It was a large thin screen that turned on as soon as Peter said, "Phone answer." On the TV, the familiar image of Neil Chen Tyson, the supreme president of AmEarth, stared back at Peter, Scott, and Barbara. He was a good-looking, half-Asian, half-Caucasian man in his mid seventies. Brianna was walking down the stairs behind them, braiding her long blonde hair as she approached her dad. Scott gestured to Brianna to stay quiet and gently caressed her hair.

"President Chen, I'm so sorry, we're just getting up for the day," Peter stammered.

"No need to apologize, Peter. I wanted to give you the good news personally. And now that you are here with your whole lovely family, here it is: I want you to become my minister of communications for alien affairs. The job has a clearance level of five, and you'll be briefed by the WPP, NASA, and NSA. But you probably already know all this. Are you up to it?"

Without taking a breath, Peter answered, "I am."

There was no hesitation or reservation in his voice. The two former American branches had kept their monikers, which began with the letter *N* for national, although they were now worldwide in their reach.

"Good, that settles it, then. Go about your job normally next week. I'll make the ministerial change in the next shuffle, which I am preparing this weekend at Camp David. Don't mention this to anyone until after my announcement. On Monday, my people will meet you at your office. Your new office will be…well I can't say right now, but I'll see you on Monday."

"Thank you, sir. Thank you for this opportunity," Peter said.

"Peter, you deserve it. Good-bye now."

"Good-bye, sir."

The image switched off. The whole family was stunned. The president of 99 percent of the world was calling their home phone! They looked at one another other and something struck Barbara suddenly.

"Washington? Are we moving?" Barbara asked.

"No, honey, no. I doubt that Communications is located in Washington. Most ministries are in New York."

"I guess we'll know soon enough," Scott said.

"Daddy, what's a minister?" Brianna asked.

"In the old days, they were called cabinet members, but now they're called ministers. Nothing to do with religion, Bri."

"Why did they change the name, Dad?" Scott asked.

"Well," Peter explained, "in the early days of the AmEarth expansion, the world was not ready for all things American, so some concessions were made to ease the transition. Words like minister were more common worldwide than cabinet member, so the AmEarth intelligence community changed things like that. The supercomputers developed for NASA were used to determine how best to achieve the desired outcomes of any given situation."

"Was that how the name AmEarth got picked?" Brianna asked.

"You're quick, Bri, but I'm actually not sure how AmEarth was chosen," Peter admitted.

"Well, I think we should celebrate!" Barbara said.

"I'm so tired. Can we just stay in and celebrate here?" Peter implored.

"Absolutely, darling."

Peter went back up to his room and lay down on the Egyptian cotton sheets, resting his head on a down feather pillow. He remembered being selected for his first Foreign Affairs job back in 2017, when the second Trump administration had started its power. Every year, he had moved through the ranks of Homeland Security, even as it changed into the Foreign Affairs Ministry. When he had started, the secretary of state had been Bernard Sanders but in

2022, when AmEarth created the ministries, his position had been moved to America's greatest ally, Britain. For the next twenty-year stretch, Peter worked under former Prime Minister Cameron. He was an affable and good man and had run the department well. Cameron had stressed the importance of the alliance, obviously making sure that British interests remained in focus. He strove to make his people happy and this position helped Britain to retain many of its interests around the world.

As the years passed, Peter was cleared into ever-higher levels and passed all the required courses that AmEarth imposed on high-ranking officials. It was very important for the governing entity to jockey individuals with credentials up the ladder and Peter was excellent at this particular game. His only problem was that the ceiling in Foreign Affairs was the ministerial position, which would always go to a Brit. As things progressed in AmEarth, it became an unspoken law that the world was happy as long as everyone felt involved. So, as an American, Peter welcomed the move to Communications that President Chen had offered, as this nudged him into a ministerial position without the geographic problem he was currently facing. It seemed like the perfect choice at the perfect moment. For the first time in many months, he felt truly happy.

FIVE

Brianna was in her sixth-grade history class, sitting with her best friend, Camilla, and her best male friend, Anton. The teacher projected a video onto the smart board and asked all the children to be quiet and pay attention. Most girls were secretly using their phone wafers, but the teacher hit a button on his desk and they all started ringing, calling out the culprits.

"Anyone with a wafer ringing needs to turn it off right now."

"Phone off," Camilla said.

"Phone off," Brianna said to her phone, just as many others did the same.

The video began with the seal of the president of the United States. Then, the audio came on, and the class could hear gradually diminishing clapping followed by the voice of Donald Trump, the forty-fifth president, as he began his last State of the Union address, back in 2024.

"Listen, listen carefully, please. I am here today with a momentous announcement that goes well beyond my tenure as president of the United States. It is about the Truth, with a capital T. In the early part of the space race, all of us saw the competition between two powerful nations with opposing political systems attempting to master space. When we reached the moon, we were a jubilant and excited country, but that fifty-six years ago. I was only twenty two! Since that proud moment, America has sped past all of its neighbors..."

Clapping and smiles of approval interrupted President Trump. She paused and gestured with her hand for the crowd to stop.

"As I was saying, America has sped past all of its neighbors at great economic cost. But the reality behind the aim of this massive space program was not only to reach the moon or to launch satellites; it was about our survival as a species."

There was a hushed mumbling and then silence fell over the entire hall.

"We have been sending unmanned spaceships to another planet in our galaxy twenty-three point five eight light years away. We have been sending these unmanned ships with cultural and technological information from mankind for over sixty years. Furthermore, we have been communicating with alien beings on this planet through radio frequencies, but the response time is twenty-three and a half years! Therefore, we only have a fractured conversation.

America has kept this information secret from the world, but today, I am afraid that it must be shared. Some of America's technological prowess and superiority can be attributed to controlled leaks of the information shared with the aliens. Although America has profited in some ways from the technological advantages afforded by this knowledge, we did not keep these secrets solely for our benefit! We have done so because our greatest interest is the survival of our species. Releasing this information too early could have turned our planet into a chaotic mess. Today, we finally have the tools for mass communication that are needed to prevent this chaos. Ninety-nine percent of the world has some connection to information and we have been in communication with over two hundred governments so that this speech can play live and be translated on all television stations and Internet sites. The Internet is also going to force people to view as they connect. By this time tomorrow, we expect ninety-nine percent of the world's population to be aware of this important truth."

A sudden buzz of voices and commotion erupted on the floor and balconies of Congress.

"Calm down, calm down. We are in no imminent alien danger. We are simply confirming to the world something that we have all known for a long time."

Trump paused for effect.

"We are not alone in the universe...but I must stress this: no ship is going to arrive carrying aliens to the Earth and we have not sent anyone there. That is simple math. There is no science fiction warp speed or wormhole that can magically connect our two

planets. Our fastest rockets traveling to Kepler 3763, the alien planet so named by astronomers, move at half the speed of light, and they are small vessels carrying tiny payloads and lots of fuel. Imagine a USB drive traveling at 100,000 miles per second, on a predetermined course. We're not even sure if our ships will make the journey and no confirmation of their arrival is possible until roughtly twenty four years after the forty-seven-year journey. Some inklings of confirmation exist and we believe contact was successful but it is still unconfirmed."

"Let me be very clear about this next point; no life form could withstand that journey. It is as impossible for them as it is for us. It takes forty-seven years to get there, and there is no ship that could hold a live human being with all his needs supplied that can also travel at 100,000 miles per second!

"We expect alien ships traveling at roughly that same speed to arrive in our atmosphere at some point. We cannot know where they will land and the odds are that they will hit water and not land, but we are prepared to retrieve and study these ships. We expect that they will have cultural and technological information that will be of interest to everyone on the planet and we intend to share it. Of course, it must be quarantined to first ensure that no biological or nuclear threat exists, but we do not expect hostility from this advanced alien society.

"Both planets have a commonality and from our communications, we have been able to decipher some of their language and music, and we have sent ours to them as well. We are going to begin a sharing process with all the countries on the planet of these technologies and cultural discoveries. Most of the world's leaders, as well as a select group from

Congress and the Joint Chiefs of Staff, have known about this for some time. America is uniquely positioned as we have the communication line to the alien society and the expertise to study whatever they send us. We have entered into agreements with most countries of the world to be the firsthand responders at the impact point to examine any alien ship."

Mr. Edwards, Brianna's history teacher, turned the video off and turned the lights back on. Brianna was interested in the video, although many of these words seemed like old news. She knew about the alien threat, but Trump had been playing it down back then. She had seen this video a few dozen times; they all had. She raised her hand.

"Yes, Brianna?" Mr. Edwards said.

"I was wondering what happened. Why are we so afraid of the aliens now? Trump said that they couldn't hurt us."

"Good question, Bri. It's called fear-mongering. Has anyone here heard President Chen Tyson espouse the view that the aliens are dangerous?"

"No," many students replied.

"Exactly! We have no certainty that the aliens will pose any threat to humans. All of their ship landings have proven to be harmless and technologically interesting to humanity."

"Then why are we building the honeycomb protection system? My dad is an engineer working there," Anton asked sincerely.

"It is merely for prevention, just prevention. It doesn't imply an imminent threat," Mr. Edwards said robotically, as though this was his established pat response.

"Well, I'm scared." Camilla said.

"So am I," Bri agreed.

"Listen up, boys and girls. It is simply an insurance policy. It is there 'just in case.' It is only being built for a very unlikely scenario. Are you afraid of flying in a plane? No, of course not. Because the odds are in the millions to one that something bad will ever happen. Well, this time the odds are in the billions, so we shouldn't have anything to worry about."

"I don't like flying," Camilla whispered to Bri and Anton. They both laughed, but quieted down at Mr. Edwards's stern glare.

SIX

(Monday, March 31)

Scott and Peter were having cheerios with fresh blueberries and milk at the kitchen counter. Peter was reading a large flexible wafer with the news on and Scott was texting Cate on his wafer. They seemed not to talk much during their morning routine, but Scott had an itch.

"Dad?"

"Yep?"

"When Trump announced the alien situation, it seems like the earth fell pretty quickly into compliance with AmEarth. Why weren't there more countries like Bolivia?"

"Hmm. Where is this going?"

"No. It's just history. I'm trying to understand for my final report in Mr. L's class."

"You're not going to start some conspiracy theory like yesterday, are you?"

"Nothing to do with that. This is for Mr. Landon's class."

"Well, even before Trump confirmed the existence of other beings in the universe, the world was experiencing massive technological breakthroughs—one after another. It was a flood of technological capabilities that humanity could never have imagined. In retrospect, it feels like we should all have known that something was going on," Peter began.

"That's funny. Mom said the same thing about NASA yesterday. I asked her and she said, 'We should have known.' Who's this 'we'?" Scott asked.

"'We' is all of us. People in general. Well, smart people in general, that is," Peter said.

"You mean *common sense*?"

"Yes. We should have seen it. Now we have the information and everything makes sense," Peter finished with a sigh.

"I seem to be confused about so much of it. In class, Mr. L always talks about the Finnish example and Nokia. What's the story with Nokia?" Scott asked.

He kept eating his Cheerios.

"Nokia, Google, Apple, Cisco—gosh, there are so many examples! Nokia, however, is probably the best one, which is why it's used in school. In the early days of telephone communications, there was no way of even imagining that we would all have cellular phones, let alone these flexible wafers with GPS attached to our clothing. It was all wire and copper cables to send messages. Humans were still installing copper wires by dropping them from ships all across the oceans, followed by fiber optic cable, as late as the year 2000!"

Peter paused and ate a few bites, staring off into space and planning his next barrage of information.

"The communications between the US and the aliens started about sixty five or so years ago. The first reply from the aliens was captured on a dish in Nokia, Finland. This fact was kept from the world by an agreement between the Finnish and American governments known as the "Nokia Accord." In it, the technological exchange was supposed to have been kept secret. Well, after a few decades, from this tiny country in the middle of nowhere, out comes the strongest cellular phone company in the world! It was ridiculous. Everyone had a Nokia phone; they were tiny and worked ten times better than anything the world had ever seen! They called them Nokia, which really pissed off the US, because not only did they break the accord, but they even had the gall to call the company by the name of the city where the first contact was made!"

Scott could see that his father knew the history of AmEarth better than anyone else in his life.

"So the US was behind in its technology?" Scott queried.

"Exactly. So the government leaked secrets to US tech companies to see what they could do with the information. In a few years, Nokia was on its knees to the likes of Apple. We got Google and faster Wi-Fi, faster routers, faster everything. Even solar energy, which had been written off as a pipe dream, suddenly became profitable."

"Amazing."

"It's nice talking to you about all this, but I have to go. It's the last day of my Foreign Affairs job and the first day of my job with President Chen."

"But you didn't explain why the countries merged so easily."

"Another day, Scott. I did digress, but it all ties in."

"Thanks, Dad. Break a leg!"

"Thanks, son."

Peter left his home and drove his new Audi-S8 toward the Saw Mill River Parkway and the perpetually slow West Side Highway. He arrived at his office building's underground parking lot and used his reserved spot one level down. He went in the elevator and up to his office. It was his last day as Foreign Affairs deputy of the ACA. That thought resonated with him as each floor passed. His office was on the fifty-first floor of the building and faced the west skyline of Manhattan, providing a wonderful view between the tall buildings. He called in his assistants and all his staff. As soon as he saw the entire staff present, he began.

"Welcome, everyone. Thanks for taking the time to gather here. I wanted to announce that President Chen has offered me the position of minister of communications for alien affairs. I wanted to inform you all that I have accepted the position," Peter stated.

His announcement was met by a round of applause. A chorus of congratulations followed.

"Bravo!"

"Well deserved."

"Congratulations."

Many approached him and shook his hand.

"I do not know if I can bring any of you along to my new post," Peter added. "I am not even aware of the precise situation, but it is a ministerial position with high clearance level, so I expect that it's an improvement, although I will miss this job immensely. Truly, it has been an absolute pleasure to work with you and I enjoyed every minute of our collaboration to make AmEarth whole. We all helped to deliver on a promise to the human race."

Amid the applause from his staff two men in dark suits suddenly appeared and made their way forcibly through the ten or so people between Peter and the door.

"Mr. Peter Johansen?" one the Secret Service agents, a squat, serious-looking individual, asked.

"Yes. That's me," Peter responded.

"We're here to escort you to your new office. Please follow us."

"Nice to meet you; and you are?"

"That is not important."

"It is to me."

"Barnes, sir."

"Well, Barnes, I do need to take some of my personal belongings. Can I have five minutes?"

Thrown off by Peter's humanity, the Secret Service agent was confused as to how he should respond; in that pause, Peter began to pick up the framed photos off the desk. After he had placed a few more items in an empty cardboard file box, Peter looked up and noticed that Barnes was not happy. He looked at him with questioning eyes.

"You can send for the rest of it later. We need to go, sir," Barnes insisted.

They took Peter down the elevator to the basement executive parking area and into a large black SUV. Agent Barnes and his assistant entered the van and Barnes told the driver to depart. Peter had been driving through this parking lot every day for years and did not expect them to go down the ramp, as opposed to going up and exiting to the outside. The van circled down five more flights before going straight to the end of the lowest parking level. There, it was dark and lonely; rarely did anyone park way down there, and the SUV signaled ahead. Peter was speechless. A great wall of steel began to slide open, revealing a dark tunnel. The car entered this tunnel and the concrete door immediately closed behind them.

"Where are we?" Peter asked.

"All in good time, sir," Barnes responded coldly.

Only when the concrete door closed did the lights return and Peter was able to see the full length of the tunnel ahead. It was unbelievably long; in fact, the end was not visible because it ramped down for a long distance and obviously ramped up farther away. The SUV driver gunned the accelerator and they began traveling through the tunnel at high speed.

"We're moving east, right?" Peter asked.

"You're a genius."

Barnes pointed to the rear view mirror that sported a red E in the LED display.

"Oh. I didn't see that," Peter mumbled, thoroughly confused.

They traveled under the East River in a private tunnel that must have cost tens of millions to build. Peter later discovered that it connected the former United Nations, now the ACA, to Brooklyn. He wondered when they had built it, and more importantly, why. From the car's side window, he could see that the lighting and the concrete walls looked ageless and sterile.

At the end of the tunnel, they reached a wall that they signaled open once again with a sequence of flashing lights. The lights in the tunnel turned off and a matching steel door slid open onto another subterranean parking lot. The van went straight into this parking lot toward the area nearest the elevator.

"Go to the main floor. You will be greeted there," Barnes declared, opening the door.

Peter grabbed his cardboard box, but Barnes stopped him.

"We'll take that to your office, sir." Barnes said.

"Thank you."

Peter entered the stainless steel and marble elevator car and rode up to the L level. When the doors opened, he was blinded by sunlight streaming directly into his eyes. He could not see what was happening until he heard the recognizable voice of Supreme President Chen from directly in front of him. As his vision cleared, his first emotion was slight embarrassment. He hadn't expected him to be so short. President Chen was dressed in an impeccable gray suit tailored to fit his small size, and he wore a white shirt and striped blue-and-red tie. He looked exactly as he always did—meticulous and presidential perfection.

"Peter, how are you?" President Chen said.

"President Chen! I'm a bit confused, to tell you the truth."

"Welcome to the Shadow White House. It is in this building that most of the critical governing happens. I don't mean to say that your job at the ACA is not important; it is—or *was*—but this is where the real decisions are made."

They walked through the modern concrete, marble, and glass lobby of the building. President Chen escorted Peter alone, with no security detail in sight. Peter followed him outside through the main revolving doors so that he could appreciate where they were. The building was a skyscraper, facing Manhattan without any obstruction. The exterior was magnificent, made of glass and wood colored marble that looked solid, yet light. Architecturally, it had a single feature that made it ultra-modern—it was twisted in the middle. It was similar to a long rectangular block of Play-Doh that had been twisted right in the middle. It created an amazing effect. Those offices in the shrunken middle would surely have some tangled and interesting-looking windows. Peter had seen and loved this building before; it was beautiful. He wondered if his office would have a view of the UN building.

"*Architecture Parlant*," President Chen said with a perfect French accent.

"Excuse me?" Peter asked.

"The building, Peter—the building is saying what it is. The simplest example of *Architecture Parlant* would be a hamburger shop that looks like a hamburger."

"I see. I get it. But how is this skyscraper doing that?"

"AmEarth is strong, yet flexible; you see?"

"Ah…very nice. Very nice, indeed."

Peter contemplated the beauty of the architecture, but doubted that many would see this meaning as plainly as President Chen did.

"Who was the architect?" Peter asked.

"This was the last creation of I.M. Pei. It was found in his notebook as he was contemplating an idea for AmEarth. He was 103 when he conceptualized it," President Chen said proudly.

"He was Chinese?"

"Chinese-American, a little like myself."

"Interesting."

"In my case, being half-Chinese was useful. It helped ease the entry of the largest economy in the world to AmEarth."

Neil Chen changed his facial expression.

"Excuse me, Peter," he said. Then he touched his right ear delicately. "What is it, Rosemary?"

He looked away from Peter and talked into a minuscule headset that coiled automatically from behind his right ear to his mouth.

"Set up a meeting of the Joint Chiefs as soon as possible. We will begin the operation. Thanks, Rosemary."

President Chen hung up and the coiled microphone retreated behind his ear.

"Follow me, Peter."

President Chen led Peter to his office on the building's ninety-seventh story. In the elevator, he pushed a code into a pad, and then pressed his thumb on the glass panel. The elevator opened to reveal that the entire floor was the executive office. The few walls and pillars were veneered in book-matched marble slabs. The marble gave the space an ultra-elegant and executive feel. The doors were glass and the partitions were floor-to-ceiling glass, so everyone could share the exceptional view. President Chen's office was in the corner, facing the UN to the west and south toward Staten Island. When he sat in his office, everyone in the floor could see him through the glass walls. As he motioned to Peter to sit, he pushed a button on his desk and all the walls of glass, as well as the glass door, changed to a dark wood color. There was a nano gas in the vacuum between the glass panels that changed depending on the frequency the user chose. President Chen liked this wood-like brown and privacy was immediately established in the office.

"Peter, we are going to clear you to level five. At this level, you will know everything there is to know about the true nature of AmEarth. You will be cleared to learn about alien events and information not anywhere in the public domain. You cannot share any of this, even with your spouse or children. I know you have sworn to this type of secrecy in the past, but you will need to do so again," he explained.

"Of course," Peter said.

President Chen handed Peter a glass wafer that was lit with a circle in the middle.

"Do you solemnly swear to uphold and defend AmEarth, as well as its rules and regulations, so help you God?" President Chen said.

"I do."

Peter placed his thumb on the glass, effectively registering his print for the new clearance level.

"You are entering the highest structural level of AmEarth, and you will need to be loyal. As you are aware, treason is unacceptable and remains the only crime punishable by death in AmEarth. You understand this?" President Chen said.

"Yes, sir!"

"All you will see and learn here must be used to serve the greater good, and we must trust AmEarth to place the best interests of the world as its highest priority. The survival of our species depends on the next and last phase of the World Protection Project. We are close to closing all the gaps."

Peter remained quiet, sensing that at this point, he should answer, not ask.

"I hired you because of your skill in communications. No one had cracked Peru, Costa Rica, and Bolivia, but you did it! Now, let me ask you, if you knew that the Keplerian species was going to send a nuclear bomb our way, what would you do?"

Peter was shocked. Here was the president of AmEarth, asking him for advice on a potential doomsday scenario.

"First, I would need to be certain that the threat was real, but how could we confirm it? I don't know if we could until it was too late. Second, I would dedicate all resources to finishing the WPP, so the honeycomb could stop the device from entering our atmosphere. Third, I would keep the information bottled up, as mass chaos and hysteria would ensue if people knew." Peter answered as rapidly as the thoughts came to his mind.

"Bravo, Peter. I knew you were the right man for this job," President Chen said with a hint of pride.

He pressed a button and his assistant entered with a tray of small sandwiches, scones, and a tea set.

"Please, Peter, let me offer you some tea. This is really the only English pleasure I enjoy," President Chen joked.

He motioned to Peter as he moved to the large living room on the other side of the office.

"Thank you," Peter said.

Peter sat and was served tea. President Chen remained silent until the assistant left and closed the door. Then he took a small sip of tea and continued.

"Peter, nothing we discuss can be communicated unless we decide to do so, which is why I need to pick your brain. We have knowledge of the potential threat that I just mentioned," President Chen continued.

Peter gulped and choked on a scone. He had not been prepared for such a serious hypothetical situation becoming a reality in the space of a second. He went white and felt the blood rush to his head. He struggled, but remained cool.

"We know this not because we can see a spaceship coming with a bomb, no…It is something awful that happened in our past. And as you know, we can't undo our past," President Chen said.

There was a silence, which Peter used to imagine wildly what President Chen was hinting at. President Chen seemed calm, but wreathed in mystery. A lightbulb went off over Peter's head.

"Preemptive measures? Was that our preemptive measure?" Peter trailed off, his confidence from moments earlier somewhat dissipating.

Peter suddenly looked pale, and expressively revealed his disappointment in humanity.

"I'm afraid so. Yes," President Chen confirmed.

"Who?"

"Reagan."

The fortieth president of the United States. Of course. Peter knew of the man. Peter wondered why he was being thrown into the path of fate at this particular moment. President Chen had some Reagan-like qualities about him and Peter remembered the famous quote.

"Trust, but verify," Peter said softly, almost inaudibly.

"Did you say, 'Trust, but verify'?" President Chen asked.

"Sorry, I didn't mean to say it out loud, it just sort of popped into my mind. You know it was a famous Reagan quote."

"Yes, of course I know. It is just that we can't trust—not with this situation."

"Exactly. So what will we say?"

"That is exactly why you just became my new minister of communications. AmEarth needs a fresh face, a fresh language, and some modicum of trust. You have all that, which makes you the man for the job. We want to communicate and inform so that people react with trust."

"But how can we verify the threat?"

"Like I said, we cannot. So we must assume that it exists. You understand?"

"Yes, sir. You can count on me."

"Here is your brief. I expect the text of your announcement by tomorrow."

President Chen handed Peter a file and clicked the button that turned his office into an instant fishbowl. They could now see all the personnel working busily at their different stations and offices.

"Thank you for this opportunity, sir," Peter said.

Chen nodded and smiled. "Get to work."

President Chen's secretary, Rosemary, escorted Peter to his new office. It was on the northwest corner of the forty-eighth floor and had windows wrapping around at an angle, like draperies in the wind. This level was in the "flexible" part of the Shadow White House skyscraper and the corner was rounded, making his office the shape of a baseball field. This office was also in an area of the building that overhung the footprint of the square below, so close to a window that the view was vertigo-inducing as there was no continuity below. Peter realized that the building was as large as one of the twin towers destroyed in the infamous 9-11 tragedy. Those towers had been enormous, just like this one, and even had their own zip codes. Here, in a single building, all of the top personnel of the government could be in a meeting with the president at the push of an elevator button. It was brilliant and efficient. He wondered why this had never been done in the past. After all, skyscrapers had been around for centuries.

In his office, he found all his papers and personal effects from his prior position, as well as his cardboard box with his family portraits. He pulled out a frame with all four of them smiling in front of the lake and mountain background of a trip to Jackson Hole. A familiar voice greeted him.

"Mr. Johansen," Mary said.

"Mary! Hello! I'm so glad you agreed to move with me," Peter said to his long-time secretary.

"Rob and Sandra are already here."

"Good. I could only keep you three. This will be a fresh start for all of us. I don't want things to move exactly like before."

"Okay."

"Can you get me a cup of coffee?"

Peter sank into his chair with the full weight of the information that had just been given to him. Ronald Reagan had taken preemptive measures that would only reach their destination well after his death. How selfish and stupid that had been? However, in his defense, what if the aliens were aggressive and had attacked first? Wasn't offense the best defense? Weighing these kinds of scenarios was a pastime of Peter's, but now that it was really happening, he realized that the outcome was bad in both cases. The only solution would have been a truce with a standing threat, like the Cold War and its mutually assured destruction. Only then would the two parties survive. How could this be stopped from happening? If only he could communicate in real time with them; why did they have to be so far away? Twenty-three point five light years was more than his mind could even comprehend.

He looked around and found that the bent window wall was beautiful, despite its unsettling view. His office had a small living room in it, with one nice wall where he could hang a painting. He considered bringing his old rusted steel sign that read Franklin St., which was holed up somewhere in his garage. It would look amazing and would blend the memory of Benjamin Franklin with his love for the subway station near his New York City apartment. Now, he hoped that Mary would be bringing him as good a cup of coffee as she usually had in the old Foreign Affairs office.

"Your coffee, Mr. Johansen," Mary announced.

"Thanks. It smells delicious."

"You have a call on line one. It's President Chen."

"Thanks Mary; give me some privacy. Hold all my calls."

"Of course."

Mary left and closed the door behind her.

"Mr. President?" Peter said.

"Peter?"

"Speaking."

"Before I forget, I want you to bring your family to the White House Correspondents' Dinner. I think they would really enjoy it."

"They certainly would. I appreciate it, Mr. President."

"I will send the invitations to your home."

"Thank you."

"Have you read the brief?"

"Sir? I'm sorry, but I just sat down in my office."

"Read it. Don't wait any longer."

"Yes, Mr. President."

Peter heard the click of President Chen hanging up. He immediately opened the brief envelope and found the first document stamped boldly with the title: TOP SECRET. He took a sip of Mary's perfect coffee as his eyes fell on the first lines. The brew was even better than the ones at Foreign Affairs.

TOP SECRET

Problem: President Ronald Reagan, during his tenure from 1981 to 1989, began a campaign of hostility toward the aliens in Kepler 3763, despite there being no evidence of any hostility from them toward us. The first alien communications, representing a response to our friendly contact, were received by Earth once Reagan turned on the policies of his predecessors and sent faster rockets with more aggressive payloads. The Freedom of Information Act of the United States kept this Reagan Era information locked up for nearly twenty-five years. To the best of our knowledge, the Reagan Administration used NASA to deliver biological viruses and electronic computer viruses in the hopes of eliminating the alien society. The payload of those rockets was not capable of sending nuclear weapons.

Solution: Communications campaign to be launched, informing the public that NASA will finish the WPP honeycomb to prevent the passage of any hostile rockets launched by the aliens. Also, an information campaign is to be initiated with the aliens to discredit Reagan and distance AmEarth from the policies he began. Unfortunately, this campaign will not reach them for 23.5 years. We hope this campaign with the aliens will eventually repair the relationship and allow us to revert to a more peaceful interaction with them.

Potential Issue #1: Alien attack or attacks come to earth. We have no way of knowing what kind of threat this will be.

Potential Issue #2: WPP fails to provide adequate protection for Earth.

Conclusion: Inform the public as to the alien threat; prevent panic by using the WPP honeycomb structure as a safety net, and by stating that the threat is not known to exist as a fact.

Peter was practically hyperventilating; the information that had just been handed to him represented his wife's fears to a T. The channels and personalities that preached hatred and fear would all be proven right. How could he make people feel safe while revealing this threat? That was the challenge he was now tasked with solving. He took another sip of his coffee and looked out of the angled window. It was an impossible one-of-a-kind situation he had been thrown into and it was oddly fitting to be staring out of those skewed windows at the twisted gravity of the world.

SEVEN

April arrived quickly that year. Scott Johansen and Cate Richardson were sitting in their twelfth-grade history classroom, where they were studying the effects of global warming and the advantages of a central world government in dealing with planetary crises. About twenty-five kids sat in a pre-adult stupor of boredom and hormonal rage. Mr. Ted Landon stood in a brown jacket with leather elbow patches, a white t-shirt beneath it, a pair of blue jeans, and desert boots. He looked across the classroom, fitting the part of a clichéd academic professor, except for one thing; he was actually good-looking.

"In the early decades of the twenty-first century, mankind reached a critical point, as billions of humans all over the world began to prosper and to desire everything that the developed societies had already afforded their citizens. Societies like America, Japan, and Europe were the envy of the less developed and highly populated countries, such as China, India, and Brazil. You will need to know at least ten countries in these two categories for the final exam, so go to your wafers and find them. You need to use chapter twenty-seven of the authorized book on this. No Google search answers!" Mr. Landon said.

"How did AmEarth reverse this?" a student asked.

"Good question. I was just getting to that. If the populations of these less developed nations had become consumers of energy to the same extent that Americans and Europeans had, then the level of carbon in the air could have exterminated our species. However, the world was fragmented with different governments, so it was very difficult for western powers to force the emerging powers to stop their growth and consumption. So how could we tell them that growth and wealth through fossil fuels was bad, when we had all profited from them so much? Having them develop through the use of clean energy was a problem because of its high cost. Only when AmEarth became a world government could regulations be imposed on the entire planet to stop the insanity of global warming. Today, we have scientific evidence that the warming trend has stopped; perhaps not reversed, but stopped. We have high hopes that it will begin to reverse soon."

Mr. Landon took a drink of water.

"So, AmEarth decided the fate of the emerging countries?" another student asked.

"Yes, but they are no longer countries. There are no more 'emerging' and 'developed' labels when we are all in the same boat. The world is now a single country, in essence. So, the high cost of solar power became a priority that was centrally financed to avoid mass extinction."

"But this was achieved because aliens threatened our planet, not because of the global warming issue, right?" Cate asked.

"I see your point, Cate. All global issues, such as global warming or the alien threat, could now be addressed by practically the entire planet through the central government, which became proactive in eradicating many worldwide problems, including poverty, disease, and war. Having a single governing entity changed our planet forever. And for the better. A great example is money. In the old days, there were competing currencies and currency wars that sometimes were more destructive than bombs. Today, there are only Orbs. Their value is regulated by a single central bank and we have a specified inflation rate and a steady interest rate that will not change. We no longer have fluctuations and we all can save our Orbs safely with guaranteed interest. There used to be great uncertainties in life, which made humans overcompensate in savings; or even worse, they could lose all their savings, resulting in poverty and misery. In Mexico, there was one infamous currency devaluation that literally halved everyone's savings overnight!"

The school bell rang, signaling the end of the class period. It was at that point that many students sprang to life. Scott was not paying much attention, as he was using his electronic wafer-book. In it, he could access tons of information that sometimes made boring teachers unnecessary. He was searching for information on the Sucre landing, but there was nothing on the usual search engines. He needed to access restricted websites that were frowned upon by the school system, but who could help him? At that moment, he looked up to find Mr. Landon looking at him, but that also reminded him that Mr. L was somewhat of a free thinker. In a previous lesson, he had criticized the AmEarth Central Authority's decision to monitor the traveling of all humans across the globe. He had said that this was an invasion of privacy.

"Mr. Landon, can I ask you something?"
"Yes, Scott."

Scott got up and approached his desk while the other students left the class.

"Do you know how to find newsfeeds that are restricted by ACA?" Scott asked.

"Why would you need that? Are you looking for trouble?" Mr. Landon asked, somewhat teasing, but with a hint of serious intent.

"No, I just know about something that happened recently, but no one is reporting it. It's censored. That one detail shows us that AmEarth is not as open as we are led to believe."

"What do you know?"

"Can I trust you?"

"Of course."

"I promised my dad that I wouldn't tell a soul, so you have to keep this absolutely secret. Even if you think I'm talking crap. You have to promise not to tell anyone. If my father finds out, he'll kill me…or lose his job."

"Okay, Scott. I promise."

"No, swear on your kids' lives."

"You know I can't do that."

"Then I can't tell you."

"Scott, I can't do that because I have no children. And if you don't want to tell me, that's okay, too. It was you who approached me, remember?"

Scott looked around to be sure that no one was listening. Most students had left and a few others were standing in small packs, talking and looking at wafers, showing no awareness of Scott at the front of the room.

"An alien ship crash-landed in Bolivia," Scott whispered.

"Whoa…what?"

"Yes. You know that my dad works at ACA, right? Well, so does Cate's and we both heard the same thing on the night that Bolivia agreed to join AmEarth."

"Yes, I heard that Bolivia finally conceded."

"Yeah, after the alien ship crash-landed in the city of Sucre."

He was showing his Google search page, but there was no mention of the alien landing. Mr. Landon was stunned and didn't know what to say. History was written by the victors, so why hide the fact that another alien ship had landed? Many had in the past, so what was special about this one? Then something clicked in his brain.

"What are the odds of an alien landing in one of the last bastions of rebellion?" Mr. Landon said slowly and quietly.

"Exactly. The odds are astronomical. It can't be a coincidence."

"There is only one way to find out, but we need to be careful. Meet me at three p.m. in the teachers' lounge."

"I'll be there."

Brianna Johansen was always late to leave the school and Scott always told her to stop being so social. Today, Scott counted on Brianna's perennial tardiness. If she got to the car before him, she was sure to text him before the cold weather got to her. Scott walked briskly to the very end of the school commons. There, a final office housed the only place the teachers loved in the whole school.

Scott and Mr. Landon met in the teachers' lounge, which was completely empty. School had ended and everyone tended to leave as soon as they could. Mr. Landon pulled a very old laptop from his locker. The thing looked prehistoric—a proper personal laptop with a fold-up screen and everything. Scott could see that Mr. Landon was something of a rebel. With the laptop open and plugged into some network, Mr. Landon used a chat program to call someone. He placed the call and hoped for an answer, but the computer just rang incessantly. He stood up and filled two cups of coffee from the hot glass pitcher before turning the coffee machine off.

"Do you take sugar?" Mr. Landon asked.
"Yes, please."

Mr. Landon grabbed a packet of sugar and a plastic spoon and placed the heavy ceramic mug in front of Scott. He sat with his sugarless black coffee and stared motionless at the screen. An image appeared. It was the face of Pat Jackson, an older man with a goatee beard and pulled-back hair, giving him a ponytail in the back. He wore dark leather clothes and looked rough, like you would imagine an aging member of a biker gang.

"Hi Pat," Mr. Landon began.
"Hiya Ted," Pat replied in a Kiwi accent.

Scott wanted to get in the frame of the computer to say hello, but Mr. Landon held him back with a simple hand signal.

"Listen, have you heard of a landing at Sucre? Last night at some point?" Mr. Landon asked.

"We have a landing recorded in the southern hemisphere, so yeah, Bolivia could be right. What do you know?" Pat inquired.

"A rumor that ends up being a strange coincidence."

"You know what they say about coincidences, Ted…"

"Yeah, only suckers use that word."

"So then, what do you think?"

"Only that I'll need to hang up soon. I don't want to get either of us in any trouble here."

"If an alien ship lands here, we'll be ready. We're not Bolivia!"

"That I know. Yours is the only country left, Pat. *The last*. I wouldn't rule out a full military invasion. It won't take much to turn the tide. World defense is the only reason they need now."

"I know, but it'll end up as a genocide. Everyone here wants to be independent! That isn't going to change."

"Good luck, old friend. I have to go."

Mr. Landon smiled and clicked the computer shut before turning to Scott.

"You were right. Confirmed." Mr. Landon said.

"What should we do?" Scott said.

"Nothing. You can do nothing except tell no one."

"But…this Pat person knows that we know. Can we trust him?"

"It's not like he'll tell anyone in AmEarth! He's on an island far, far away."

"New Zealand?"

Scott's teacher seemed taken aback. "Yes, how did you know?"

"Cate."

"What about Cate?"

"She said that only a few places in the world were still missing from AmEarth, and she mentioned New Zealand. She must have heard her father say something."

"Yes. He's there. And they're still free."

"Free? Aren't we?"

Mr. Landon shrugged his shoulders.

"To an extent. Some of the new laws that AmEarth has been issuing are restrictive, but there is no way to confront them. We are given these rules that are 'for the greater good,' but frankly, some of them are boilerplate authoritarian regime. It's something I'm not at liberty to teach, which is another indication that we're not 'free,' per se. Do you get it?" Mr. Landon said.

Scott sensed that Mr. Landon was afraid to sound too rebellious. After all, Scott could blab all of this to his father and spell the end of his career with a single phone call.

"Yes," Scott said.

"I don't know if we can or should do anything with this information." Mr. Landon said.

He looked at Scott with a worried frown.

"I need you to stay quiet about how we confirmed the landing. Is that clear? I need to be able to trust you. Not even your father, okay?"

"Mr. Landon, I really appreciate your help. I'll never speak about Pat to anyone. Word of honor! But

I really do want to find out what is going on. I don't know, but I don't like it. I don't like being lied to by the government."

"Calm down, Scott. As far back as we have recorded history, governments have lied to their citizens. Some less than others, and some more. Now, we have a regime pretending to be truthful, but it was essentially founded on lying about NASA's true purpose for more than half a century!"

"So, they're not being as truthful as they pretend?"

"Exactly."

"I have to go, Mr. Landon. My sister will be waiting and I need to drive her home."

"Not a word of this to anyone. Promise me."

Mr. Landon gestured meaningfully with a finger over his lips.

"Scout's honor!" Scott shot back and offered a strange little salute. He felt that they had just begun something…something important.

Scott picked up his backpack and left. New Zealand was stuck in his mind. What did they know in New Zealand that they were willing to die for before joining AmEarth? Scott was curious, but needed to slow down and let the rest of his life come back into focus. Either that, or he would flunk his math final the following week. He was walking back to the parking lot when his wafer vibrated. Bri was standing by the car, looking irritated. As usual.

EIGHT

(THURSDAY, APRIL 3, 2045)

Barbara Johansen was having lunch with her best friends at the Darien country club. They were dressed exquisitely, as always, and had a table reserved by the windows facing the golf course. The four females discussed everything except aliens.

The room was filled with ambient babble from the many tables replete with retirees and club-goers. The dress code was elegant and the china service was set on white linen tablecloths. The waiters wore dark suits and the atmosphere smacked of money and success.

In the bar area, adjacent to the club dining area, there was a large TV turned to the sports channel. The staff in the room all seemed to be watching the TV; no one was paying attention to the guests. Subtle waves and clinking glasses weren't getting their attention. Little by little, the entire club was gradually drawn by the intense attention of those watching the screens in the bar area. Barbara and her friends were the last ones to arrive, but they managed to catch a glimpse of the screen. Even before she could see the figure speaking, Barbara recognized her husband's voice on the TV.

"...there is no reason for panic. We are only responding to a potential retaliation, not verified and possibly not even there," her husband's voice cautioned.

"How long has the government known this?" A reporter asked.

"The Freedom of Information Act of the United States forbids any national security information to be released for a minimum of ten years, and in many cases, that was extended to twenty-five. The government of AmEarth did not discover these facts until now. There is no conspiracy, and you should know that the transformation into AmEarth did not make former governmental secrets public. Otherwise, there would be no alliance. The future of the human race is dependent on the trust we have in AmEarth to maintain the greater good."

"Barbara, that's your Peter!" Esther exclaimed.

"Yes, yes, let me listen," Barbara retorted with a tight smile.

"Peter, Peter!" other reporters clamored for his attention.

On the scroll beneath Peter's face, CNN's banner read: *Breaking News: Earth is Under Threat of Alien Attack.* Barbara read that and a deep feeling of fear surged into her gut. She pulled out her wafer and began texting Scott and Brianna. She told them to stay in school and wait for her. She told them not to drive home. She looked around to see that everyone in the clubhouse was on their devices, and many were leaving with barely hidden urgency. She rushed back to her own table, grabbed her purse, and returned to the TV.

"*What should we do?*" another reporter asked Peter.

"Our supreme president has asked everyone to go on with their lives as usual. There is a threat, but we are dealing with it. The WPP honeycomb barrier will protect us and we are not expecting anything to happen immediately."

"What kind of bombs are they sending?" another reporter asked.

"*Bombs! No one said the aggression was specific. Bombs! Please—don't make the situation worse than it already is. What I said was this..."*

Peter read his prepared statement once more.

"*During the Ronald Reagan administration, the United States reversed its alien policy. Remember, at the time, only the US and a few allies knew of the existence of the aliens. Some Republicans in the administration distrusted the intentions of the aliens. They began preemptive plans and undertook actions against the alien terrestrial planet, Kepler 3763. They assumed the alien civilization would be doing the same. They launched various aggressive ships on newer rockets that would arrive in 35 years instead of 47 years. These strikes were unilateral and Reagan took full responsibility. AmEarth has been ensuring our future, and was building the World Protection Project honeycomb structure even before this was revealed. This WPP structure was designed because there may be other aliens we don't know about, and we can also protect the earth from asteroids."*

"Reagan sent bombs?" a reporter raised his voice over everyone else's.

"No; once again, I didn't say anything about bombs!" Peter said.

"Then what the hell are we talking about?" a random voice from the crowd demanded.

"Well, they were aggressive packages, but not bombs. The rockets carried computer viruses and biological viruses. Small packages that packed a punch."

"Are the aliens going to send us viruses or bombs?"

More questions leaped out at Peter.

"First things first! We do not intend to let any more alien ships into the Earth's atmosphere. Period. In space, we might analyze or destroy the content. Unfortunately, for all of humankind, the paranoia of the Reagan administration soiled our relationship with the Keplerian aliens."

Peter stopped talking and took a sip of water.

The clubhouse broke into immediate discussion. Former Democrats cursed Reagan on the spot. You could hear insults like "paranoid imbecile" and "warmonger" among other less polite comments.

Barbara barely said good-bye to her friends as she went to her car to start her drive to the school. When she arrived at the lobby, all of her friends were directly behind her and there was a mess of cars all leaving at once. The valets were completely swamped. Mr. Post, the owner and director of the country club, saw Barbara on the line and gestured to her.

"Barbara, Peter was so eloquent, but no one seemed to be paying attention," Mr. Post began.

"Not even me! I should listen and stay calm, but isn't it awful?" Barbara replied.

"You don't say…you don't say. We sure pissed off the aliens, huh?" Mr. Post offered.

"Stupid. It's just plain stupid." Barbara looked at the sky as though it was going to fall on her at any minute.

"What can we do? Nothing! I'm going to get me a drink!" Mr. Post replied.

"You do that. I'm going to get my kids and make sure they're okay. Oh yes, and maybe kill Peter at some point!"

***

Peter finished his interview at the media center in the lobby of the UN building, but he was not sure that it had all gone as planned. He had tried to calm the crowd, but the mood of the reporters was hysterical. This was an admission of a real threat to the public and asking politely for people to be calm was not working. Thank God he was making the announcement on a Friday afternoon. People could flock home to be with loved ones, and by Monday life would hopefully be back to normal. That was the plan. He took the secret tunnel back to his new office at the Shadow White House across the river and reassured the many people sending him desperate text messages. He was relieved that the tunnel existed, as he could avoid the countless reporters that would probably be waiting outside the UN building. Upon entering his new office, he found President Chen sitting casually on the corner of his desk, waiting for him.

"So you saw the disaster! I'm so sorry," Peter began to apologize immediately.

"Sorry? It was perfect. I'm here to congratulate you," President Chen responded.

"Huh?"

"Peter, you did exactly as you were told and the media frenzy was ideal."

"But the world is in a panic. I thought we wanted the opposite. I thought you wanted people to be calm. I tried to reassure them that there was no imminent danger."

"And there isn't. But what we really wanted was a controlled frenzy. Something we can use to our advantage."

"I'm sorry? Perhaps you should fill me in. I'm now being seen as the bad guy from New York City to New Delhi!"

"All in due time, Peter. I need you to be vigilant. We want some mass hysteria. We want some concern, just not full-out panic. Okay? You did good out there. Keep up the good work, and be ready for the next announcement."

President Chen walked out of Peter's office. Peter fell on his chair, exhausted, and looked out at the Queensboro Bridge, which was completely filled with cars at a standstill. On the three monitors in his office, he could see the breaking news scrolls and news channels running repeats of his morning press conference. The alien threat was the top story on every channel. He hadn't considered that he would become a household name the world over. As President Chen left his office, Peter's secretary allowed calls to pass in again and all the lights on his phone blinked into existence. Peter placed his head in his hands and waited.

"Your wife is on line one, sir," his secretary informed him through the intercom.

"Thanks," Peter said. "Honey?"

"Peter…you could have warned me!" Barbara started without any pleasantries.

"I couldn't. You have to understand that. I just couldn't."

"All these days you've been telling me not to worry and now you are the one to announce this! What will I tell Bri and Scott? That their father has been lying to them for years?"

"Calm down! I mean it when I say that you're not in any danger. You must believe me! I was just with President Chen and he said the same thing to me in plain language. There is no imminent threat! None."

"I don't know what to believe anymore."

"Where are you?"

"I'm at the school, waiting to see the kids. There is mass chaos over here. Every parent flocked to the school. The traffic is terrible."

"Scott has his car there. I'm going to text him to go home. You go home, too."

"Not without Bri. I want her with me."

"Fine, but I'll see you at home later tonight, okay? Barbara?"

"Yes, Peter?"

"I love you."

"You sound strange. Now I'm really getting worried."

"No, honey, please believe me…nothing is happening. Everything will be just fine. Don't let the kids worry. If you take Bri out, then Scott will be worried and who knows what will happen then? Just go home and let the kids get there on their own, okay? Please, just do that for me," Peter pleaded.

"Fine, okay…I will," Barbara replied.

Barbara made a U-turn and headed home slowly and carefully along the back streets, stopping for longer than usual at every intersection. It was the long way, but there was no traffic. She got home and sat at the kitchen counter, where she texted Scott.

Take Norton Ave—avoid route 1—see you at home—Mom

NINE

Pat Jackson sat in his Christchurch apartment's small bedroom office. He used an old oak armchair with four wheels and was surrounded by walls layered with newspaper clippings concerning AmEarth. On his TV, the image of Peter delivering the last message of the AmEarth government was being broadcast—the same image and words that were being shared all around the globe. He knew that this was the moment. He prepared a backpack with camping equipment and tools, as well as his laptop computer. His office was disheveled and grungy, and even his telephones looked like they were from another era. All of his furniture was coated with a thick layer of dust and grime, as though they belonged in an antique store or at a garage sale. Pat got up, ready to leave, when the phone rang.

"Pat? It's me, Ted," Mr. Landon said.

"Ted, I can't talk right now. What is it?" Pat replied shortly, clearly irritated.

"Did you hear the news?"

"Of course we heard. It's a blatant use of misinformation! You know what this means, right?"

"I think so."

"Well, then let me go about my day. Every man, woman, and child will need instructions in the days to come, so I need to go. Good-bye Ted."

Pat hung up before Ted could say good-bye. He left his apartment and got in his old Range Rover. His mission took him out to Mount John and the University observatory, about three hours away from Christchurch. He needed to meet with Professor Oliver Cook as soon as possible. The only way out of this predicament would be to mount the offensive communications attack they had planned to deliver to the world. He regretted for the thousandth time that the New Zealand Parliament had rejected the project in the past by citing the possibility of an invasion. Now, New Zealand would probably be invaded anyway and the information campaign had never been launched. Who knew how close AmEarth was to invading?

On the way to the observatory, Pat noticed that many people were standing on the side of the road, looking up in a bewildered daze. It was working even here! Alien fear was gripping the country, which would make the takeover all the easier for AmEarth. He drove as fast as he could, speeding down Tekapo-Twizel Road and then onto Godley Peaks Road before finally arriving at the deserted mountaintop where the observatory building sat. It was a hangar-like steel structure with a multimillion-dollar observatory attached to it. It was almost comical to contrast the two buildings that composed the complex. Pat parked, entered the huge metal doors of the building and made his way toward the part of the building that connected with the round wall of the observatory. Inside the observatory there was another entry door and a staircase going up and around and into the main observation room.

"The end of the world," Pat said with what little breath was left in him.

"Literally or figuratively?" Professor Oliver Cook's voice emanated from behind the huge telescope, seemingly unconcerned.

"Both! You should have seen what I saw," Pat said.

"What?"

"People on the streets looking up at the skies, worried about nothing but the infinite threat of a hundred billion galaxies. I'm afraid that it might be too late for our campaign now."

"It's not in our hands any longer."

"Have you heard from the government?"

"Not yet, but I expect the worst."

Pat did not realize that the knowledge Oliver had on Kepler 3763 was as impossible to grasp as the story being told by AmEarth. The truth was that Oliver held differing views on many issues that were rapidly becoming religion throughout the world. They sat there waiting and silently pondering their individual helplessness. Then the phone rang.

"Mr. Prime Minister?" Oliver said.

He motioned for Pat to keep quiet and his face became stone cold serious.

"Oliver, I can't...No, I won't enact your mandate," declared Robert Smith, PM of New Zealand.

"But sir, the truth is not what we're being told. I have proof," Oliver argued.

"At this point, the people of New Zealand would suffer the wrath of a world in mass psychosis, and then we would be blamed for all their ills. How can I force our men to fight against the world? It's mass suicide. I can't do it! I trust your knowledge, but I regret that I can only use it now—when it's too late.

"Where are they?"

"They have taken the port of Christchurch."

"Damn!"

"I have arranged an online meeting with President Chen; I wanted to give you warning to lock up the information that you have on Kepler 3763. They must not get their hands on this information. It might be useful as leverage in the future, understood? It might be our only leverage with AmEarth in the future. Secure it as soon as possible."

"Yes sir. Of course. Yes."

Oliver hung up the phone and looked directly into Pat's eyes.

"New Zealand will be joining AmEarth," he stated in a complete monotone, shocked himself.

"Holy mackerel!" Pat uttered, as he could think of nothing else.

"Another bloodless coup by AmEarth."

Pat fell into his chair, sickened by the feeling of defeat.

"What now?" he asked.

"We need to keep all of the information on Kepler 3763 as secret as possible!" Oliver replied.

Pat agreed and began moving data from the main drives of the Mount John Observatory to Pat's laptop and other small computer drives.

"Whatever you do, do not tell me where you hide your laptop. I won't tell a soul where I hide these," Oliver stated as he gestured at the USB drives.

"Okay."

"Now go. I'll leave here after you call me from your apartment. That way, the copies will be safe in two locations."

With that, Oliver hit the delete button and the hard drive of the observatory computer began to erase the contents of all information regarding Kepler 3763. Pat and Oliver parted ways. New Zealand's PM was signing the online treaty around the same moment, and AmEarth's invasion of New Zealand resulted in a pen-led coup that lasted less than two minutes.

The prime minister of New Zealand was offered a new position as the minister of Parks and Wildlife, with its headquarters in New York and staff in every continent on the planet. He was entrusted with the welfare of millions of acres of open land. He did not seem to realize what a powerful job this was, as AmEarth managed all of the world's wildlife and its habitat. Despite that fact, the entire proceeding was no great consolation to a truly independent man with firsthand knowledge that any "New World" government was based on a hoax.

TEN

On that same day, Ted Landon was preparing to leave the school, but he was frustrated by the traffic and the pandemonium. Being a bachelor and not having to get home in a hurry, he decided to go back to the teachers' lounge and wait out the situation. He took out his old laptop computer and made a call to his mother. She didn't answer, so he left a video message.

"Mom, I hope you get this soon. I want you to know that I'm fine. You probably heard all about the alien invasion and the escalation of the situation on the news. Please don't worry, okay? There is not a real threat. Call me whenever you can and I'll explain what I can. I love you."

Mr. Landon clicked the laptop off and the connection was terminated. Then he entered the information to contact Pat and find out what was happening in New

Zealand. For some reason, the program was no longer functioning properly. It seemed like it was going to work, but then the image began to blur.

Meanwhile, Scott and Bri were sitting in the parking lot waiting to exit the school. They found themselves frozen in place, not going anywhere. They were not even able to pull out of the parking space they occupied. Bri was texting away to her friends about the bubbling fear of an alien attack. Scott was beginning to get anxious and looked nervously at all the other parents and students in their cars, panicking. He turned the car off and texted his mom.

Still at school. Too much traffic—will be home later—one hour.

Then he unlocked his door and looked at Brianna.

"Bri, we're getting out," he stated calmly.

"Why?"

"Because."

He exited the car and waited for Bri to do the same. She took longer than he expected and he had to practically coax her out. Once she was out, he locked the car and began heading back toward the campus.

"Where are we going?" Bri asked.

"Follow me. It's pointless to sit in the car," Scott said.

Scott walked in the opposite direction of the flow of students leaving Darien Country Day, the K-12 school everyone in Darien went to. He went to the teachers' lounge, hoping to find Mr. Landon; he figured that if that failed, he could wait there with a cup of coffee. On the way, he saw throngs of hysterical parents picking up their middle-school wards and treating them like babies. Scott thought to himself that people were so strange—always showing their affection at the wrong time.

"Scott, I'm scared. What's happening?"

"Bri, please don't worry. I don't think there's any sort of threat. I have a feeling that we are all going to be fine."

"Okay."

Scott said this while looking straight into her eyes. His words rang true to Brianna and she felt reassured, but he wasn't sure if he felt the same. Scott led the way through the high school commons to the teachers' lounge. Inside, he found what he was looking for.

"Scott, you can't bring her in here," Mr. Landon said.

"But Mr. L, I need to watch over her. This is my sister. Anyway, she's cool," Scott vouched.

"Yeah, I'm cool!" Bri chimed in.

"Listen, Bri, please just sit over there and stay quiet," Scott directed.

Scott pointed to a chair far from where Mr. Landon was sitting.

"Scott. You need to come see this," his teacher said.

"What is it?"

"It's some sort of bug. I can't get this to work."

Scott saw that Mr. Landon's computer was showing all sorts of visuals that seemed wrong, like something was corrupting the processor. It was making the screen look like a green and black mess of gibberish. This was one virus that Scott had never seen before.

"Has this ever happened to this computer before?" Scott asked.

"No."

"That's a weird one. I think your computer is fried. Try to restart it."

"Okay."

Mr. Landon pushed the "Off" button, but the computer did not turn off; the screen maintained its crazy mess of colors and error boxes. Scott held down the "Off" button for nearly a minute, attempting to force a restart, but nothing happened.

"Were you trying to call Pat?" Scott asked.

"Yes. I wanted to see what the reaction was to the latest news down there," Mr. L said.

"Let's use mine, instead."

"Scott, this one is special. It's old as dust and there is no serial number that can be traced back to me."

"But mine is…well…it's mine. I'm just a student and my dad has some important job in the ACA."

"He's a minister now, Scott!" Brianna said, her tone a bit sassy.

"I told you to stay out of this, Bri. Yes, he's a minister now. So this is the computer of the son of a minister."

Mr. Landon knew that this might all be ill-advised, but his curiosity outweighed the safety issue for the moment.

"Okay, but only for a few minutes."

The laptop that Scott owned was ten times faster than the antique relic that Mr. Landon had been using. In under a minute, the screen was ringing, connecting to Pat.

"Pat! How are you guys holding up?" Mr. Landon said, having no time for small talk.

"New Zealand conceded, Ted. People got scared. We joined AmEarth. It's unbelievable! Fucking unbelievable," Pat responded, his voice annoyed.

"No, no…" Ted said, disbelieving what he was hearing.

"Yes, my friend, it's already done. The news broke as the AmEarth Navy began docking in Christchurch. It was planned perfectly."

"You were the last hope. Now AmEarth has control over a hundred percent of the planet. This is the first day of a single world, single government. There's no escape." Landon's voice began to crack, as though some great resolve had finally been broken.

"Now there is nothing to stop them from abusing their power! All in the name of unity and defense! Unbelievable! Un-fucking-believable! Ted, this is madness, but before anything else happens, I need you to download a file. It's some of the evidence that we have already and it's *damning*. If something happens to me, I need you to show it to the world. Okay?"

"What is it?"

"It's scientific information on Kepler 3763. Astronomers and physicists can certify the findings. If you can get it into the right hands, it is priceless!"

"I can't have you send it."

"Why not?"

Scott gestured to Mr. Landon that sending the information should be fine. This might be the only chance to get the download; he didn't understand Mr. L's hesitance.

"No, nothing, it's okay. Go ahead and send. We need to do this now…and fast. Pat, good luck and good-bye; we'll need to disconnect as soon as it finishes downloading."

"Okay, good-bye Ted." Pat signed off with a grin.

The file-sharing between the two computers began. Scott looked on and Bri pretended to understand, but was mostly awed that Scott was friends with adults. *Maybe Scott is actually cool,* she thought.

"Finished. Now what?" Scott snapped.

"You can't have anyone find this. I think that you should make a copy to a USB and then delete it from your computer," Mr. Landon advised.

"What? Why? This might be something that my dad can use. He's in the administration now, so he could use it to show them that NASA was wrong or something…" Scott's idea petered out before it could ever properly develop.

"Are you out of your mind? If your father gets this, both of us will go down! The government is not in the business of proving itself wrong. The government would just condemn it and get to the bottom of how you found all of this out," Mr. Landon whispered. "Not a good plan."

"Maybe."

"Just get it off your computer."

Barbara Johansen entered the teachers' lounge. She had an app on her wafer that allowed her to locate her children.

"Mom!" Bri shouted when her mother's face appeared at the door.

Brianna ran into her mother's arms and hugged her for what seemed like an eternity. Then she looked at Mr. Landon from over her mother's shoulder and winked at him, too—an exchange that meant that she understood not to talk about what she had seen. Brianna felt cool, and keeping her parents out of that particular loop made her feel rebellious, even though she didn't understand everything that was happening.

Scott closed the laptop with a decisive slam.

"I'll send you a copy via email," he said.

"No. The file is too large. Just put it here."

Landon handed Scott a USB drive.

"Okay, you'll have it tomorrow morning," Scott said, without a hint of doubt.

"What, honey?" Barbara asked.

"Homework, Mom. You remember Mr. L, right?" Scott said.

"Mr. L also has a real name, Scott," Barbara chastised.

"Mr. Landon," Scott said.

"Yes, of course, I remember you. History, right?" Barbara said.

"Yes, that's right," Mr. Landon replied with a grin.

"Well, I think we'll be going now," Barbara said, cutting off the conversation awkwardly.

She embraced her offspring, locking one hand across each of their necks and shoulders as she walked down the school commons at a rapid pace. Scott carried his computer in his backpack.

Scott arrived home from school after following his mom's car down Norton Avenue and immediately went upstairs to his room. He called Brianna on the house intercom, summoning her to his room. He sat her down on his bed and took a spot next to her. He leaned back and looked at the flat white ceiling of his bedroom. She copied his pose.

"That was strange," Scott said.

"Yep," Bri agreed.

"I think we need to keep this whole Kepler 3763 business quiet."

"What Kepler 3763 business? What are you talking about?"

"Nothing…I just mean the stuff that went on with Mr. Landon. We should keep it a secret until I say so, okay? Please, Bri."

"Absolutely, you can count on me." She was forever trying to prove herself in the eyes of her brother.

"I mean it, Bri…I won't talk to you for like…*ever* if you say a word about that to anyone. Swear it."

"I swear!"

With that, Bri left Scott's room and went to her own little bedroom, where she used her wafer to text her best friend Camilla.

Met Mr. L with Scott—super hottie—call me

Bri would tell everything to Camilla, as best friends do, but she focused on Mr. Landon's good looks and how Scott had been super cool about fixing computers and communicating. None of the information that had been exchanged interested her in the least.

Meanwhile, Scott called his best friend.

"Cate? I need you to come over."

"I can't. My mom is freaking out. If I leave she'll go berserk!"

"So is mine, but you won't believe what happened!"

"What?"

"Not on the phone."

"What? Who are you, James Bond?"

"Seriously. Come over as soon as you can."

"You're scaring me, Scott."

"Baby, come over. Please."

"Okay, as soon as she lets me."

"Thanks!"

Scott sat at his desk chair and opened his laptop. He opened the downloaded file, which was on the stationery of Mount John University Observatory, New Zealand, and was titled:

Preliminary findings on the composition of Kepler 3763, taken over a period of 17 years.
Researched and Published by Oliver Cook

A chart with headings and check boxes followed. Above it, the titles were labeled clearly: Mass, Orbital, Flicker, Density, Color, Luminescence, Position, Date, Time. Sometimes, tiny handwriting was visible in the boxes. It was small, meticulous, and quite hard to read.

It seemed complicated to decipher, but the title suggested that it contained details over a period of seventeen years, which explained why there were so many pages with categories checked and unchecked in boxes, as per the observations and the evidence. It contained at least a hundred pages; the first few were scanned versions of written papers, and then hundreds more that had been typed. Scott didn't know what to make of it until he scrolled all the way down to the final pages. It was the final statistical compilation and conclusion that actually mattered most. He read page 111 of the report.

Conclusion

Kepler 3763 is a nondistinct planet of class C. It is approximately 23.5 light years away. It is nonterrestrial and has a probability of holding H2O. The surface temperature has an average of 300 Kelvin putting it in the "goldilocks" temperature range due to its distance to the nascent red dwarf star at the center of its system. However the analysis of shape taken over seventeen years concludes that it is stationary. This fact rules out the possibility of life. The dark half of the planet has temperatures of 10 Kelvin.

Scott went online and looked to see why other astronomers had not picked up on the Kepler issue in the past. He read and discovered that the cosmos is so large that astronomers across the world actually vie for time to observe minute slices of the sky. But Kepler 3763 was in the news since the Trump state of the union in 2025, so many would have flocked to see Kepler 3763. Of course a quick look would seem like it was in the perfect zone, and few would have the time needed to study it in detail. On top of that AmEarth controlled most the worlds telescopes. Oliver Cook was probably the only astronomer actively studying this planet in the past two decades. This information unequivocally proved that AmEarth was based on lies.

***

That morning, Peter had driven to work along a new route. He took the ferry in Darien across the Long

Island Sound and drove from there down to Brooklyn. He loved that drive, since it involved no entry into Manhattan, which was basically an impossible city for cars. Throughout the drive, he allowed his mind to fantasize over his new job and what it meant to be a minister. He had now been given the proverbial bucket of water to the face. On arrival, he sat behind his desk and kept replaying the way he had released the information to the public. He wondered if he could have done things differently. All of those facts were already known by Parliament members and ministers in a top-secret setting, but that was quite different from what the common man was led to believe.

His new clearance level had allowed him to read about the details, and President Chen had sent him various files that made plenty of references to the subject. It was a bold move by AmEarth to allow the whole world to receive this information, as it damned the United States and its past choices. So why had they done it? As far as Peter could see, President Chen was happy if the vast majority of the world was worried about an alien attack. But why?

"Mr. Johansen?" his secretary said through the intercom.

"Yes?" Peter replied.

"It's your son on line one."

"Thanks, Mary…Scott?"

"Dad, I need to talk to you. It's important."

"What is it?"

"Not on the phone. When are you coming home?"

"Tonight. Scott, what is this about?"

"Not on this line."

"Scott!"

Scott hung up. His teenage kid had enraged Peter yet again. Scott could push him into a rage zone so easily that it often scared him. Things had gotten better in recent years, but even lately, Scott could make his blood boil up over the stupidest things.

***

Cate stepped into Scott's room looking frazzled. The events of that afternoon had impacted everyone, but some more than others. Her mother had driven Cate the short ten blocks to Scott's house and was in the living room with Scott's mom. They didn't like each other, but the day had caused people to flock to one another.

"My mom is here, with your mom," Cate said ominously.

"Oh my god! Why?" Scott asked.

"She didn't want me to walk here, and she needed to talk to somebody. She's going nuts. She's terrified."

"So is mine. Things are getting out of control!"

Scott pulled up a chair next to him at his desk, but she did not sit.

"I don't think there's any danger. Actually, I'm pretty sure it's all a lie," Scott said.

"Scott, please don't start again with your crazy theories."

"But Cate, just listen. I have proof that there is no alien attack!"

"I don't want to hear about your proof. My dad said that we're in imminent danger and that the whole world has finally united to stop the attack. You're not in a position to make me believe otherwise. Please, Scott."

"Okay, okay…just relax, I'll just keep what I know to myself."

"What do you think you know?"

"I thought that you didn't want to know."

He wrapped his arms around her waist and pulled her closer to him. They kissed deeply, and he tried to comfort her with that simple gesture. In his mind, Scott was torn between trusting Cate and leaving her out of this altogether. He weighed the options and chose the latter, which would ultimately be for the best.

"You know something, Cate?" Scott said.

"What?"

"I don't think I'm going to convince you of anything. I just want you to remember something that I said to you once in the past."

"And what was that?"

"People high up in the ACA aren't worried. Just keep your eye on your dad, okay? If he starts seeming panicked, let me know."

"Are you really not afraid?"

"No. Not in the least."

ELEVEN

Peter Johansen was sitting in his office with the strange draped windows at his back. He was still questioning what the intention was behind yesterday's news report. He left his office and went to the water cooler, where many bureaucrats shared their thoughts and shot the breeze. They all hushed when he arrived, so he grabbed a cup of water and continued on his way. He entered the empty elevator and pressed the L button. On the way down, the elevator stopped at floor 39, where Peter caught a glimpse of what appeared to be a military strategy meeting through the glass partitions.

A general entered the elevator, and Peter exited onto the same floor without looking back. As he reached the glass doors that separated the elevator lobby from the central room, he could see the door's keypad green light flicker on as he approached. His clearance level allowed him free rein in the building. He entered the room and saw a crowd of military personnel manning computer terminals, staring intently at the large wall of monitors. The engulfing of New Zealand was the clear focus of this military nerve center. Peter saw an empty computer terminal and sat down to watch. He fit in perfectly, and the personnel didn't even blink. They were busy going about their own important business.

On a centrally located screen, an image had been taken from the sky of Mount John University Observatory in real time. Helicopters had landed on the same road that Pat Jackson had been traveling earlier. The operators around Peter gave orders to different military personnel in seemingly random ways. One operator close to Peter was talking calmly, instructing a team on what to do at the observatory.

"Do you have him in custody? Good. Now, get the computer hard drives and disable the station…Well, ask Roberts, he knows how to do it…Get the telescope disabled," the operator ordered into a headset.

Peter could not understand everything that was going on around him, but it was interesting. Why were they taking astronomers and observatories instead of military bases? On a map, seven different observatories had been marked, but Mount John University was the main focus. Peter knew this because the monitor blatantly said "Primary Target" in red letters across the bottom. Telescopes were obviously an important aspect in defending the Earth from an alien attack, but it was strange that they needed the military. He kept listening.

"Roger that…Get Professor Cook into the transport; he is to be taken to H.W.

immediately…Once the telescope is out, leave a surveillance unit in place until further instructions…Good. Roger that."

Peter got up and discreetly left the room. He had a vague sense of the military capability of AmEarth, but he was now experiencing the immense power behind it firsthand. He strode to the main hallway and noticed a set of stairs. He went up another flight to level 40. There, he found more of the same, but the monitors were not focused on New Zealand at all. There were monitors showing images of different parts of the world, also in real time. Many images showed doomsayers on street corners and personnel being sent to quell these agitators. The control that AmEarth had was obviously worldwide, and the sudden sense of Big Brother made him uncomfortable. In this room, the monitors had colors on their borders that ranged from green and yellow to orange and red as they approached the center. This visually showed the places of greater interest to AmEarth based on their emergency level. Peter saw that there was one map on a monitor showing Germany, Poland, and Russia, ringed by a big red circle. The protests and guerrilla issues in the central area of Eastern Europe were clearly a top priority for AmEarth. Peter hadn't been aware that the Central European area was so problematic until that moment.

Russia, Poland, and Germany were historically war-torn, and now AmEarth was having problems there, as history would naturally have predicted. Peter was leaving the theater when he noticed a final image. On one monitor, a crowd of protesters held signs, one of which read "Außerirdischen Lüge!" Peter had never seen those two words together, but could make out what the intent was from his high school German lessons. *Alien Lie*, or *Extraterrestrial Lie,* to be more precise. It was obvious that in Germany there was dissent. From the monitor board, Peter clearly discerned that Europe housed most of the AmEarth dissidents.

Peter left and made his way to the lobby. From there he called Scott, who was making out with Cate in his bedroom while their mothers engaged in a joint panic frenzy in the kitchen. As Scott's wafer rang, he peeled it off his jacket hanging from the swivel chair.

"Scott? We need to talk," Peter began quickly, trying to convey the importance of his request in his tone.

"Where and when?" Scott asked.

"How about a miso soup?"

"Only if it's Han's."

"Exactly. Half an hour?"

"It will take me an hour, Dad. I'm not in the city."

"Okay, see you in an hour then."

They both knew that Han was the owner of Zutto, their favorite place for miso soup, and they referred to no restaurant name during the conversation in the event that it was being monitored. Peter was giving his son the opportunity for a chat with full privacy, well away from Barbara and Brianna. He knew that it was a whim, but he missed spending time with Scott, and a father-son chat would do them both the world of good. He called his secretary and cancelled all of his appointments for the next two hours. He took the secret tunnel across the river and parked at the UN headquarters, from where he could walk to Zutto and leave enough time for Scott to get there. When his son finally arrived, Peter was standing outside the restaurant on the corner of 52nd Street and First Avenue.

"Hi, Dad."
"Hi, son."
"Dad, I need you to listen to me with an open mind."
"I always do," Peter asserted.
"No, Dad, you don't! But this time, I need you to really listen closely. Let me just say it and then you can tell me how wrong I am. Okay?"
"Okay, Scott. I'm here because I know that you've been trying to say something to me, and I've been out of touch. You are the most important person in the world, Scott, besides Bri and your Mom, of course. You can tell me anything. Come on, son."
"Not here."
"What?"

Peter rolled his eyes, but Scott stood up and walked away on the sidewalk.

"Please, let's just walk. I'll talk as we walk."
"Okay."
"It all started with Bolivia."

Peter rolled his eyes again.

"Bear with me, please. I'm taking a statistics course and my homework was to find the odds of certain things; you know, like what the odds are of landing on a zero in roulette."
"One in thirty-eight."
"Dad, let me finish. Basically, I calculated the surface of the earth, and the odds of anything landing in a major city in Bolivia are astronomical. The Earth has 510 million square kilometers, and Sucre is about thirty-six square kilometers. The landing in Sucre represents a coincidence of fourteen million to one.

You said it was lucky because it helped tip the scales of public opinion, remember?"

"Yes, it was lucky."

"Have you ever heard of anyone that lucky? Or an entire planet being that lucky?"

"Scott, have you been discussing this with anyone? Did you tell your math teacher about the landing?"

"No, dad. No. I did this exercise for my own knowledge. Only you and I know this."

"Good."

"Dad, that's not all. Please listen. I was online with a friend on wafer chat—a friend from really far away. You know how I play online with people all over."

"Yes."

"Well, he is in New Zealand, and they were being invaded by AmEarth as I spoke to him, at the same time you were on TV. It was happening at the exact same time. They were told on the news of the imminent threat to places without the WPP. Do you know what that means? The news of the new alien threat and their hostile intentions was timed to match up with the invasion of the last free country in the world!"

"Scott—"

"Wait, Dad, you said that you would listen…"

"Okay, is there much more? The last "free" country…my god!" Peter was shocked by his son's bold conspiracy beliefs, even though they hadn't been the first.

"One last unbelievable thing also happened, but you have to promise that you won't ask how I learned about it."

"Scott, if I can't verify the authenticity of the information, then it's worthless anyway."

"Oh, this can be verified, but you just need access to a sixty-inch refractor telescope and a scientist who can use it."

"What? A large telescope like in an observatory?"

"Yes."

Peter was a bit aghast that his son could know any of this, let alone all of it. They continued walking north on First Avenue, ignoring everything around them.

"Dad, please let me finish. I got my hands on a document from an observatory in Mount John, New Zealand," Scott played his trump card triumphantly.

Peter listened intently, but feigned disinterest. He knew that his son was onto something, but this could be dangerous, so he needed to stay cool. Hearing about Mount John University in New Zealand twice in a single day was too much.

"This document is a study of Kepler 3763, and it says the planet is uninhabitable. You are aware that astronomers don't study the full scope of the cosmos; they vie for areas and time on telescopes and only get to study certain angles. Space is huge, like…ridiculously huge. So very few astronomers have ever studied Kepler 3763. You understand that, right?"

Peter stopped and looked at his son intently.

"Is that it?" Peter asked.

"Yes, sir."

"Has it ever occurred to you that this information reached you because you are a minister's son? That someone with the desire to hurt AmEarth might feed false information to you?"

"But it was Cate's father who mentioned the landing in Sucre."

"Yes, and that part is a strange coincidence, but that's all it is. We can't prove otherwise."

"What about the invasion of New Zealand? Don't you think it was timed perfectly with your announcement?"

"Does that mean that there is no threat? New Zealand is a rather small peanut in the scope of the whole world. I don't think AmEarth announced the alien threat to cover up an invasion of that tiny island, do you?"

Scott seemed less certain of his thesis as his father parsed out his arguments, unraveling them before his eyes.

"And the Kepler 3763 document?" Scott said.

"I think that one got to you because of who you are. They want you to get to me. Kepler 3763 has been seen by every astronomer in the planet and they all know it is the source of the alien communications. You should give me the document and tell me exactly how you got it."

"Spam."

"What?"

"It came in my junk mail."

"And you brought it up like this to me? Please, son, drop all of this. We are an AmEarth family. We work for the government and we need to trust it. Okay? I want you to study…don't let these crazies get to you."

"Do you want a copy of the document?"

"Of course not; you should just delete it before it drops a Trojan into your computer and affects things that actually matter! It might be selling you things that you don't need based on your location and habits by data mining your computer. Please, son, just delete it. Promise? Not a word of this to your mother."

"Scout's honor."

They finished their chat with some familial small talk before Peter shifted to a happier topic.

"Let's get a grilled cheese and a milkshake…what do you say?" Peter said.

"Not healthy at all, Dad. Mom will kill you," Scott replied instantly, relying on his upbringing to know the right answer.

"So now you're a snitch?"

"Nope."

"Then let's go."

In the coffee shop, Peter sat and ordered for them both. They talked about other things while waiting for the food. When the meal arrived, the waiter took out a white wand device that shone a white light directly on the food. He moved it slowly over the plates and they all saw the wand turn a slight green hue as the light changed. The waiter quickly removed the wand from view and left the table. The device had scanned the food for any living organisms at the microscopic scale. Green meant that the food contained nothing harmful. Peter and Scott ate their sandwiches and drank their milkshakes quietly.

"Son, do you have your laptop with you?"

"It's in my room."

"I don't want you to forget to delete that crazy stuff. I can't be exposed to subversive information like that. Remember, I'm a minister now…"

"I'll do it as soon as I get home. I promise."

"Okay," his father agreed.

A few minutes later, they parted ways, and Scott drove back to Connecticut, where he went upstairs and opened his laptop. He dragged the Kepler document into a hidden file in the operating system of his computer by going to Applications > Stuffit > Documentation and making a new folder simply called 01. He moved the Kepler file there. The location made it difficult to find, and renaming the files by number made them look like a boring part of the program. Scott could tell his dad that he had erased the file, and his father would never find the documents. Even if he pried with a full search, the Kepler reference would no longer show up as part of the search. His wafer rang.

"Mr. L," Scott answered.

"Hi, Scott. Did you read the file?" Landon asked.

"Nope, not yet."

"Did you copy it to the USB I gave you?"

"Doing it now."

Scott copied the file to Landon's USB drive, which he fished out from the bottom of his backpack.

"I'm outside your home. Bring it to me," Landon ordered.

"Where? You're outside?"

Scott looked out of his bedroom window at a silver Toyota Corolla sitting in the driveway. The USB finished copying and he plucked it from the side of his computer.

"I have it. I'll be right there," Scott said.

"Scott, delete your copy first."

"Okay, I'll delete it now," Scott lied.

"Wait!"

"What? Why?"

"I need to make sure that the information is on the drive."

"Too late, I just emptied the trash!" Scott lied again.

"Damn. Well, bring it down. I sure hope it's on the drive."

Mr. Landon sat in his car with a white laptop computer on his knee. Scott entered the car on the passenger side to get out of the cold. He glanced down at the white laptop, which had a pink decal covering the Apple logo.

"It's my girlfriend's...don't ask," Landon said when he saw Scott's gaze.

"No worries."

Mr. Landon inserted the USB drive into his computer and accessed the file without downloading it onto his girlfriend's computer. He opened the file. The report that Scott had already seen was there, and he began to read it.

"Just skip to page 111," Scott advised.

"So you did read it," Mr. Landon glanced sidelong at him, suspicious.

"Yes. Sorry..."

Mr. Landon read the conclusion, and Scott watched his expression. Kepler 3763 was evidently uninhabited by any life form.

"Scott...Are you sure that you deleted this from your computer?"

"Absolutely."

"You just lied to me about having read it. How can I know that you're not lying now?"

"I did delete it. I swear!"

"You're too close to the government to be messing around in this. You shouldn't be engaged in any of this. Have you told anyone about this document?"

"No."

"No one in your family?"

"You mean my dad? Even if I did tell him, he wouldn't believe me," Scott admitted with a shake of his head.

"Just forget about everything that's happened recently and go back to your normal life. Please, Scott, get this out of your head. Okay?"

"Okay."

"So…have you heard back from any colleges yet?" Landon tried to change the subject, with genuine interest in Scott's future.

"Nope, still too early."

"Where did you apply?" Landon asked.

"The usual—Stanford, Yale, Harvard, Columbia, Brown."

"Don't worry, you're a shoo-in for the League."

"I hope so, or my dad will lose it."

"Well, your dad may be the reason you'll be accepted. He's on everyone's radar now."

"I guess that's true."

They looked at each other over a strange extended pause. Scott pulled on the door handle and stepped out of the car.

"See you in class."

"Yep." Scott walked slowly up to the house, not looking back.

TWELVE

President Chen Tyson sat behind his desk, contemplating the whirlwind of political victories that had recently yielded the first world empire. This was a major victory for America, and few knew that better than Neil Chen Tyson, whose family had become one of the wealthiest on the planet. His father's interests had global tentacles, as he controlled the vast majority of the world's supply of pork. The family also had interests in solar power and electronics, having diversified back in the first decades of the twenty-first century to avoid the volatility of the financial markets.

However, President Chen was not only happy with his family's fortune; he was also happy with having total political and military control of the planet. New directives concocted by the central computer had resulted in gun control on a planetary scale and had criminalized the deadly use of force. No one else on Earth could match the forceful hand of a world army with its satellites and cameras everywhere. Powerful computers, both in the Shadow White House and in other capitals where AmEarth had established them, could identify the perpetrator of any crime from images taken on the streets. Added to this was the identification of pings left by people when they used their wafers, as well as identification through DNA signatures and traditional fingerprints. New babies being born worldwide received mandatory DNA sampling, and upon reaching the age of eighteen, they would receive their first government-issued wafer. In essence, everyone on the planet was being tracked, and the movements and habits of every individual were documented from very early on.

The powerful computers would identify any unusual behavior in a person and send real-time notices to their wafers and nearby authorities. All of this was viewed as a service, rather than as the intrusion and invasion that it truly represented. The AmEarth system allowed people to have a sense of freedom, but there was an invisible fist controlling everything else. The same applied to business; entrepreneurship was highly rewarded, as long as it remained out of the political arena and didn't violate "World Security." "Freedom through Regulation" would be one of President Chen's lasting legacies. To some, this all felt heavy-handed and a breach of rights, but those were mostly operators of businesses in that gray area where regulation is impossible—prostitution, drugs, and other illicit activities.

The thorn in the side of AmEarth, like all empires of the past, was rebellion. Empires die shortly after their military budget becomes bloated and unsustainable. This time, however, AmEarth had achieved its goals without putting any boots on the ground, but the military cost was still quite high. President Chen had made it a priority to quell any doubts of the alien threat wherever they appeared and as quickly as possible. Now that the world knew about the alien threat, it had to remain in the minds of civilians. Any doubts would need to be dealt with efficiently. The Keplerian enemy must be perceived at all times as a clear and present danger.

"Get me Johansen," President Chen spoke harshly into the intercom.

"Right away, Mr. President."

Peter was in his office, hoping that Scott would drop the whole subject of AmEarth's legitimacy, but he couldn't stop thinking about it. He thought that someone might be getting to Scott, but that paranoid thought did no good for anyone, so he shook off the idea. He was a new minister at the highest ranks of power and would not start peeking around corners just yet. He noticed Mary, his secretary, rise from her desk and rush toward his door. His heart began to pound. *Oh no, what now…?*

"What is it, Mary?" Peter said.

"The Executive wants you—up there," Mary said quickly.

"So you run at me like the building's on fire?" His pulse slowed a bit, but not by much.

"Sorry," Mary looked down at the ground.

"It's okay, Mary. Did they say when?"

"Right now. President Chen said *immediately*."

Peter got up and walked to the elevator, stepped in and pushed 97. Only when he had a legitimate appointment would the elevator begin to move. Entering level 97 without an appointment was impossible. In a few seconds, he was back in the glass world of the executive office. He saw President Chen sitting in his office, apparently reading something on a wafer hanging before him.

"He's waiting for you," Rosemary informed him as she led him to the inner office.

"Thanks," Peter said.

He walked in, and President Chen instantly changed the walls to wooden privacy once more.

"Good afternoon, sir," Peter said.

"Hello, Peter! Sit down, please," President Chen instructed him with a calm, measured voice.

Peter sat and waited for President Chen to speak. President Chen continued reading something on his wafer, which was hanging from its wiry stand. He turned the wafer so that Peter could see the information on it. It was a bio on Peter with his face on it, as well as a picture of his family.

"Peter, your name is constantly being selected by our central computer," President Chen said.

"I don't understand, sir…Have I done something?" Peter replied, suddenly nervous.

He began to perspire, as he feared that Scott's information on Kepler 3763 might have something to do with this.

"No. You have done everything," President Chen said.

"I don't understand," Peter answered dumbly. "Can you be more specific?"

"You have done everything right."

"Right?"

"Yes, Peter. You have done everything right. Let me explain. We've been struggling with the maturity of AmEarth. You see it is a marvelous achievement, and with Bolivia and New Zealand now in, we are asking Essie to determine what is best for AmEarth as we move forward," President Chen explained.

Peter silently sighed with relief, trying to remain as cool as possible, he had heard the nickname of the super computer before but pretended not to know.

"Essie?" Peter asked.

"Essie is the nickname of the Super Computer, S.C. you get it?"

"I do."

"We asked her for the best system of succession for the presidency, among other viability questions, of course. Succession to the role of supreme president must not be a problem as it was in other—for lack of a better word—empires. AmEarth has the advantage of knowing history and all of its failures, in addition to having Essie to help avoid those failures," President Chen continued.

"What has this got to do with me, if you don't mind me asking, sir?"

"Everything. Essie determined that supreme presidents of AmEarth should come from the ranks of civil servants; they should be in power for an average of fifteen years, and they should be from America by descent, birth, and belief system. As you can see, the US is the founding entity of AmEarth and its values need to be preserved. After all, what is the purpose of a global system if it doesn't come from the best political and economic system the world has ever had? Essie also determined that the best candidate should have studied and excelled at history, have pursued higher education, have a family with two to three kids at most, have good looks, have no interests in financial affairs that could corrupt him, and finally, have global fame."

"You're not saying that…"

"Yes, Peter. Essie continues printing your name as my possible successor."

Peter felt that he had to sit down, but he was already sitting. His mouth was open and his emotions were everywhere, despite his inability to form words.

"But you don't think this is right…Right?" Peter asked, wishing he had phrased that question a bit better.

"Oh, but I do. This job is tiring, and my family interests make the job nearly impossible at times. My daughters are not interested, and their husbands are not good men. I have never thought that any of them could succeed me in this post. Also, I am constantly accused of having made my fortune larger, as if having a global market was going to make it smaller. Everyone knows that the computer is programmed to favor business, as long as it is fair business. I have done nothing wrong, but the criticism and the rumors are a constant pain. I'm tired, Peter. I want to retire and enjoy some of my wealth while I can. The role of this office is more like that of an overseer. Remember, Essie always finds the best way," President Chen finished.

"When?" Peter asked.

"Not immediately, of course. We need to deal with some problems first and to make sure that you're on board."

"Oh, I am."

"And your family?"

"I'm sure they will be, too."

"It won't happen for some time, but you need to start your training as soon as you confirm that your family is okay with all of this."

"I will let you know by tomorrow."

"Good."

Peter walked down the corridor to the elevator, but had no feeling in his legs or feet. He didn't know whether to cry, laugh, run, or collapse into a pile. This wasn't happening to him.

He felt like he was floating and sensed that everyone was somehow aware of what President Chen had told him. Looking around, he saw that people were busily working; the few who saw him smiled politely. It was surreal; the world had just been knocked off its axis, and no one seemed to be affected but him. Suffice it to say, it would be an interesting night at the Johansen home.

That evening, Peter broached the subject gently to get a response from his family. They all sat in the elegant dining room at four places near one end of the long Queen Anne-style table, being formally served by the housekeeper. Barbara had opened a bottle of vintage Heitz Cellars Beaujolais from 2011; the wine helped Peter to roll out the words he needed to say.

"Now that we're all together, I wanted to share something rather amazing that happened to me at work today," Peter began.

They all kept eating and paid him very little attention. Brianna's wafer kept making clicking sounds as messages stacked up.

"Wafer off, Bri," Peter said, interrupting his own flow.

"Wafer off," Brianna dutifully said.

Peter held Barbara's hand and looked into her eyes.

"I was offered the presidency of AmEarth."

"What?" Barbara squealed.

"Come again?" Scott's eyes perked up, and he sat up straighter than he had in years.

"That's fantastic, Dad!" Brianna said.

Peter didn't say much after that. That's all he really knew. After their initial reaction, the questions began to come fast and furious.

"But Peter, you're not an elected official. How can you be the next President?" Barbara inquired.

"Yeah, Dad, why you? Did you ask for this?" Scott said, his curiosity already budding.

"No, and yes. It seems that Essie keeps choosing us as the ideal presidential family. Something about my face recognition, the number of kids, our looks, the fact that we're American, my education…" Peter repeated the list that President Chen had mentioned.

"Who is Essie?" Scott asked.

"Essie is the super computer, its a nickname."

So the computer chose us? Like it chose the name AmEarth?" Brianna asked.

"What will this mean for us?" Scott asked over his sister's question.

"Secret Service?" Barbara tagged on to her son's question.

"Everyone just hold off. This was just a comment that President Chen made to me, and I wanted to see what all of you thought. Would you be okay if we became the first family of AmEarth?" Peter asked.

"Ummm, of course it would!" Brianna said without hesitation.

Peter turned to his wife.

"I'm okay with it if you are," Barbara, the ever-supportive love of his life, replied.

Scott was silent. His father looked at him and could tell that he was thinking hard. Inside Scott's head, there was the huge contradiction. One side had the bug of the Kepler 3763 document and the hoax, the other the possibility of living in the White House and having his own father in the history books.

"I'm fine with it. I think it's great, Dad," Scott spoke, knowing that this was a moment to be supportive of his family, not bold and brash with his beliefs.

They all sighed with relief, and Peter turned as the phone rang.

"Rosa, can you get that, please?" Peter raised his voice so she would hear in the kitchen.

After a short pause, Rosa came back into the room, looking pale and panicked.

"What is it, Rosa? Are you okay?" Barbara asked.

"It's, it's…President Chen on the phone. For Mr. J," Rosa said.

"Thank you, Rosa," Peter smiled, amused at the thought of Rosa answering the phone to find the president on the other end.

He went to the wall wafer in the kitchen, but returned to the dining room a few seconds later.

"Honey, it looks like I have to go in. There's a crisis, and I'm needed," Peter confessed sadly to his family.

"What is it?" Scott asked.

"Nothing important. Good night, all. And honey, don't wait up for me."

"Bye, Peter."

"Bye."

As soon as Peter had left the kitchen to get ready to leave, they all began to chat and speculate about the possibilities of being the first family. Peter, having grabbed his coat and car keys, reentered the dining room.

"This is important: All of you, not a word about this to anyone. Anyone! This includes you, too." Peter directed that last comment at Barbara.

Then he heard the familiar clicking sound of Brianna's wafer.

"Bri, stop that. Delete whatever it is. You are not to send anything relating to the presidency. I'm serious. I will take your wafer away for a month! Do you understand?" Peter shouted. Privacy was of the utmost importance now.

"Yes, Dad. Geeeeze!" Bri whined and rolled her eyes.

"Bye! Not a word!"

"Honey?" Barbara called.

"Yes, dear?"

"Can I tell my mom, at least?"

"No."

Peter headed to his office, wondering what emergency had arisen that had caused President Chen to need him. This was not the first time he'd had to deal with an after-hours crisis. As a Foreign Affairs deputy, he'd had to routinely deal with time differences, but this was the first time he couldn't deal with it from his home phone. President Chen had been specific; he needed to come to the Shadow White House in person.

THIRTEEN

“Prepare the nuclear warhead to launch back at five p.m. I want it to go off at exactly six thirty p.m. Warsaw time,” President Chen said.

He was standing at the head of the war room’s long table, at which ten generals also sat. On the large white computer imaging board was an animation of the Earth with Poland at the center and several satellites hovering over it. The clock on the wall read 11:00 p.m. New york time and 7:00 a.m. in Moscow. The Joint Chiefs of Staff were all aware of the gravity of the mission and knew that if anything went wrong, it would be very, very bad. The greatest dissent came from General Redford of the Air Force, whose voice carried weight, as the operation was in the air, or rather, in space. The NASA Director, Dr. Larry Kanter, was communicating on his earpiece with his headquarters, where the operation was being conducted.

"Operation AA1-25 is a go. Repeat, we are a go," Director Kanter said into his mic.

"I know that I have said this in the past, but I'm worried that contamination will fall back to earth," General Redford stated.

"General Redford's opinion is noted, as is the opinion of my astrophysicist, who calculated that entry into our atmosphere requires mass plus force, and this explosion has no mass, so it will not penetrate our precious atmosphere. We can assume that the detonation will remain in the stratosphere," President Chen countered.

"Have they considered that it might nudge the earth off its orbit, or anything like that?"

"They have."

"And?"

"General Redford, next time you come to a meeting of this importance, please read the material fully beforehand. The estimate is quite tolerable. It is in the inches, which will not affect the Earth at all. At most, time could be altered slightly, but the estimate of a clock differential is 0.001 seconds! That is a thousand times less than the movement recorded by the Earth when the Russians detonated the fifty-kiloton in Siberia."

With that operation, Alien Attack Number One began in April of 2045. President Chen was confident that this would quell any and all dissent, but only if reported and experienced correctly. He pressed the button on a remote control to view the animation of the attack one more time.

The 3D image of planet Earth with Poland at its center showed a series of shuttles in space and a few satellites. The animation zoomed in and showed a large shuttle opening its bay doors, ejecting a projectile into the atmosphere, and then taking off. The projectile sat there, and the camera zoomed back out to show the full-size Earth. Then the explosion occurred. It was massive, about one-tenth of the earth's size, right over Germany, Poland, and Russia. The animation was a computer estimate, and Redford looked at it with distrust.

"Now for the other half of this directive. Gentlemen," President Chen said.

Everyone stood as President Chen left the room. He went to the elevator and stopped at Peter's forty-eighth floor. There he found a few workers whom Peter had called in to help him, as well as Peter himself, sitting at his office desk, looking a bit frazzled. Everyone noticed President Chen enter and stood up as he passed. Some greeted him and others shook his hand. President Chen entered Peter's office and closed the door.

"Peter, I need you to be ready to go live in the next twelve hours. Here is a brief. There is no time to delay, and I won't revise it. I trust you. Are these the staff members you will need to transmit?" President Chen asked.

"Yes sir. They're all in technical departments," Peter replied.

"Good, good…please be aware that I fully trust the WPP to work, even though it is incomplete. NASA is sending a video animation of how we believe we will be protected. Of course, there is always a danger, but I think it's minimal. Do you have family in Poland?"

"No, why?"

"Read the brief and we will discuss everything later. I'm going to my office. I need a nap."

"Yes sir."

President Chen left. Peter opened the folder on his desk and began reading.

TOP SECRET

Problem: Alien missile directed to Earth projected to land near Warsaw, Poland on 4-15-2045 at 6:30 p.m. Warsaw time. Actual coordinates put the impact over the small city of Plock.

Solution: NASA will track device and detonate by missile defense honeycomb before entry into atmosphere. Explosion is expected to yield twenty to thirty kilotons of power and the WPP honeycomb should rebuff the explosive force, effectively protecting the Earth.

Potential Issue #1: WPP honeycomb system is unfinished and areas where pieces are missing will create a weak link. Impact is expected in the Northern Hemisphere, far from weak links.

Potential Issue #2: Nuclear device penetrates honeycomb and detonates over Warsaw, killing millions.

Potential Issue #3: Radiation poisoning is likely if radiation penetrates Earth's atmosphere.

Potential Issue #4: Panic is created if the population finds out in advance and thousands lose their lives unnecessarily due to mismanagement of the media.

Outcome: NASA, the NSA, and WPP all concur that the device will be stopped at the periphery of the Earth over Poland. If the rocket has a nuclear device, given the calculation of its size, the explosion should be visible as far as Portugal to the west and Uzbekistan to the east, Norway to the north, and southern Italy to the south.

Peter was scared. This was far worse than anything he had imagined. The alien threat was real, and the honeycomb would be tested for the first time in a matter of hours! He began to brainstorm the text and realized it would be hugely incendiary, just like his last release. While considering what that meant for him, he received an electronic communication from NASA. He downloaded the animations for Earth's defensive safeguards.

He played the first animation on his large screen wafer. It was similar to the one President Chen had shown at the meeting with the Joint Chiefs; it was the earth in a 3D representation, but in this version, Spain was at its center. In this version, the honeycomb was present and there was no shuttle ejecting the warhead; this animation showed an alien rocket making its way toward Earth, but various corners of the honeycomb sent laser beams toward the rocket, making it explode before it ever reached the honeycomb.

The second animation showed the potential breaking of the honeycomb, as it was weak in certain areas. The video showed the animation of the honeycomb falling to Earth, along with the rocket. The animation finished with an explosion at ground level—very destructive.

Peter worked and prepared his message. He felt ready by 9:00 a.m., but President Chen gave the explicit order that nothing was to be released until noon. Peter found it uncomfortable, but understood that six or eight hours of advance notice would create a panic in cities with millions of inhabitants. Being responsible for something like that was not something he had planned for, nor did he think he could handle that responsibility. The brief he was about to read also explained that fleeing was a terrible strategy. This message was for all of AmEarth, even though it concerned central Europe more than any other area. Germany, Poland, and Russia were the larger territories involved, and they would have to brace themselves for what was to come. Peter decided to try to sleep for a few hours before it was time to start. He lay down on his office sofa, but was unable to get anywhere near sleep, so he called Barbara.

"Honey?" Peter said.

"How are you doing? Did you sleep at all?" Barbara asked.

"No."

"What is it? What's the crisis?"

"First of all, you shouldn't worry. All of it is happening over Eastern Europe."

"What's happening?"

"Barbara, you mustn't tell anyone—not even the kids."

"Okay, Peter, but now you're scaring me."

"You had better just wait till noon and see me on the news."

"If you want to come back to this house tonight, you had better tell me now!"

"Okay, fine…the first alien attack is being countered by the WPP tomorrow at 12:30."

"I don't understand, Peter. Attack, counterattack…can you explain it to me? Are we in danger? Yes or no?"

"No, we aren't. This is happening far, far away, so relax. Watch the news at noon and don't tell anyone what I just said."

"Okay. Get some sleep; you sound terrible."

"I will, honey. Just be calm. Nothing is going to happen to us."

"I hope you're right. Love you. Bye."

"Big kiss."

Peter immediately felt better that Barbara knew. He was pragmatic, but needed that one release that could only come from his wife. He went to the media room, where his cameraman was waiting. The set showing the AmEarth logo was ready. They sat there waiting for noon to arrive, eating donuts and drinking coffee. The clock moved in slow motion until 11:55, when they all sprang to action. Peter placed eye drops in his eyes to remove all the redness and straightened his tie. His assistant applied powder all over his skin to prevent it from shining on camera. Sweat was one's worst enemy in the communications business, and he was happy that the room was cold.

Peter began the newscast intervention behind the Breaking News TV graphics on the lower third of the screen all over the world at exactly noon on that April day.

"Good evening, citizens of AmEarth. I am Peter Johansen, minister of communications for alien affairs. Only two days ago, I announced the potential for an alien attack. I explained that this was due to a preemptive strike launched back in the 1980s by the former United States of America."

He paused for effect.

"Today, AmEarth has discovered a new kind of alien rocket moving toward our planet. We cannot know if it is hostile or what type of payload it is bringing. The World Protection Project, with its honeycomb design, will shoot this vessel with its laser system to establish whether or not the ship is aggressive. We cannot know this right now. These are stock images we have from NASA, along with an animation of the honeycomb protection system doing its job."

The animation played on every TV on AmEarth. People in Europe were particularly concerned, as the image showed the northern hemisphere with Spain at its center. Evidently the makers of the computerized animation chose a random area of Europe when making the video. Panic began to strike Madrid and the surrounding cities of Spain, but before this actually began to take root the screen went on to explain further.

"These images are not current, nor real. I repeat, this animation is stock footage—a simulation. We believe that the rocket will be destroyed over the city of Plock, Poland, in exactly twenty-five minutes. The most important aspect of this is that we must trust the WPP honeycomb and have faith that it will protect us. We don't want people to panic. We ask that people stay at home and wait. Images will be shown live on this station as the rocket is disabled. This will happen at six hundred kilometers above the Earth in the exosphere. The danger is very, very low."

An animation of the honeycomb failing then came on the TV, but the gaps over the southern hemisphere suddenly appeared ominous.

"We debated at great length whether or not to show the following NASA animation. However, we want to be truthful and let everyone know that there is a possibility that the rocket could be destructive enough to harm the honeycomb itself. If this were to happen, everyone on Earth could be harmed by debris from the WPP structure itself. We do not, I repeat, *do not* anticipate this happening. If the honeycomb had been finished and all of its gaps were closed, it would be far stronger, as a blow to any of its areas would dissipate throughout. Unfortunately, the gaps over the last remaining countries to join AmEarth put us all in jeopardy, but we should all be thankful that the rocket is not following a path that would lead through any of those gaps."

Peter looked solemn and sat there with the clock behind him, which was counting down meaningfully.

"Now we will turn to images in and around Warsaw, where we have asked our anchors to show the night sky to see if the rocket will be visible from Earth."

On the screen, images began to appear showing people who had taken to the streets all over Warsaw. Knowing that a nuclear bomb would annihilate them, even if they began to flee, they had opted to go out and look up, contrary to the recommendation Peter had made. The atmosphere was something between panic and a street fair frenzy. Everyone was either cursing Ronald Reagan for turning the aliens hostile or praising AmEarth for the honeycomb, their only hope. Everyone had a wafer pointed at the sky to record the moment, even though it could be their last.

The clock reached 12:30, then 12:31, and then 12:32, at which point a huge flowering explosion could be seen over Warsaw, then an eerie silence ensued. The only sound was Peter's voice on TV and in wafers across the globe.

"This is incredible. We have just witnessed a nuclear explosion over the European plains. I am waiting to hear back from NASA on what exactly just happened."

Images kept feeding out onto the screens, as people who had just witnessed a ball of fire appear in the sky now looked up at a night sky no different from any other night. There was no debris falling from the sky, no ash, just…nothing.

"The WPP honeycomb has worked. We are seeing no immediate aftereffects of the explosion. I'm just getting confirmation from NASA that the explosion was the result of a thirty-megaton nuclear warhead. They are telling me that we can expect a loud explosion in the next twenty-five minutes, because the detonation happened so far away and the sound will be delayed. Please do not panic when the explosion is heard, it has already passed. NASA expected a smaller explosion, given the size of the rocket, but the technology the aliens possess is clearly superior to our own. We can report that the Earth is safe, and that NASA will send us an update of any possible damage to the honeycomb."

The street images coming in now showed a wild party in Warsaw, as well as in other cities around the world. Peter had an idea that he knew was off-script, but the moment's adrenaline had him in a frenzy and he shot from the hip.

"I think April fifteenth should be declared a holiday! This is truly the first global party I've ever experienced. People all over the world, in all different time zones, have a reason to celebrate!" Peter touched his earpiece, where he was being fed updated information. "This just in: NASA reports that all areas of the honeycomb are intact. The WPP honeycomb will keep us safe from the alien threat! Brace for the noise coming, it will be heard all over the world."

Scott, Cate, Barbara, and Brianna were glued to the TV wafer. The world had gone from terror to a global celebration. Not only had the WPP worked, but Peter was the sole source of information on the largest news story of the century. He was fast becoming the world's best-known human being, next to President Chen Tyson, of course.

The boom sounded loud over Poland and could be heard live as far as northern Germany and Southern Switzerland. The whole world heard it via TV exactly as Peter had announced.

"And there is the sound, boy it was strong. I think we should all thank AmEarth for the WPP it worked! We are safe!"

FOURTEEN

President Chen was very pleased with the nuclear detonation. His advisors had been right. The Earth had not been in danger. Now, all the detractors and disbelievers were in a tough position. He knew that he needed to seal the deal, so AmEarth would be respected. He summoned a meeting of the Joint Chiefs and called in his possible successor.

"Peter," President Chen spoke to him in a serious tone.

"Yes, sir? Did you approve of my reporting?" Peter asked.

"Of course. It was fine, fine. I'm calling on the other matter."

"What is that, sir?"

"The issue of succession that I mentioned."

"Oh…well, my family is fine with it, and I'm still very honored and excited."

"Good. When I became president, there was no choice or plan for the next one. We did not maintain the US system of elections, as that would jeopardize the continuity of the WPP and NASA's benevolence. We have been careful not to politicize the actions of the defense of the Earth, so elections were suspended. Now, Essie is saying that the succession should be based on merit, arguing that humans should not elect via popularity or good looks or even political tendencies. Instead, the successor should be chosen by the data analysis. In other words, she will find the best person to keep AmEarth running smoothly."

"And that's me?"

"Frankly, yes. But it can't be announced that you are suddenly the winner and replacement. Essie will select the top ten candidates and then a worldwide popular vote will elect the best candidate. Essie will insure you are singled as the top contender. I don't expect that you will fall out of favor with her anytime soon, but the process will familiarize humanity with ten candidates, then three or four favorites, and finally the chosen successor. This way, by the time you become the next supreme president, the Earth will be ready for my departure and your arrival."

"But I might still not be the president, right? I mean, there is a chance that the popular vote might leave me out?"

"Yes, but that's highly unlikely. In fact, Essie can't seem to find people with your level of recognition in public service, meaning that you have reached the entertainer level. Only well-known actors, sportsmen, and rock stars rank above you in terms of recognition level."

"Mr. President, may I be candid?"

"Surely."

"Do you know how long a president's tenure will be?"

"No. Essie will be calling the shots from here on out. It will be best that you don't know, in line with the rest of the world. You will have no reason to change your priorities due to the end of your tenure, and so forth. It is akin to being a king, but the interests of AmEarth will be inseparable from your own interests. You might serve until your death or for only a year. We cannot know. I spent the latter part of this decade designing this program. If a better suited person arrives on the scene, the computer might begin to track this individual and then make the decision to begin a successor process."

"Are we leaving everything up to Essie?"

"No; there is the Supercomputer Committee, of which I am the chairman, but we do respect the findings. After all, we wouldn't have ministers from around the globe working in New York had it not been for the solution that Essie found to political integration. Essie can manage an enormous amount of information that no human could possibly control, and it has guided AmEarth toward the best use of the world's resources. Yes, it has made some humans immensely rich, while some are still not living that well, but the purpose is for improvement—the gradual improvement of all. Essie has deciphered that capitalism is the best system for growth, and we agree that the American Way works. However, it is also benevolent and has prevented most of the world's ills from the past, like famine and disease, not to mention war. Overall, it has worked to improve AmEarth and our lives."

"So the president just follows her directives?"

"Kind of. We ask her what to do and plug in the parameters of our desired outcomes, and she helps us to make decisions. Say you want to help Sri Lanka, for some reason; perhaps you think it has been neglected or that they have something new to contribute. As president, you have the power to request a computer review of Sri Lanka's assets and plug in the new parameters. Imagine that they have discovered a new flower with a new aroma. Well, Essie would guide you to make directives that would regulate the planting of said flower and the value of its resource so that it would not be manipulated by unregulated markets. Overnight, you could have a new industry in Sri Lanka. Maybe the press of AmEarth could run stories on the new scent, helping those citizens reach billions of consumers who wanted to experience the new smell. You see?"

"I do. That sounds fantastic."

"If you think of the progress of AmEarth in the past two decades, you couldn't call it anything other than fantastic. You have no idea of the power contained in the supercomputer. However, you won't be able to run against it. If she determines a course that you oppose personally or morally, you won't be able to stop her."

"That sounds ominous."

"It is. I've had to approve directives that I don't support, but the outcome has been better than I imagined every time. Essie might steer you in a direction you disagree with, but she anticipates the reaction by the counterpart, and the threat is simply that…a threat. You see?"

"I guess she has learned to bluff."

"Not exactly, but she has learned to anticipate moves. It's more like chess than poker. We will start the succession effective immediately."

"Excuse me?"

"We have begun the process already. Expect an announcement from me tomorrow at 1700 hours."

Peter was in a state of shock, but all he could say was, "Yes sir."

"And Peter, don't forget that the communication skills you have are skills needed for the presidency. You are the physical embodiment of the AmEarth mission and the human voice of Essie's directives. You're not a traditional politician, vying for votes and pandering to the masses. You're something more."

President Chen clicked off the phone and left his office for his appointment with the Joint Chiefs of Staff. Peter was stunned and confused. The succession pattern would now be computer-chosen and massaged for a public-approved yet computer-chosen outcome. He was not too happy with the idea that people could be so easily manipulated by Essie. This new presidency felt empty; not nearly as powerful as President Chen's term had seemed. Having a Essie operating behind him with the objective of helping the "greater good" was not so bad, but considering that he couldn't imagine what she would determine going forward, Peter was essentially like anyone else in AmEarth.

President Chen knew what to expect and how to manipulate it. The Joint Chiefs were celebrating in the conference room as the sun was setting on the New York skyline. The slightly drifting windows of the building's thirty-ninth floor made the room look like it was turning along with the Earth. President Chen entered, and they all clapped for what seemed like minutes before he stopped them with a wave of his hand.

"Director Kanter, please give us your report," President Chen said.

"We have detonated the thirty kiloton warhead over Poland at 600 kilometers above the surface. All the fallout remained in the exosphere, where no human will ever come into contact with its radiation," Dr. Larry Kanter, director of NASA, explained.

"General Roberts, report."

"We have seen diminished activity on subversive social sites. Our main focus in Eastern Europe has observed an immediate drop in participation at the rallies. Immediately after the explosion, a massive anti-AmEarth rally dissipated. Most people no longer doubt that aliens exist. We believe that subversive leaders will continue espousing these views, but most ears will be deaf to them. We're going to determine who these leaders are and try and integrate them into society," General Mark Roberts of the AmEarth Army reported.

"Good. Perfect."

"Mr. President," General Roberts said.

"Yes."

"I just wanted to apologize for having doubted the operation. It was flawless. Your scientists were right on the mark."

"No problem, your uncertainty was understandable. Nothing like this has ever been done before and we were all preoccupied."

General Roberts was worried that he might be perceived as a threat to the inner core of AmEarth. The Joint Chiefs and the executive had a special relationship that relied heavily on Essie and her directives. He was, after all, one of twelve core members of the Supercomputer Committee. The top secret information contained within that committee was so sensitive that any minimal inkling of rebellion could be seen as treason.

Blind trust was not something with which any of these individuals were comfortable, but it was usually difficult to go against Essie's directives, as they always seemed to work. Experience was making these men rely on her more and more, and their trust had not only yielded the greatest empire in history, but also an improvement for humans around the globe. It was hard to find a flaw with the system, although they all knew that there could be a scenario in which Essie could fail. It was for this purpose that President Chen had created the committee to oversee the computer's questions and answers. It would be important that this committee knew all the realities of AmEarth in a highly classified manner. The committee was composed of the five chiefs of staff, President Chen, two top NASA scientists/officials, the director of the NSA, and a man by the name of Sergio Ramirez-Bulatov. This last member was a brilliant art director whom President Chen had recruited to conceptualize and create the alien look and feel. These twelve people knew that AmEarth was founded on a lie; not about whether aliens existed or not—the existence of generic aliens was not in question—but rather the lie of contact and reciprocal aggression with them.

Essie was not located at the Shadow White House building. It was a sensitive issue to President Chen, and he knew that any threat directed toward AmEarth would probably be centered on New York, so he had placed the servers for her very far away. After all, it was the brain of AmEarth. As in any organism, President Chen had decided to place Essie at its head. To him, this should be far from the extremities—the cities. The computer needed a nice cold climate and a powerful satellite system to connect to the Internet, so the northern regions of Alberta, the former Canada, had been chosen. Deep in a concrete bunker, protected by a system of locks that Essie herself opened and closed, and powered by geothermal energy received from the earth beneath it. The work of the committee centered on fulfilling the directive of finding a new supreme president who did not know the reality of AmEarth. It was Essie's solution to a problem that had vexed President Chen. The leader of the world must believe that the alien threat was real. Otherwise, he would need to avoid the media, as President Chen now did. It was a serious problem for AmEarth, because lying was difficult. It was not that President Chen couldn't lie; he was actually quite good at it, but software programs in every police department could now detect facial lies. No one could outplay that technology without looking psychopathic.

AmEarth needed a Peter Johansen to maintain its continuity just as much as it needed aliens threatening the Earth. Without such a threat to galvanize public support, the viability of the AmEarth empire was impossible. Essie had prognosticated these necessities and had begun spewing directives to achieve this outcome.

"Gentlemen, we will begin my succession by announcing the ten candidates for the presidency of AmEarth tomorrow. Of course, you all know that whoever is chosen must not know the truth behind AmEarth, but must be open to following the directives. It will be a powerful position, but limited by Essie to a great extent. I believe that she has selected Peter Johansen, so barring any popular backlash, he is slated to be the next AmEarth president. Any objections?"

No one uttered a word. The imprimatur of Essie was enough.

***

The work of Sergio Ramirez-Bulatov was not known to humanity. He was responsible for the appearance of the alien technology, its rockets, computer chips, and the physiology of the aliens themselves. Of course, no alien had ever come to Earth, but humans had "received" images of them and had "sent" their own.

The images received by these "aliens" had to have a completely different environment. To mask the problem of a reality that would involve many workers and potential leaks, Sergio had created a low-resolution solution.

His aliens were out-of-focus dark brown creatures that seemed to live in round rooms where they floated. President Chen had sketched the idea of a society in which advanced creatures would be self-reliant and alone. Sergio had come up with the idea of a large amniotic-like sac that kept the aliens happy, each like a child in the womb. This image was easy to manipulate with different size aliens having different features, unclothed and happy—always in a similar space. The insularity of the housing avoided the problem of having to show the planet or its fauna, and mankind seemed to accept this. It was a point brought up only by the alien deniers, but as issues grew, so did the solutions. In one episode, President Chen had asked Sergio to show a peek of the planet by permitting a slit of a round room to allow the exterior in. Sergio had created a sky with a red sun and large puffy pink clouds that did not allow the horizon to be seen. It was an abstract image that quelled deniers, as it showed a different size sun with a different quality of light.

Sergio Ramirez-Bulatov had been discovered by President Chen and vetted by Essie as the perfect candidate for this delicate task. He had been born to a Russian mother and a Mexican father. His parents had divorced when he was thirteen because his father was an incorrigible cheater. His mother's brother had been a famous Russian graphic artist turned pop artist by the gallery system back in the 1990s. His father was a Mexican entrepreneur who ran bars and discos and who could charm a ladybug into marrying a scorpion.

Sergio had studied art in London before working in New York, and was recruited into New Zealand's Weta studios at the turn of the century by filmmaker Peter Jackson. He had worked at Weta and had become involved with Robbie Taylor, the daughter of the duo owners, Richard Taylor and Tania Rodger, essentially ending his career. He had been fired by Mr. Taylor on the basis of an old trick used to fire art directors he no longer wanted—namely adding retardant to latex so that a project was late to set. Through no fault of his own he was out of work, and without knowing that his dismissal had been unjust, he had tried his luck at many careers and had attempted to continue his relationship. He had worked odd jobs, but eventually had to leave New Zealand because there was simply no reason for an art director to be on the island unless he was working for Weta. His relationship had failed, and he'd entered a mild depression. It was at this point that the president of AmEarth had called him.

Recruited by President Chen to create a body of work that could have no signature, he had essentially traded all of the rewards of individual fame for immense fortune and a position on the most powerful committee on Earth. The blow from being fired from Weta, plus his parents' divorce, had yielded the perfect personality that President Chen and Essie needed. Sergio was quiet, hardworking, and a loner. He crafted and sculpted in completely secluded warehouses and only opened the loading dock to deliver his work directly to NASA director Larry Kanter.

Unknowingly, his work could in itself be a clue to be used against the system. He had created the artwork as originally as he possibly could, but any creation is always a representation of its artist. Of course, this could only be done by people who were familiar with his work, and those were few. His mother could recognize the work, but she swore that she would be quiet, and he kept her in regal conditions—she wouldn't risk losing her only source of income. If he was outed as the creator of the Keplerian race, AmEarth would think that he himself had leaked the news, which would constitute treason—the only offense punishable by death. His only comfort was that he worked completely alone. No one other than President Chen and NASA knew the whereabouts of his studio, and he did all of the work himself. The first set of artifacts he crafted with extreme precision and where sent to the Smithsonian Museum as the true originals.

Ramirez-Bulatov then proceeded to make a multi-million orb empire because his companies held the rights to fabricate all of the replicas of the aliens for sale to museums, schools, and universities. He would make these a grade lower in quality so they looked fake, this way keeping the Smithsonian works looking authentic. He also received a handsome paycheck for being on the supercomputer committee. Because Ramirez-Bulatov had invented and designed the aliens it was important to keep the source material from other manufacturers, otherwise the risk was high that they could detect foul play. His empire of replicas was anonymously held through shield corporations and the name most people knew for where these products came from was Roberta, LLC.

FIFTEEN

That June, President Chen took to the airwaves for the first time in many months. The citizens of the world had not seen President Chen speak publicly in almost a year. His script had to be perfectly truthful. No mention of aliens was the key element to ensure that his speech worked. This event was announced days earlier on a constant commercial rotation, so billions would be watching. President Chen was particularly popular around the world, but rumors said that he had lost his vocal chords or worse. Presidential speeches always took place at the huge terrace in front of the UN building, and it was packed to capacity that night. President Chen stood before the front row of a bleacher with five long rows of government ministers that included every continent, race, language, and fashion style on the planet. Peter Johansen was sitting directly above President Chen, three rows up.

"Ladies and gentlemen of AmEarth...As you all know, the government of our world now encompasses one hundred percent of the globe. We are a single world with a common interest—the survival and well-being of our species. The human race is better now than it has ever been. Despite the amazing strides we have taken, it is time for change. I must announce that this twentieth year of my presidency will be my last. I believe there is a need for a successor to my post."

Sounds of shock and dismay rose from those gathered in the bleachers nearby.

"It has been a great honor for me to have overseen so many important developments, and to have experienced them with you, my fellow citizens of the world. I personally asked the supercomputer at NASA to craft the best system of governance with excellent sustainability so that AmEarth can grow and prosper for all. The supercomputer scanned and found the best available candidates for president in the world. It accessed everyone's IQ, age, health, education, career path, and financial records. It found individuals with selfless dispositions and great credentials to serve AmEarth honorably. Not all individuals are made to be leaders, but those that are can be found. We have received a list of ten potential candidates for president. The vote will take place a month from now. Please study the candidates at your leisure, as they all have a wafer site for your use. All humans over eighteen years of age anywhere on AmEarth have the right to vote. The top three candidates will go to a final vote one week later."

Some noises emanated from the audience and Chen continued...

"Ladies and gentlemen, the tenure of the next supreme president will be defined by the supercomputer based on his or her performance. The next president will be in charge as long as the responsibilities of the position are met. If there is any inkling of corruption, favoritism, nepotism, or improper conduct, it will end the term. You must know that my tenure was ended by the supercomputer as she determined that I was aging and becoming tired. This has been an extremely stressful job, and without the computer's directives, it would have been an impossible one. The directives pointed at my retirement, and I have yet to find fault in those directives. I will not go against the supercomputer!"

People began rumbling comments, asking for him to stay. He felt the warmth in the voices of the crowd.

"I can't thank you enough for your kind words. I truly can't thank you enough."

People continued cheering for President Chen and this time, he waited for it to die down.

"One important issue that everyone must understand is that technology in our era has enabled the ultimate analysis of the world's resources and has optimized these things for mankind to thrive. We are at the threshold of a promising and wonderful reality, and I have been lucky to see it in my lifetime. It will be a wonder to see the world ten or twenty years from now. To those who disagree with the use of our powerful supercomputer, I say this: Do you want to go back to a world of wars? Famine? Racism? Disease? Chaos? Financial ruin? I say no, never again!"

The crowd went crazy, and for a while, it looked more like a party than a press conference.

"I have a list of the names of the people who have been selected, and as I call them, I would ask them to come down and share the stage with me. General John Redford of the air force, Mr. Alvin Messersmith of the Interior, Mr. Peter Johansen of Communications…"

The crowd cheered wildly for Peter, something that had not happened with the other two names. The cheering lasted for quite a while and President Chen smiled, knowing that Essie had been right again. Seven more names were called, but the cheering was never equal to Peter's moment. The ten figures stood in front of the UN Plaza, blinded by the lights and swept up in the madness of the crowd. History was being made.

SIXTEEN

The voting took place one month from that day via wafers online. It was a twenty-four hour process to reach all the time zones on Earth. The three top candidates were selected and announced the following day:

Peter Johansen, minister of Communications
Jonathan Richardson, minister of Finance
Sasha Obama-LeVaughn, minister of Cultural Affairs

The following week was a flurry of news reports and commercials that cast a favorable view of Peter. Essie steered the best times to interrupt people's television viewing with positive messages on Peter and mediocre takes on the other candidates. Peter Johansen was then elected supreme president winning the popular vote by an unprecedented margin exactly as President Chen had anticipated. He was the most recognizable human on the planet and the first worldwide elected supreme president of the world. President Chen had been elected in the United States before AmEarth became the empire that it was now, so there was a difference having eight billion humans voting. These citizens now knew Peter Johansen's name by heart.

Neil Chen and Peter spent many days together transitioning the government. Peter read more than he ever had in his life and learned the system of AmEarth governance from the top down. However, many ideals of democracy held dear by him were missing from the structure. This was a top-down system with the paternalism of an authoritarian regime.

The main difference between this and previous authoritarian regimes was semantics and the pretense of goodness. Evidently, the owners of the means of production remained in power, but now their wealth had increased exponentially. The only check on this mercantile force was the ocassional Essie directive that allowed AmEarth to redistribute some wealth to the bottom half via jobs. Having a huge anti-alien army was expensive, but Essie kept it as a fixed percentage of taxation and now that every human paid taxes to the same government it was a large number. Peter studied and toiled hard through this learning experience, which lasted only sixty days.

The time passed quickly and Peter was not sure he was ready for such a daunting task. August first came like a whiplash. The official ceremony had been promoted like a blockbuster movie and it took place at the UN Plaza. Peter was sweating, as it was a hot and humid day, but he looked the part perfectly as he was sworn in by the Chief Justice of the Supreme World Court. He had been flown in via helicopter from Washington, DC, where the court was located.

"Do you swear to uphold the charter of AmEarth?" Justice Rodriguez asked.

"I do," Peter replied.

"Do you swear to place 'the greater good' over all other interests?"

"I do."

"I now declare you supreme president of AmEarth!"

The crowd cheered and waited for Peter to speak. He had prepared a speech, but words momentarily failed him. Then, with the dignity of the most powerful man on the planet, he began to speak.

"Ladies and gentlemen, ministers, Supreme World Court justices; I have been chosen to become the second supreme president and fully understand the enormous responsibility this job represents. I want you to know that my career was not on this path, but I am here because of our system's directives and because you desired it. I don't feel uniquely qualified or special. I am just a regular human, like any of you, and I am standing here today much to my own surprise. Perhaps that is a better way to get here than through the bickering and backstabbing of politics. I can promise you this: I will make every day in this office count toward humanity's continued success on this beautiful planet. I will place all of my effort in working with world leaders and the supercomputer to achieve the best outcomes for our entire world. I will take all grievances seriously and address them promptly. I am at your service. We are a world that has great advantages, so let's make the best of that and foster the well-being of the human race!"

Peter paused as the cheering began.

"I come from a background of hard-working people. A few years ago, I felt special to be American and I loved this soil. Now, I feel a much greater connection to humanity, and we are all going to love our soil, our Earth, because it belongs to all of us. People around the globe will all be able to enjoy all the promise of a great future, just as America uniquely felt in the past. AmEarth will deliver a better life to all humans."

Peter believed these words, even if most of the eight billion people listening had few of the luxuries to which he was accustomed. The crowd continued cheering until Peter motioned for silence.

"We finally have the directive and resources to finish the WPP, which is expected to close fully by 2046. The protection it afforded us has changed the state of our planet, and we are all overjoyed that the recent act of aggression was contained so successfully. However, let's not become complacent. We cannot know if the alien race is determined to continue these attacks, so we must always prepare for the worst. We have begun a campaign to communicate our peaceful intentions to the aliens, but all of these efforts take twenty-three-and-a-half years to receive a response. Our only path is to be strong and protective of our precious human species. Let's remember that there might be other alien species out there, so any effort to stay safe must also account for those other possibilities. We must all work together to continue the WPP and meet the needs of our governing system to maintain a happy and healthy world."

The crowd cheered again.

"I want to finish by saying that a major breakthrough in technology has been achieved through the Ministry of Engineering and Alien Technology. Minister Oliphant has informed me that we have mastered the weight-to-energy ratio of battery technology. From now on, we have the ability to power all commercial aviation with lightweight batteries and powerful new motors. We have begun to deploy new vessels into space that will capture solar power and self-sustain their batteries to power the rockets we send to Kepler 3763. We will be faster and better in terms of our packages, and we have determined to send only friendly payloads to the aliens. I will be discussing these technological advancements in detail as we receive more information. May the world be safe, may it be free, and may all of you have a wonderful tomorrow!"

A spontaneous cheer erupted and Peter motioned for Barbara, Brianna, and Scott to stand beside him. They joined him and the first computer-selected first family stood in front of billions of people around the globe.

The world felt protected. The WPP honeycomb had worked. The first worldwide holiday was proclaimed. People were happy. Essie had found a human with attributes connecting him to most of humanity. He was tall, but not too tall; strong, but not too strong; handsome, but not intolerably so; smart, but not a geek; wealthy, but not rich; and he had two kids and a beautiful wife. They made the perfect picture of the desires of humanity. They saluted the crowd.

***

The next day, Peter sat in the supreme president's chair in the glass office that had once belonged to Neil Chen Tyson. His picture was being printed and would be placed in every government office from New York to Patagonia, from Ecuador to Vietnam! It was all still surreal to him. The speed of his rise from deputy of foreign affairs to supreme president had been a process of only months! There had been none of the insane years of a president's career as in the past, no election name-calling, and no dirty political campaigns. It was a civilized process now that humanity had a shared interest—survival. It was humans as a race against the alien threat, which meant no more territorial disputes or infighting.

AmEarth under President Chen had left a legacy of fear directed toward aliens, which was indisputably terrifying, but it had united humanity. It had worked to create an empire and a single government. Many of Essie's solutions had felt un-American, such as the government health care system, which had broken many corporate backs. If a man contracted tuberculosis in Cairo, the World Health Ministry would isolate him and take care of the threat. President Chen had never foreseen that Essie would push toward government-run systems like this, but as long as his committee could keep her directives away from other industries, like those in his family, he was fine.

It had been a funny twist of fate that had caused New York and Washington to flip. New York was now the political capital of the world and Washington held up the financial sphere. The power of the Federal Reserve had become enormous, as it converted all currencies to Orbs and enacted rules and regulations for inflation and interest rates. It was an electronic currency, and all global operations emanated from Washington, DC. Paper money and coins had been eliminated in 2027 when the Orb was introduced. This had been the single hardest directive to follow for

President Chen. The world still remembered the riots from back then, but the move had resulted in enormous savings and increased efficiency for the financial system. Illicit financial activity had fallen to a minimum and the greater good had been served.

Peter began his presidency with his first briefing by the Joint Chiefs in the War Room. The meeting was uneventful, as they repeated the same old WPP gap-closing necessities. The meeting finished with a great deal of handshaking and congratulating. The Joint Chiefs seemed aloof, and Peter had a strange feeling that he was being left out. He guessed that they all missed Neil Chen being the president, or they weren't yet sure whether he would turn out to be a wise choice. He hadn't exactly proven himself.

On his desk was the first electronic communication from the supercomputer. Having a directive this quickly was unexpected. In fact, it was a list of one hundred top directives that had not yet been accomplished. The top one was in red.

"Mr. President?" Rosemary said.
"Yes," Peter answered.
"It's ex-president Chen on line one."
"Thank you, Rosemary."

Peter picked up.

"Mr. President," Peter said.

"Peter, did you see the computer directives?" Chen said, skipping the pleasantries and getting down to business.

"Yes, they are in front of me."

"Are there any red ones?"

"Yes, one."

"If the directive is red, it must be priority one and it must be fulfilled. The computer will not function until you have cleared the red ones. Do you understand?"

"What do you mean, it won't function?"

"It won't like it."

"And?"

"It will make your life hell. In 2030, I tried to prevent the World Health Ministry from breaking up the control of the pharmaceutical companies. I'm a capitalist and feared that if the supercomputer wanted to regulate the health system to such a degree then it might also go after other industries. I failed to recognize that health care is totally different from other industries, like consumer goods or tourism. The greater good principle required health care to be managed by a single player. Period."

"So the computer felt leftist to you, but you couldn't stop it."

"I tried, but it began to shut down. Powerful forces can be unleashed if you try and act against it."

"So in the end you accepted the demise of those companies?"

"And I lost many personal friends. There are people with whom I had great friendships who would kill me today. Being president is not for everyone. You, on the other hand, will be able to direct without allegiance to any industry or group. But don't forget, the red ones must be followed."

"Yes, Mr. President," Peter responded robotically.

"Former president. Call me Neil. Bye."

The phone clicked as Peter looked down at the first red directive of his tenure.

TOP SECRET

Directive 25853: Population Limit to Planet Earth.

Problem: The total population sustainable by planet Earth is 8.5 billion people, give or take 100 million inhabitants. The total area of arable land, the population of farm animals, and the sustainable fishing of marine protein are at full capacity with this limit. Moreover, at this level, the population cannot live with an equality of consumption of these life-sustaining substances. The optimal population for the planet would be between six and seven billion inhabitants if they all desire access to equal and optimal consumption of life-sustaining foods. Overpopulation started before this computer began its operations.

Solution: Directive 25853 requires the legislation of licenses for the privilege of reproduction. Human males will be the control group and each male will be limited to two live births during his lifetime. The necessity of a male vasectomy after the birth of the second child will become a directive for the World Health System. DNA printing of all human births in any location on the planet will prevent that human from further reproduction.

All men are to be informed that their moral obligation is this limit. If a male impregnates more than one woman during the nine-month gestation period, his promiscuity will be deemed an act of treason against the sustainability of AmEarth.

All women will be required to achieve a college-level education before reproducing. No woman can reproduce if uneducated, unless she has reached the age of thirty. The penalty for transgression will be a choice between termination of the pregnancy if discovered before the first trimester, or adoption. If the pregnancy is caught after the first trimester, there will be no termination choice and adoption will be mandatory.

If a family wants to have more than two children, they can adopt, provided that they can prove they have the income required.

There can be no exceptions to this rule.

End of DN 25853

Peter was stunned. Had this been Chen's plan all along? Get out right before this incredibly invasive and sensitive directive? He would be hated by religious groups, and the strong separation of church and state would not be enough of a buffer to protect this directive. AmEarth had established a strong separation from religious organizations, but this would not be taken lightly by many faiths. God, after all, was not completely dead in the minds of many humans. Women would also hate the forced adoptions. These penalties seemed very severe.

He called Rosemary on the intercom.

"Rosemary, get me Dr. Rosencrans at Health," Peter said.

"You want him on the phone or in your office?" Rosemary said.

"How did Chen ask so that you would know right away?"

"He would say, 'Rosemary, get me such and such in here.' Or he would say, 'I need such and such.' So I guess 'get me' meant send up, and 'I need' meant call. How would you like it?"

"Get me Dr. Rosencrans."

"Yes sir."

Through the glass, Peter could see Rosemary dialing the call and probably speaking to Dr. Rosencrans's secretary. Behind her, he could see out of the windows to Queens and beyond. He began to miss his former life, but Barbara was on cloud nine and loved living in the Shadow White House. The apartment occupied floors 98 through 100 and was decorated as an exact replica of the actual White House, including stairs, high ceilings, and the identical floor plan. Even the windows were old-style double-hung wooden windows, but they were directly in front of the actual windows of the skyscraper's exterior. This was a bit surreal, as the view did not match the style of the home, but it worked visually, even if the windows did not provide air when opened. The old White House had been open to the public year round and had become a national monument where governmental proceedings no longer took place.

Barbara had her own First Lady's office on the sixty-ninth floor. She had a staff and a secretary to deal with all aspects of her public affairs. Her only regret was having to move her daughter to Trinity Academy in Manhattan. She did not want her daughter being raised in the city, but her new Secret Service detail would drive Brianna to school and back from the Shadow White House every day.

Brianna was thrilled, even though she did miss her best friends. The boys at Trinity were much cuter than the Connecticut crowd at Darien, and they all acted with such maturity. They were funnier, too, and she was courted like a new species of flower, a fact that she loved. Her friendship with Camilla was still great, and they chatted on their wafers constantly. Brianna could also visit Camilla whenever she liked. This new chapter in her life made her feel powerful, although she did not know how to use this newfound asset.

Scott had been accepted at Columbia University, Harvard, Yale, Stanford, and Brown. He really wanted to go to California, but his parents forced him to go to Columbia for security reasons. He was accepted by the Sigma Chi fraternity and tried his best to play down the fact that a Secret Service agent was always nearby. Being the president's son had its ups and downs, and he did not like being brown-nosed. He kept in touch with Cate and as many of his high school friends as he could, but he felt torn inside.

Peter knew that being President would be a huge task, but having the supercomputer calling the shots was quite strange. He was beginning to feel used, like a puppet or a king in the modern-day UK, and that was not a position he wanted. He needed to know more about how his office actually worked.

Dr. Rosencrans appeared on the elevator landing, and Peter could see him walking toward the office. He was a strange-looking man with glasses and such disheveled hair as only a doctor can sport in such an environment. However, even if he'd wanted to, there wasn't much that could be done with his curly white hair.

"Mr. President," Dr. Richard Rosencrans began.

They shook hands.

"Please, sit down," Peter said.

Peter then pushed the button that made the room instantly private, as if encased in wood.

"Rich, I have a problem," Peter said.

"How can I help you?" Richard answered cautiously, still trying to determine what kind of supreme president Peter would be.

"I have a directive from the supercomputer on a—how can I put this?—on a Malthusian issue."

"You are referring to Malthus, the overpopulation economist of the eighteenth century?"

"Yes."

"Let me guess; the supercomputer agrees with Malthus?"

"Yes."

"Wow…"

"Exactly. It has determined the limit of Earth's food supply at 8.5 billion people. Actually, it is requesting a reduction to a sustainable 6.5 billion if everyone wants to eat well."

"A reduction! How in the name of God is it asking us to accomplish that!"

"It isn't, Richard. Relax. It's not calling for an immediate reduction. It is, however, calling for a Chinese solution. And that is where you come in."

"It wants to limit our reproduction to one baby! Like in China during the twentieth century?"

"No…yes. Well, two."

Peter held up two fingers.

"Well, that's better than one," Richard said.

"Yes. I think the computer assumes that a maximum of two per couple will have a diminishing effect on the population, as statistically, there will be couples with one or none, so the outcome is reductive. In time, we will reach a state where all humans can share the same level of health and lifestyle," Peter said.

"And my department is expected to achieve this how?"

"All males will have to limit the number of women they impregnate. This is a directive for Communications, not you, but you will enforce the tracking of all births by the same father. In other words, if a man has two live births, he will be called in by Health and given a vasectomy."

"And if he refuses?"

"It will be considered treason."

Richard paled noticeably.

"We also need to give licenses to people who want to have children. This will ensure that they are aware of their responsibilities to AmEarth and the world. Health Department licenses will be the best, as that is really your area."

"But we don't have the bureaucracy for something like that. We're not the DMV!" Dr. Rosencrans said, but checked his tone as he realized that he was raising his voice.

"But you do grant inoculation cards, right? Please, Richard, we're all in this together. Having children is a huge responsibility."

Peter looked down at his computer and saw Richard's bio, which gave him something to work with. Richard got up from his chair and began pacing the floor, thinking.

"You have kids; you know this," Peter continued.

"Well, I guess that nurses could administer the licenses," Dr. Rosencrans agreed. "So it would take some of the strain off doctors and the system."

"Good, then that settles it. I'll send a copy of the directive to your inbox."

Peter called Rosemary on the intercom.

"Rosemary, get me Bergman," Peter declared, moving from one problem to the next.

Peter stood up, at which point Richard stood as well.

"Richard, you'll need to collect every DNA record of every citizen in the world, Bolivia and New Zealand included. If you need more people, let me know. The army is at your full disposal to help gather all the samples you need. The directive also asked for minimum education levels for mothers. I'll be speaking to Bergman next, and he'll get back in touch with you. Thank you for your time."

"Thank you, Mr. President. This is a hefty directive," Richard responded, still with a cautious note in his voice.

"I know. And it's my first one! I know I don't need to tell you this, but you need to keep this under wraps until I make my announcement. Then you can put your plan in place to follow it. Is that clear?"

"Crystal. Top secret."

Richard made a hand gesture to indicate a key locking his lips. Peter pushed the button that immediately turned his office back into a glass bowl. As he did that, out of the elevator stepped the slim and elegant Janet Bergman, minister of education. Dr. Rosencrans left the office, and they greeted each other in the hallway. Bergman entered the office.

"Minister Bergman, what a pleasure," Peter welcomed her. "Please sit down, Janet. Would you like some tea or coffee?"

"Coffee would be great," Janet said.

"Two coffees, Rosemary," Peter spoke into the intercom.

He pushed the privacy button, turning the walls brown once again.

"Janet, we have received a directive that is both ominous and complicated. The supercomputer has calculated that we are reaching the Malthusian limit on the level of our population. Essentially, we must prevent the famine and calamity that this could bring down on humanity's collective head," Peter stated matter-of-factly.

"Oh my God," Janet said, unable to control her surprise.

"I know. It's shocking, but also fairly obvious."

"Yes, I guess that's true."

"I need you to follow the directive and coordinate with the minister of health so that all births are recorded. You will need to conduct a full crosscheck to achieve this. Furthermore, all women must obtain undergraduate college-level education before they are allowed to reproduce."

"What? How can we force them to do that?"

"We're not forcing them. It is only if they want to reproduce before the age of thirty. The directive is lifted at age thirty or when a degree is obtained, whichever comes first. Now, let me give you the full idea before you panic. The supercomputer will limit all human males to contributing to two live births. The Health Department will monitor all births and determine the father through DNA. This way, if a male has two recorded births, he will undergo a mandatory vasectomy. If he impregnates more than two, say, during the gestation period, then he will be punished as a traitor to AmEarth."

"No!" Janet exclaimed, her face contorted in shock.

"Yes. And you will handle the mandatory education of women. As we both know, the best contraception ever devised has been education, but culturally, it has been difficult to achieve. Now, AmEarth will legislate this."

"So if a woman cannot complete schooling for whatever reason, then she cannot start a family until she turns thirty?"

"Those women will be in the minority if you do your job correctly."

"Is this a punishment to them?"

"I don't know. It might be a reward. I think it's a greater punishment to have a child when you're still a child yourself, or when you can't take proper care of it. I suppose that the computer identifies thirty as a more responsible age for most people. After all, we need to lower the number of inhabitants without mass famine or utter chaos. This imposed limit, in addition to those people with one child or no children, will eventually reduce the world's population to a sustainable level."

"This does make some sense, but I don't think men will like this at all…nor women."

"It won't be easy, but it's necessary. I know that treason will spike on my watch, but no one said this job was full of easy decisions!"

Rosemary knocked and entered, followed by a staff member who brought in a large tray with a beautiful coffee service in elegant china. They left quietly and Peter and Janet were left to enjoy their coffee, sipping in silence for a moment.

"You certainly have a beautiful view," Janet said casually, making small talk as she stirred in the sugar.

"Yes, it's one of the perks," Peter joked back.

"I sure hope this directive works."

"We've had tough ones before. Remember the Orb?"

"Whew, that one was crazy. Riots. AmEarth almost broke up after that…it was shaky for a long time. At least now, AmEarth includes one hundred percent of the planet; that should make things easier."

"I don't know how men will react to this, Janet. I expect that the southern hemisphere will be much harder to convince, but your department has made great strides there."

"It's really thanks to the wafer distribution, which has made sizeable inroads in teaching. The directive that pushed for "entertainment education" was one I didn't initially agree with, but it has been amazing. Having great programming that is customized to pause and teach while keeping the viewer engaged was a revolutionary idea. Education has never looked back."

Peter was enjoying the conversation and the articulate intelligence of Minister Bergman. She was ten years his senior, but he could still see the beautiful, youthful spirit within her. Her Chanel suit looked as if it had been tailored to her body by hand. At eighteen, she must have been a knockout, Peter thought.

"Please keep this to yourself until I make the announcement. Then, you should immediately coordinate with Civil Affairs so that no marriage is permitted outside of the new directive laws. You must also head up the Education Services side of things to monitor all women who stray from the education path," Peter explained.

"What happens to women who are in the middle of their education when they get pregnant?" Janet asked.

"The punishment needs to be severe; this whole thing needs teeth. They will be given the choice, in the first trimester, between abortion and adoption. In the second and third trimesters, adoption is their only option," Peter outlined that part slowly, knowing that it would be one of the most controversial.

"Very severe, Mr. President. There will be lots of backlash, but consider it done. That supercomputer sure is something!" Janet said.

"Indeed it is."

Peter stood up. Janet kissed him politely on both cheeks and left the office. He had begun a very dangerous process and was suddenly questioning his role; was he the president or Essie's slave? He looked at the computer. The red directive glared at him from the screen. In empty slots, he began checking off the steps of the process he'd already completed. Meeting with Health, check. Meeting with Education, check. Announcement…he inserted the following day's date for that one. No need to rush everything.

He thought about what he would say in his announcement, and his mind was filled with a barrage of delicate phrases and sensitive ways to break this global news, but he couldn't settle on an opening line. Instead, he opened a line of inquiry to the supercomputer. He locked his office door and enabled speech recognition on Essie.

'Who am I?' Peter said.

'You are Peter Johansen, supreme president of AmEarth,' the supercomputer answered instantly.

'How far away is Kepler 3763'

'Kepler 3763 is 23.5 light years away.'

'Is Kepler 3763 able to sustain life?'

The computer did not respond immediately. It gave enough time for Peter to repeat the inquiry.

'Is Kepler 3763 able to sustain life?'
'Information unavailable at your clearance level.'

Peter was immediately shocked. The computer knew that he was the supreme president, so how was it possible that he was not cleared on all levels?

'What is my clearance level?'
'Level five'
'How many levels are there?'
'Information unavailable at your clearance level.'
'What is Neil Chen Tyson's clearance level?'
'Information unavailable at your clearance level.'
'Is Neil Chen Tyson at a higher level than Peter Johansen?'
'Affirmative.'
'Wow.'
'Is that a question?'

Peter disabled Essie's speech function and logged off.

"Rosemary, I need Neil Chen Tyson," Peter ordered into the intercom, his mind racing once again.
"Yes, sir."

Peter took another sip of coffee and tried to choose a way to approach this conversation with the previous supreme president.

"Ex-President Chen on line one," Rosemary announced.
"Thanks," Peter said.

He picked up line one and took a deep breath.

"Mr. President," Peter began, remembering that Neil Chen was no longer in that office.

"Peter, you can call me Neil," Chen replied, sounding calm and relaxed.

"Neil, I just used the supercomputer terminal in your—my office to ask some questions. It seems that I have clearance at level five, but it says that you are at a higher level. Can you explain why the current supreme president has a lower clearance than the former president?"

"I'm still on the Supercomputer Committee, Peter. You know that."

"So the Supercomputer Committee is cleared to know certain things that I don't?"

"What do you want to know, Peter?"

"I was asking the computer how many levels of clearance there were."

"And Essie said?"

"No, she said, '*Information unavailable at your clearance level.*' Do you know how many levels there are?"

"Six."

"Six," Peter repeated, uncertain where to go with the conversation from there.

"Yes, six. What else do you want to know?"

"Don't you think that the president should have full access to the supercomputer's information?"

"Peter, let me be frank. Before the committee was formed, I was cleared at level six. As supreme president at level six, Essie begins to reveal contradicting visions and facts in a way that is not always linear and is very, very complex. It is easy to start questioning reality, so your effectiveness as president diminishes."

"Why? Because you know the truth?"

"The truth is not all that it is made out to be. Truth is relative, Peter, and in time, half-truths become full truths simply because they work. Do you understand?"

"Not really. You're being deliberately vague."

"I know. I'm not going into specifics, and you shouldn't look to find them. As president, you cannot doubt the truth of your statements or you will lose your position. Essie can and will replace you."

"What?"

"Peter, why do you think I could no longer speak publicly? My clearance level showed me facts that conflicted with certain directives. Citizens could see that I was not speaking truthfully. You get it?"

"So Essie wants me to lie?"

"No. She needs you to believe in AmEarth and all of its potential without digging around into the intricacies of how this world works."

"So ignorance is bliss?" Peter flippantly replied, slightly annoyed at the logic behind what Neil Chen was saying.

"In a way, but it's much more than that."

"I feel like a puppet in this office." Peter wished he hadn't said it, but it was true.

"A puppet? Peter…you're the most powerful man on earth! You have a great life, a helicopter on the roof to take you to Camp David whenever you want, an entire planet looking up to you for direction, and you feel like a puppet?"

"Yes."

"Then quit."

"I didn't say that, Mr. President."

"Peter, there is nothing sinister going on here. Do you want to be cleared for level six?"

"Frankly, I think that would be the best way to move forward."

"Let me talk to the committee."

"Actually, I would like to talk to the committee. I don't even know who is on it."

"That's a valid point. I'll get back to you soon."

"Thank you, Neil."

"No, Peter, thank you for your service to AmEarth. I hear that you're getting ready to give your first major directive speech. A big one, eh?"

"Yes, I'm working on it. I wanted to ask you something else about Kep-" Peter cut himself off, not wanting to show any more of his hand to Neil Chen.

"What?"

"No, nothing. I won't bother you with anything else. Good-bye, Neil," Peter said.

"Good-bye, Mr. President," Neil Chen replied.

Peter thought about confronting Neil Chen with more questions, but perhaps that was enough for one day. This new directive would be explosive. There had been many in the past and President Chen had been amazingly calm and reassuring through them all. Peter needed to learn from ex-president Chen, not make him his adversary. He also wanted to access level six clearance so that any of his questions could be resolved. He needed to quell the doubts rolling around in his head thanks to Scott and the events unfolding in New Zealand.

He began scribbling out his speech for the population control directive and suddenly felt a wave of depression sweep through him. As he read the words, he saw that there was no way to make the directive any softer. It was a punch in the gut. He called Barbara on his wafer.

"Honey, can you come up?" Peter said.

"Of course, what is it?" Barbara answered, immediately concerned.

Peter explained the situation briefly on the phone and what seemed like a minute later, Barbara was striding purposefully down the long hallway toward his office. He met her at the door of the office and embraced her gently. He realized that many eyes around the executive floor were on the pair, so he led her back to his desk, behind the privacy walls.

The whole staff had seemed giddy at the encounter. It was the first time they had seen Barbara Johansen with the supreme president together since the ceremony. Of course, Peter had shown Barbara his office earlier, but the office staff hadn't been there.

"I might have a solution," Barbara said, having apparently thought of a way out of his current predicament in the previous minute or two on her way up.

"What's that?" Peter asked incredulously.

"Find another directive. Pick one that is more positive and less controversial. Then, make both announcements at the same time. They will at least cancel each other out a bit."

Peter considered her words and realized that she was right. People were quite easy to control, as long as you knew how to do it.

"That just might work! See? This is why I need you."

"Oh, honey, you're just too close to these problems now. You need to see the forest, not just the one tree. What other directives are on the list?"

"Hundreds. Come here and take a look. Help me find one that might lift some spirits instead of inciting a global riot."

Barbara sat casually on Peter's lap and started to read the list of directives in black. In less than a minute, her finger stabbed down at one.

"This one," Barbara declared.

"DN 25801: The creation of a worldwide lottery. All humans participate in a daily lottery, which rewards the winner with one billion Orbs. One human per day will win and become wealthy; that winner will be announced every day during the evening news. Any human that already have more than one billion Orbs will be excluded from this lottery. Only adults over twenty-one years of age are allowed to participate," Peter read aloud, nodding as he went.

"I love it. People have always loved lotteries."

"You're the best."

Peter kissed his wife in a way that he hadn't done in years. Their hands began to roam and the pair clutched one another, warmly at first and then progressively more passionately. Peter did love this woman, and she clearly wanted to celebrate with the supreme president in his personal office.

"President Chen on line one," Rosemary's voice came through the intercom, disturbing their moment.

"Thanks," Peter said.

Barbara stood up and fixed her appearance as Peter picked up the phone. She walked out of the office and gave him a wave and a blown kiss, knowing that he needed to get down to business. Peter turned the privacy setting off only to find everyone in the office looking in their direction. Barbara was still fixing her dress when the walls emptied of their color. Peter mildly blushed, and when Barbara turned around to find twenty or thirty pairs of eyes on her, her flush of red was impossible to miss, and she walked back to the elevator with a slight urgency in her steps.

"Hello, Peter. I wanted to let you know that I've arranged for a meeting of the SCC for September third," President Chen began, right down to business again.

"Where?"

"They take place with the Joint Chiefs. You've been there. Thirty-nine."

"The War Room."

"Yes, but we might as well call it the Peace Room."

"I'll make a directive for that."

"He's an ideal candidate to lead the world, *and* he's funny," President Chen replied with a laugh.

"What time?"

"We'll all meet at noon."

"How many people are in the committee?"

"Twelve."

"Twelve?"

"Yes."

"Don't you need an odd number to prevent ties?"

"No," President Chen replied naturally, as if the idea was ridiculous.

"Then what happens?"

"Most decisions have been voted in unanimously, but if there ever came to a tie, the tie-breaking vote would be given to Essie."

"I should have seen that coming."

"Peter, please remember…she is not your enemy. She is AmEarth's best asset. There would be no AmEarth without Essie."

"I had always hoped that AmEarth was the result of mankind uniting and becoming better on its own. This seems somehow different from that."

"Mankind created her! It is our machine, our achievement. We are the supercomputer. See you at the meeting."

"Of course. May I ask, why the delay? Why can't we meet now?"

"Many of the members are out of town. I thought it best to meet after the summer vacations. You do want to meet all twelve members, correct?"

"Yes, definitely. That timing makes sense."

"Good-bye, Mr. President."

"Good-bye, Neil."

The next morning, Peter took to the airwaves. He wore the distinctive blue suit and white shirt that President Chen used to wear, as well as the elegant gold presidential pin on his lapel with the honeycomb globe logo on it. He looked good; he looked presidential.

"Ladies and gentlemen of AmEarth…Today, I will be announcing the first two directives of my term. Before doing so, I would like to explain something very important to everyone listening. There was a study of the Pacific Islands explaining how most were settled by Chinese sailors in the Middle Ages. We know that certain islands were able to support more men than others. As the Chinese retired their navy when they built the Great Wall of China, these different islands were left to fend for themselves. They did so for centuries and each of them developed their own societies. On some small islands, humans tolerated infanticide, a practice that we would abhor, but given that the population of this tiny island societies could not support more than a few thousand inhabitants, it became morally appropriate for them to practice it. Infanticide is repulsive to us now, but it was a necessity for their survival," Peter explained.

He could see some of his staff with confused looks on their faces.

On TV screens around the world, you could almost see him sweat, although he never broke. It was his mannerisms that made it look as though he was about to break into a sweat.

"Our planet is like one of those tiny islands in the Pacific. We had reached the peak population of our planet even before the rise of AmEarth. In the divided past, we faced multiple forms of population culling through acts of nature, war, disease, and famine. We no longer tolerate the barbaric and painful methods of population control used in the past, but it is obvious that we must still control our population. The directive I am announcing will change your lives, and we hope that it will change them for the better. The supercomputer has devised a system that allows for large families, as well as optimal-size families, and is not going to impede our happiness and lifestyles. It will, however, place strict limits on human reproduction based on statistical analysis and logic. From now on, men will not be allowed to have more than two naturally born children. Any deviation from this directive will represent an act of treason. Women will not be allowed to have children until they obtain a college degree or reach thirty years of age. There will be no exceptions. Any deviation from this will require women to offer their additional offspring up for adoption. There will be no exceptions."

Peter paused slightly, he could hear his own staffers and technicians whispering, so he launched into the second half of his announcement.

"I am also announcing a second directive that will create the first worldwide lottery. It is a free drawing that will make one person a billionaire every single day. This applies to all citizens of AmEarth who are twenty-one years of age or older. You do not need to buy a ticket; your DNA is automatically entered into the draw and on any day of the year, *you could become a billionaire!"* Peter put some extra emphasis on his delivery, trying to make this announcement stronger than the preceding one.

It was the first week of August when Peter announced both directives. In the days that followed it was clear that the lottery distraction had essentially failed. All over the globe, people of religious and libertarian beliefs joined to dissent and demonstrate. The UN building was considered the main governmental office building, even though the reality was across the street, so the demonstrations began and continued for what seemed an eternity to Peter.

People across the world began following the example of the demonstrations in New York. ACA and AmEarth buildings were swamped with groups of people, which increased traffic and began leading to vandalism. In more religious areas of the world, the riots became difficult to control.

Peter was called to the War Room, where he had previously been briefed by the Joint Chiefs. Most members of the Supercomputer Committee were there, with the notable exception of ex-president Chen. This was Peter's first emergency meeting, and not having Chen there made him feel insecure. He felt entrapped by the harsh directive and it felt like ex-president Chen was somehow foiling him. In reality, Neil Chen was recovering from a minor elective surgery and his absence was unrelated. Peter entered looking disheveled and tense and found most members there in a similar condition. Tensions ran high and the meeting began with screens all around the room showing the protests.

"The situation has escalated to a level three, and in twenty-seven population centers the army has been called in to quell the dissent," Essie said it her characteristically flat and emotionless tone.

"We seem to be gaining the upper hand and hope to see the intensity of the protests diminish as people return to the realities of their lives," General Redford said.

"The most important thing is not to harm the protesters," Peter asserted. "These are social issues and the protesters are only asking for human rights that they have enjoyed for centuries. We must be tolerant without giving in."

"We agree on that," General Roberts began, "but remember that treason and vandalism need to be treated seriously."

"I think that the main issue is the vasectomy terms," Sergio Ramirez-Bulatov chimed in unexpectedly.

"Why do you say that?" General Roberts asked, looking at Sergio as though he had never heard his voice.

"Look around. Do you see many women in the ranks of these protesters? The directive has motivated the males to act. I don't think the females are at all concerned with a directive that basically asks them to seek higher education. They welcome that. However, the vasectomy is intrusive. Physically and psychologically intrusive. Maybe there is another way."

"What do you suggest?" Peter asked genuinely.

"I don't know, maybe a voluntary vasectomy at the second live birth, and not right away. What if you have a kid that dies in the first twelve months?

That could happen, and the man might want to try again. Don't you think so? Anyway, if they don't elect to get the vasectomy and they go for a third child, then we could force those rogue elements to get the operation and give the third baby up for adoption," Sergio finished. He had obviously thought this through, as he had no known family of his own.

"I think Mr. Ramirez-Bulatov has a very good point. How can we alter the directive? What is the process?" Peter asked, looking around the table.

"We write in code the desired amendment, put it on a mini-drive and enter it into Essie's port." Larry Kanter showed Peter the port in the table in front of them for plugging in a portable drive.

"Do you want to write it?" Peter looked at Sergio.

"I already have." Sergio held up a mini-drive in his hand.

"Well, go ahead!" Peter ordered.

"One moment! We need to achieve a quorum to allow such a measure," General Redford said.

"I call for allowing my amendment to be analyzed by Essie. All those in favor, say aye," Sergio said.

"Aye!" was heard loud and clear.

"All those against, say nay." Sergio said.

Silence.

"The ayes have it!" Peter said.

Sergio inserted the drive into the port. The main computer monitor flashed small periods that moved from side to side, indicating that the computer was thinking.

'The amendment to Directive 25853 is approved. The unacceptable level of social unrest should be quelled with voluntary vasectomies.' Essie said.

"Ha! I knew it!" Sergio shouted in delight.

"Bravo!" Peter said. He approached Sergio and gave him a hug.

The Joint Chiefs looked on, as if the pair were immature children. However, a huge sense of relief struck all the members of the committee, as the worldwide tensions were immense. Peter took to the airwaves that very afternoon, and the process of acceptance of the population control directive began.

AmEarth had matured enough to be able to dictate this restrictive policy, and Sergio had written his first-ever amendment. Intelligent minorities understood and appreciated the directive as a necessary step to preserve the human race.

SEVENTEEN

The school year started in September, and students all over the world ran to their classrooms, asking questions; Columbia University was no exception. Navigating the huge campus, Scott finally found where he was supposed to go on his first day of school. He sat in the highest row of the huge classroom where American History, a core requirement of Columbia, was being taught. At first, it seemed interesting because of the new setting, but the course was going over everything that he already knew. Combined with the teacher's monotonous voice, Scott began to drift and feel sleepy. The classroom reached a peak level of boredom as the professor announced that he was giving the floor over to his new T.A. Scott was staring intently at a beautiful girl a few rows down and was not paying much attention to the class, when a familiar voice began talking about the founding fathers of the USA.

"Please turn to page 101 in your books. One of the most interesting aspects of the early constitution of the US was that its interpretation gradually changed completely from what the founding fathers intended. For instance, the phrase 'all men are created equal' really meant 'all white male landowners are created equal,' since they did not believe that all men (and women) were equal. Does anyone here know why?"

The voice was that of Ted Landon. Scott was shocked to see him here, teaching in his class!

"Because they owned slaves," one student shouted out, and Mr. Landon nodded.

"Exactly. These men not only frowned on people without money, but also on other races. It took from 1565 to 1964 for African Americans in America to receive the same rights as whites, thanks to the passing of the Civil Rights Act. Before that, African Americans were openly discriminated against everywhere they went, from restaurants and clubs to public transportation."

Scott could not believe that Mr. Landon was standing there. What was he doing at Columbia? As a teaching assistant no less! Was he following him? Scott knew that his father was the most powerful man on the planet, so he figured it had to be connected somehow. He looked at Mr. Landon to see if he would make eye contact. Any acknowledgment of him might reveal his intentions. Mr. Landon remained busy with the lesson and did not look in his direction once.

"So the initial constitution was crafted by rich white men, for rich white men, and only ended up benefiting 'all men' after 1964, because of a legal interpretation. What does this say about the American system and how it got us here?"

"It's slow as hell," another student jokingly answered.

General laughter.

"It's flexible?" another student ventured.

"It was both flexible and slow, yes," Mr. Landon responded. "Times change, and our perception of morality changes with them. We cannot go back to the unjust past, and we must strive to improve mankind's equality."

"So the original constitution was founded on the premise that only certain men were actually equal, but that was a lie back then, just as it is now. Right?" a student asked.

"It's not really that simple, but yes. The founding fathers did not mean that 'all' men were equal. To them, the term 'men' only meant a small sampling of men, and certainly did not include their slaves, but the equality for the men included was a philosophical and moral equality. Therefore, as soon as other men were recognized as being equal, both philosophically and morally, then they had to be included. It's just a shame that it took so long for society to recognize this," Mr. Landon announced dramatically.

The student bristled a bit.

"It was a lie. Even today it's a lie. Men are never truly equal. Some are rich and powerful, while others are not. Some are smarter than others, more beautiful…the list goes on and on…"

"The rights that the constitution grants are not related to finances or aesthetics. It does not say that all men will have the same wealth or beauty," Mr. Landon countered.

"Maybe it should," another student suggested.

"Well, if there was such a law, then there would be no space for difference in the world—those anomalies that make the world interesting and random. Imagine a world where everyone was identical in every respect. It would be equal, but terribly boring!"

The class continued, but Scott hardly heard the discussion. He was still trying to get over the shock of seeing Mr. Landon in his classroom. When the class was over, everyone left except Scott, who stayed and stared at Mr. Landon. He still never looked up at him. He seemed absorbed by the notes and papers on his desk as he cleaned up. Some female students went up to him and chatted briefly, almost flirting, but he quickly sent them off.

Scott walked slowly up the aisle and out of the top door. In the hallway, he decided to return and catch a last glance of Mr. Landon. Scott turned around and peeked his head back into the auditorium, only to see Mr. Landon dart through the rear door. Scott dialed his father's office, and laughed once again at how bizarre it was to have a direct line to the supreme president of AmEarth.

"Can I speak with him, please?" Scott asked.

"Sure, honey. Give me a second," Rosemary said.

"Mr. President, it's your son on line one," Rosemary spoke into the intercom.

"Thanks," Peter replied and picked up.

"Scott, how's Columbia treating you?"

"I can't complain, although it's definitely a challenge. It's so weird, Dad. You're so famous now. Everyone knows who I am and treats me like I'm going to break, or freak out, or…" Scott trailed off, not having planned to unload all of this right away on his dad.

"I'm sorry about that, son, but hopefully it will end up being good luck—an opportunity instead of a burden."

"I'll try, but it's harder than I ever expected. I don't know who I am now. I'm just the president's son."

"Oh, Scott, remember that talk we had about the tree rings?"

"The inside of the tree core, and the self?"

"Yes. Just imagine this as a new ring being made. All the others are still intact and protected; there is just a new one to consider."

"I never really paid much attention to your ring theory. Sorry, Dad."

"Scott, I just want you to know that you are still you, regardless of who I am. Even if this new chapter changes you, the real you is still in there. Don't forget that. Okay?"

"Okay. Dad?"

"Yes?"

"I'd like to talk to you about some of that stuff we discussed before. I know you don't want to hear it, but I really need to speak with you about it."

"You know what, son, I'd like to speak to you about it as well. I've been asking myself some of those same questions you posed. But we'll need some privacy. Why don't you come home tonight? I'll send the helicopter if you want."

"Dad, that's the last thing I need at this point. I can just imagine what people will think if I start getting picked up in the president's helicopter. No way. I'll just drive there. See you for dinner tonight."

"Teenagers," Peter teased. "Nothing is ever good enough. I would have killed for a helicopter valet at your age. Good-bye, son."

"Bye, Dad."

Scott clicked off his wafer and clipped it back onto his clothing. He walked to Lewisohn Hall, admiring the leaves that had turned orange in the recent changing weather. He felt different at college from how he'd felt in his former school; there was a self-consciousness that made everything feel surreal. The fact that his father was known to every human on Earth also made matters…complicated.

One example was when he had found himself in an English class, an elective, and he arrived one minute late. The professor looked at him as though he had killed someone. He sat down in the back row and tried to disappear into his thoughts of Cate, and how she had left for college in California. She was so far away and texting was just not the same as being with her in person. He suddenly noticed that the teacher had an annoying tone in his high-pitched voice and was addressing the class rather rudely.

"I will say this one last time. There will be no tardiness in my classroom. If you are late, you will not be allowed to enter, and you will miss that lesson. In this class, you will learn to appreciate the English language from its very roots. We will read Beowulf aloud, and you will all learn to pronounce it and understand its meaning from top to bottom. I expect everyone to be involved in the class reading. We will also perform one Shakespeare play in the auditorium," the professor proudly proclaimed.

For the first time in his life, Scott realized that this was an elective and that this curmudgeon of a human being might just ruin his love of the English language. He stood up in midsentence, but the professor kept speaking. Scott walked back to the front door through which he had entered only two minutes earlier.

"Excuse me?" the professor said.

"What?" Scott shot back, knowing that he was going to be reprimanded somehow.

"You have the chutzpah to come late, and now you're rudely leaving while I'm talking!"

"I'm in the wrong class."

"Which class are you supposed to be in?" the professor demanded, his pudgy face getting red.

"English."

"This is English!"

"No. This is Old English. And I still have time to change my elective," Scott said, and promptly turned around and left the room, pulling the door shut behind him. He felt empowered by speaking back to a teacher, something he'd never done before. That professor was obnoxious and deserved to be knocked down a peg or two. Behind him, the door opened and closed again and a pair of girls exited the curmudgeon's class. They giggled and followed Scott as he strolled down the hall.

Scott was not interested, as he was still loyal to Cate, so he kept walking. The only thing he could think about was getting answers from Mr. Landon. He decided to return to Hamilton Hall and confront Mr. Landon. In the main office of Hamilton Hall, he was directed to the teachers' lounge, where he was told that Mr. Landon could often be found. He walked the beautiful wide hallways of the first level, which were punctuated by thick wooden doors and Tuscan columns painted in white, contrasting gently with the walls, which were painted in baby blue. He found the lounge quite easily, and when Scott entered, he thought that he saw someone who looked like Mr. Landon ducking quickly behind a partition. Scott looked around the room, but after failing to locate Mr. Landon, he walked to the corner of the lounge where the partition was located. He found Mr. Landon on all fours, apparently looking for something under the table.

"Mr. L., can you come up from under there?" Scott asked.

"Scott, my friend, what are you doing here?" Mr. Landon said, seemingly surprised.

"Cut the crap. Are you following me?"

"What?" Mr. Landon's eyes grew wide, and for a moment, Scott thought that maybe Mr. Landon was simply a TA, but he dismissed that thought. *Coincidences don't exist.*

"Well? What brings you to Columbia University? Why are you my TA?" Scott asked.

"You're in my class? What are the odds?" Mr. Landon exclaimed.

"Stop it. My father said that someone was feeding me information to damage the government of AmEarth. It's you, isn't it?"

"Shhh…Scott, what in the devil are you saying? Are you mad? Lower your voice," Mr. Landon implored him.

"Well, explain yourself. Now."

"Listen, Scott, I'm not feeding you anything. The document you read was not intended for your eyes. Do you think back then that I knew your father would become the president? Did you honestly think that?"

"No," Scott admitted quietly, feeling some of his bravado fade.

"Please, sit down and lower your voice. I've been waiting for this position at Columbia for five years! So, no…I didn't come here to follow you! I'm trying to teach for a few years and eventually get tenure here. Did you really think that I could just follow you to your choice of college and no one would notice? Anyway, you were dead-set on Stanford. I'm as surprised to see you here as you are to see me."

"Yes, but you have to admit, that's one hell of a coincidence."

"That it is. That it is."

"By the way, that Kepler document is bullshit, right?" Scott said.

"Whatever you say. I'm not going to contradict you, Scott. However, you are in way over your head. It's best to leave it alone. Yeah?"

"Yes, I know. It's best to leave it alone."

Scott got up, feeling relieved that his paranoia had been unfounded.

"What is the Shadow White House like?" Mr. Landon asked.

"Amazing. It's an apartment though," Scott said.

"Really?"

"A huge apartment. It's so big…elegant as hell."

"In the AmEarth building? In Brooklyn?"

"Yep, Floors ninety-eight to one hundred. It's lush."

"Wow."

"It's actually a replica of the White House—paintings and all. Identical."

"That's amazing!"

"And with a view like you wouldn't believe!"

Scott had been planning to leave, but he suddenly sat down again, leaned in, and spoke quietly.

"I was wondering one more thing…" he said.

"What is that?" Mr. Landon asked warily.

"Let's say, for the sake of argument, that the alien threat is a hoax. In that case, what happened above Poland last April?"

"Scott…please just drop it. You're far too close to AmEarth."

"Just give me this one thing. The bomb over Poland was an alien attack…right?"

"Wrong," Mr. Landon stated emotionlessly.

"Hmm…"

Scott paused and looked at Mr. Landon intently. For some reason, he felt that he could trust him.

"Well, I don't believe it, either. I think we planted the bomb up there to quell dissent," Scott stated.

"Sounds about right," Mr. Landon concurred.

"What should we do?"

"We? There is no *we*, Scott. You're a member of the victorious side of the greatest power grab in the history of the world. AmEarth has a stronghold in every corner of the globe and the one country that had proof of this regime's lies has fallen. I don't know that Earth has any way out of AmEarth now."

"But AmEarth is not all that bad, is it?"

"I'd like to think that. Really, I would. The problem is not apparent now, but it might become clear in the future."

"Why?"

"Every empire throughout history has been corrupt and eventually collapsed. I see no reason why AmEarth would have a different destiny. The only difference is that its collapse could be substantially more devastating, because it is currently ruling over all the resources on Earth and is centralizing the means of production."

What? You lost me…"

"Look at it this way. Imagine that we all need widgets to eat, okay? Then, we find all the available land to plant widgets and start cultivating. Then, we need a special machine to process them, so we can consume the widgets, but only one company can make this machine. Then, we are stuck with all this land in the hands of one single technology and a global population dependent on it. What happens if the people reclaim their land, but have no access to the technology?"

"Famine?"

"Exactly, and if this type of super-specialization reaches all the products and services we currently use, then what? All the gains of AmEarth's development can disappear overnight. All of these technologies can stop working and become useless pieces of junk."

"Wow. I've never thought of that before."

Scott saw that Mr. Landon had a point. The very basis of improvement could lead to a massive failure of their entire system of living.

"If we can prove that AmEarth is based on a lie, we might get the original countries to separate again, mightn't we?" Scott said.

"Yes, just like the Soviet Union in the 1990s."

"Exactly, which means that we need to reveal the Kepler document."

Mr. Landon looked around cautiously. They had both checked to make sure no one was within earshot, but he wanted to check one more time.

"Scott, the first things that AmEarth took over in New Zealand were the observatories and the telescopes. All of them are now in the hands of AmEarth. Kepler 3763 is now basically invisible, so the document is just a piece of paper—worthless paper."

"What about the landing in Bolivia? Or the alien threat announcement? Or this hoax over Poland!"

"All would be difficult to prove."

“But there must be something,” Scott was practically pleading now.

“Scott,” Mr. Landon said seriously, “your father is the president. Do you really want to bring him down?”

“No, but I don’t think he knows that AmEarth is based on a lie.”

“You’re sadly mistaken. Of course he knows. He’s the president.”

“But I’ve asked him.”

“Do you think that presidents can divulge global secrets to their children?”

Scott’s face fell in disappointment. “I guess not.”

“Please, Scott, just drop this. There is only…”

Mr. Landon let that last remark hang in the air as he stopped himself.

“What was that?” Scott asked.

“Oh, nothing,” Mr. Landon tried to brush it off.

“Come on, we’ve already come this far. My dad won’t believe anything I say anyway.”

“Well, one of the reasons that New Zealand has been resistant to the alien theory is the aesthetics of the alien civilization. Most people there agree that they’ve been crafted by a human in order to emulate an alien race, but it is such a human-centric version. Many people actually believe that a specific art director who once worked in New Zealand is responsible for these fictitious aesthetics.”

Scott was completely enthralled.

“Art director? Like for movies?”

"Yes. New Zealand has the second-largest studio for science fiction art direction in the world. Weta."

"So they can prove that the alien life forms are not alien?"

"Yes. They think that a former Weta employee is the 'creator' of the aliens."

"Who?"

"According to Pat, the daughter of the Weta owners dated a Mexican artist there, and the owners fired him to stop the romance. The scheme worked, and the two broke up. The guy basically disappeared from the art-directing world. She became depressed and hated her parents for driving them apart, so she dedicated herself to finding him. She watched movies and commercials, music videos, plays, and scoured personal video postings in search of her lover. For years, she had no luck."

"But she recognized his work in the aliens?"

"Exactly. According to Pat, she told everyone at Weta about how the alien technology and the alien physiognomy looked like the work of Sergio Ramirez-Bulatov."

"That's his name? Sergio Ramirez-Bulatov? What a strange name…"

"Half-Russian and half-Mexican."

"What a combo."

Mr. Landon chuckled.

"If you know an artist's work, then you can recognize his hand in everything. It's like a Picasso is always a Picasso, even though his works differ markedly," Mr. Landon explained.

"I get that, but how do we prove it?"

"There's that *we* again. *We* don't do anything. Scott, don't include me in your plans. I don't want to be in your family's crosshairs. Otherwise, I'll disappear faster than Sergio!"

"Oh, stop it."

"I'm not kidding. This would be considered treason, and treason is the only crime punishable by death. Be careful of what you say. I think that in Weta, or perhaps in the hands of Ms. Taylor, the early art of Ramirez-Bulatov is the only proof of the hoax. I say it's the only proof because any possible proof from Kepler 3763 itself is gone now. The only convincing evidence might be this artist's signature in the alien creation, and it takes a trained eye to spot that."

"I can't believe this, Mr. Landon. My dad has been talking about the aliens for years. He believes in them; I'm almost sure of it. I can't believe this is happening."

"Kepler 3763 is twenty-three point five light years away, right?" Mr. Landon asked.

"Yes."

"Well, that is also a comfortable mathematical coincidence. Pat had been in touch with Dr. Oliver Cook, the astronomer who wrote the report, and he told him that the choice of Kepler 3763 was not random. They needed a planet exactly 23.5 light years away. That way, it matched up with the supposed Roswell landing and the early stages of the space race. That would make the exact time for the first landings here, about forty-seven years later…which is when AmEarth began.. You see, all the physical proof is 'supposedly' from spaceships sent many years ago that are just arriving now. If you reverse-engineer the past, 23.5 is the ideal number."

"So, mathematically, they found a planet that would give them a plausible scenario."

"Exactly," Mr. Landon confirmed in a whisper.

“This means that the rockets coming from there are our rockets returning to us to deliver the art-directed content?” Scott said.

“Indeed!”

“You’re blowing my mind, Mr. Landon! And my father knows all of this?”

“Yes, I’m afraid so,” Mr. Landon admitted, a hint of regret in his voice.

“I have to go.” Scott felt like the world was closing in on him. His whole life had been defined by a lie, perpetuated by his own father.

“Scott, don’t do anything stupid. Please. If you tell anyone, even *you* could be charged with treason. This is the type of stuff that people shouldn’t even think about.”

Scott left the building, concerned for his future, but more convinced of the truth than ever before. Later, he had to go to the Shadow White House and meet his family for dinner. Then it would be time for his father to answer some real questions.

A moment later, a text message arrived from Cate.

Call me. feeling :(

Scott ordered his wafer to “Call Cate.”

“Honey, what is it?” Scott began when she picked up the phone.

“I’m just having a really hard time. I don’t know where to start,” Cate whimpered.

“I wanted to call you before, I’m really sorry. I’ve been swamped. I have so much to tell you about AmEarth!”

‘Listen, Scott, I don’t have time for AmEarth and all your theories right now. Can I just tell you why I called?" Her tone was serious, and upset, and a bad feeling began to rise in Scott's stomach.

"Okay, sorry Cate. What's going on?"

"You know how we talked about the distance and college and all that? Well, I sort of met someone…"

"What? What do you mean, you met someone?"

"It's not like I'm dating someone, Scott. It's just that this one guy keeps inviting me to go out and I'm bored and lonely, and I want to get out and do something."

"So do you want to date this guy now? Are you saying that we should see other people? I mean, honestly, that hasn't even crossed my mind. I love you, Cate."

"I love you, too. But…"

"I get it. You like this guy and you've already gone out with him. I'm not stupid."

"I don't want to hurt you," Cate said.

"Too late." Scott hung up abruptly and felt the floor shift beneath him. Another weight had been dropped on his shoulders. First his father, and now his girlfriend. It seemed like everyone was lying to him.

EIGHTEEN

The first family of AmEarth sat at the massive dining room table with all the elegance of a state dinner. It was just the four of them, but for a cadre of servants in elegant attire that served them each course. Brianna looked as beautiful as ever, but she kept pulling out her wafer and texting Camilla. Scott was rummaging through his food, lacking an appetite, and looked troubled and silent. Barbara was happy to have them all in one room, as this was becoming increasingly rare. Peter ate heartily, but was absent-minded, thinking of the latest directive and the fallout from it.

"Dad, I need to talk to you. Alone," Scott finally piped up.

"Sure. After dinner?" Peter replied nonchalantly.

"Fine."

"Dad?" Brianna opened.

"Yes, honey?" Peter said.

"I need to talk to you alone."

"What?" Barbara said, unsure of what was happening at the table.

"Bri, stop bothering your brother." Peter read the situation properly and reacted swiftly.

Somehow, college had given Scott an instant level of maturity that Brianna disliked. They finished their dinner, and Scott followed his dad up the stairs to the TV room. They sat down on the beautiful plush couch and a waiter approached them, asking if they'd like coffee or a snack. Peter ordered chocolate popcorn. As soon as the waiter left, Scott began.

"Dad, I hate to confront you, but I can't keep going like this."

"Like what?" Peter asked, concerned.

"With you pretending not to know."

"Not to know what, son?"

"That the alien race isn't real. That it's all been a hoax."

"What are you talking about? What's gotten into you? I thought you knew better than that."

"Dad, I do. Believe me…I do, but you're the president, and I'm supposed to believe that you don't know that life on Kepler 3763 is unsustainable! Or that you don't know that Ramirez-Bulatov designed the alien race like movie characters! Or that the explosion over Poland was our own nuclear bomb! Come on, Dad!"

"Scott, slow down. Please believe me when I tell you this. I have some doubts about the alien race as well. You've put those doubts there. I've been very concerned about what you have been saying. But even talking like this is…punishable by the state. And you're my son. I need you to tell me who has been feeding you this nonsense. Or at least tell me why you're so sure. You're a smart kid, so I would expect some verification."

Peter was shocked that his son knew Ramirez-Bulatov's name. He had just hugged him as the savior of the population control directive. He didn't make a single gesture and kept his cool, not allowing Scott to sense the new doubt that had just landed on him.

"No one is telling me anything, Dad. This has all been my own research. It all started with the landing in Bolivia. Honest. I haven't told anyone but you."

"Scott, I'm worried." The president's face had taken on a dark tone. He knew that he and his son were in dangerous waters. Being the supreme president didn't feel all that secure or omnipotent at the moment.

"Do me a favor. Let's just have a talk like two adults, understanding and listening to each other. Can you do that with me? Ignoring the fact that I'm your son?"

"I suppose I can do that."

"Okay, then suppose for argument's sake that this particular alien threat is a hoax, made up by America to conquer the world? Let's just suppose that."

"Okay, let's say that's the case…" Peter agreed, but his voice was hesitant.

"So, to make the hoax work, they need to do three main things: One, scare the world with a common and powerful enemy that will unite the human race. Aliens are perfect for this. Two, they need to craft the enemy realistically and fake extraterrestrial landings. A talented unknown art director fits that bill. And three, they need to find a seldom-viewed planet at the precise distance to make the whole theory work based on our past timeline of events. Rewrite history."

"That seems pretty straightforward, Scott. But in fact, all of that would be very difficult. Are you saying that AmEarth is some great conspiracy, hidden even from me? Think about that!"

"Well, do you believe that aliens exist on Kepler 3763 and that they are sending thirty-five-year-old nuclear bombs because of Ronald Reagan? You're willing to believe that instead?"

"I do."

"You don't look like it."

"I promise you this, Scott. I will personally investigate the allegations that you've mentioned—discreetly and without alerting anyone. If you are correct, then we still might need to keep this under wraps. I'm sure you understand why. We risk losing all of this, and I mean *us*. Not the world losing AmEarth, but us losing our lives. We could be charged for this. I could lose the job just as easily as I got it, and then what? How are we going to convince anyone of what you're saying? You need to keep quiet and let me investigate on my own. Is that clear?"

"Yes sir."

"Now, let's see what we can see on the TV to take our minds off all of this. I need to rest."

"Dad, I'm going to go back to school tonight."

"Come on, Scott, just watch something with me."

"Okay, but something new, please. None of that black-and-white stuff you like."

"You're so ignorant of the big picture, Scott. I've failed you as a parent," Peter joked.

"Look who's talking!" Scott snapped back, and they both laughed.

"Touché, son…touché."

NINETEEN

Monday morning arrived, and Peter headed to his second Supercomputer Committee meeting in the War Room. He recognized most of the committee members from the military, NASA, and the NSA. Peter nodded at those he knew well. Ex-President Chen was standing at the head of the table, just where he had stood while briefing Peter a few weeks back.

"Peter, allow me to introduce you to the committee members," Chen started."

"Mr. President, I already know most of these men. Robert, Larry," Peter said and nodded to a few of his acquaintances.

"Well, then let me introduce you to Mr. Sergio Ramirez-Bulatov, a computer consultant on social, environmental, and political questions."

"We've met, Neil. Hi Sergio," Peter gave him an appreciative smile.

"Mr. President," Sergio said.

Peter was still baffled by Scott's knowledge of

Sergio's existence, let alone the fact that he was a powerful member of the committee. Was he really an art director?

"Is there anyone else you don't know?" Chen asked.

"I think that the rest of us have met a few times," Peter said casually, trying to calm himself down in the process.

"Good. Then let's start. This committee is meeting on the issue of accessibility to the computer database with level six for Supreme President Johansen. All those in favor, please say aye," Chen announced with very little introduction.

He hadn't led up to it with any sort of formal call to order, simply stating the subject that they could all feel hanging in the room.

There was absolute silence in the room.

"Aye," ex-president Chen said loudly.

No one joined Chen in approving Peter's access to the top level of clearance.

"The nays have it, then," Chen stated, not seeming upset or surprised in the slightest.

"So, that's it?" Peter questioned, shocked at how quickly he had been shot down.

"The committee has voted to leave the supreme president at level five."

"May I be frank?" Peter said, obviously irritated at the way he was being treated.

"Please do," Chen encouraged him.

Everyone paid attention, although they all sat with stoic, determined faces.

"If I am to speak directly to the world and be truthful, then I need to clear up a few things," Peter said.

"Tell us, Peter," Chen ordered him, a touch patronizingly.

"Ask the computer a question with your level six clearance right now," Peter demanded.

"That is not how this works. You cannot give orders to this committee," Chen calmly explained.

"Then I'll be forced to quit, which might reflect poorly on the computer's choice. You'll have to find a new president."

"You're being ridiculous, Peter. Essie has just gone to impressive lengths to find you! You can't turn your back on AmEarth," Chen argued, with a bit more intensity. He hadn't seen this bluff coming, if it was a bluff.

Other committee members looked across the table at one another. Some looked dismissive, others concerned.

"Watch me," Peter replied.

"Calm down, Peter. Please. You can ask your question. Give us some time to reply," Chen said.

"Why? It's a supercomputer. So it's fast. Why make me wait?"

"We need to vet the answer."

"Vet it? You mean manipulate the truth so my speeches come off as genuine?" Peter hadn't expected to drop such a loaded bomb on the group, but Neil Chen seemed oddly unfazed.

"There is that."

"Well, we're back at square one then, aren't we?" Peter snapped.

"What do you mean?" General Redford asked.

"What I mean is, *you* needed a new president who believes that what AmEarth has been putting out as the truth is actually true. However, I know that the truth is not clear. We're back to the same situation you were in when you replaced President Chen, but slightly worse."

"Why worse?" Sergio asked.

"Because I also wonder whether the foundation of AmEarth is composed of lies."

Peter looked at Neil Chen straight in the eye; he could see the uncomfortable position he had put the previous president in.

"What is that 'truth,' Peter?" Chen asked him, with an edge to his words.

"The alien threat is not all that dangerous," Peter stated without flinching.

"You know that those remarks can be considered treasonous," General Redford barked.

"Why is that?" Peter lashed back.

"Calling AmEarth untruthful about the alien threat is a form of undermining its authority."

"But I'm not doing so in a public venue. We're in a secret meeting of a secret committee that no one knows about!"

"Relax, Peter. Explain what you just said. What evidence do you have that the alien threat is not dangerous?" Chen coaxed him gently, trying to defuse the situation.

"To start with, there is the Bolivian coincidence…"

"What coincidence?"

"If you are all going to treat me like a child, then we might as well call it a day and just go home." Peter was getting annoyed. He didn't like being talked down to.

"He means the landing in Sucre," Director Kanter offered.

"Exactly," Peter confirmed

"What about it?" Chen demanded.

"The missile fell on a government building in the downtown square of the ancient capital city of one of the last countries we needed to join AmEarth. The odds of a landing with that accuracy are about one in fourteen million, and that measurement is anywhere in the city, not even right in the main square! It became even clearer to me when it was not widely reported in the news."

"You think that many people are aware of this?" General Redford said.

"How can they be? Even if the Bolivians mention it, nothing will become part of the public record unless the landing makes it on the airwaves," Peter retorted.

"That is correct," Sergio spoke for the first time.

Everyone fell silent. Chen looked at Sergio Ramirez-Bulatov with parental disappointment in his eyes. It was clear that Sergio's comments were usually frowned upon.

"Peter, what exactly do you think the aliens were intending when they landed in Bolivia?" Chen asked quietly.

"The aliens did not land in Bolivia, President Chen! Obviously, we sent a rocket that launched another rocket back at us, or it came from a station in orbit. This rocket looks alien and landed exactly where we needed it to land. This was a precisely plotted military operation. My compliments to General Redford and Director Kanter," Peter finished, nodding to the respective heads of the military and NASA.

They both looked surprised, but secretly proud. Sergio sat squirming, as though he were dying to add something. Peter was making his point using only the Bolivia information. He didn't want to compromise his son by mentioning the Kepler 3763 document or the fact that he knew about Sergio.

"Peter, what do you want to ask Essie?" Chen said.

Neil Chen flipped a switch that turned the supercomputer on in a central monitor in the room.

"Ask what is the temperature on Kepler 3763." Peter stated.

"Ha," Sergio Ramirez-Bulatov guffawed loudly, which was followed by an awkward silence.

"Okay," ex-president Chen agreed looking at Dr. Kanter.

"What is the temperature on Kepler 3763?" Dr. Kanter asked.

"Minus 325 degrees Fahrenheit, minus 198 Celsius." Essie said

"Ask if the planet is rotating," Peter said looking at the Doctor.

"Is Kepler 3763 rotating on an axis?" Dr. Kanter asked.

"No."

Peter looked at Larry. Larry knew what question was coming next, but he waited.

"Can it sustain life?" Peter asked.

There was a silent pause, Essie did not reply to Peter's question. Larry was slow in asking.

"Is Kepler 3763 capable of sustaining life?"
"No."

Peter looked around. The faces at the table looked perfectly normal, as if nothing new had been uttered.

Neil Chen stood up and looked at Peter with dead eyes.

" Essie? Are there alien life forms outside our planet Earth?" Chen asked.
"Yes." Essie said.

Peter knew this was common knowledge.

"Essie? Have we ever made contact with aliens," Peter shot in a final query.
"Turn her off, Larry," Chen growled. "Now!"

Larry turned Essie off.

"So, you've figured out that the aliens are not from Kepler 3763, but there are aliens out there. You heard the 'Yes,'" Chen argued.
"But we have never made contact. You stopped me from asking that question," Peter countered.
"The only difference is what we are doing with the possibility, Peter. We have anticipated the Earth's response to an alien threat and used it to foster our way of life and to ensure the survival of our species. It was inevitable and necessary."
"Perhaps, but even if the aliens reside only a hundred or two hundred light years away, then the entire premise of their existence simply doesn't make sense. Hell, they could be a million light years away! It would be the same as having no aliens at all. Have you ever thought of that?"

"Your indignation is healthy, Peter, but I think you need to relax. Accept your new reality as it is. America has won all the wars. We have the upper hand and essentially control the destiny of the planet. Would you rather that the Russians had their fingers on the trigger? Or the Germans?"

"But this is a difficult and dangerous conspiracy to bottle up."

"Is it?"

"I figured it out. Others might figure it out, too."

"Peter, you were at the very heart of AmEarth, with access to privileged information when you figured this out. You are very bright, and we obviously underestimated you. You must remain as president until the computer determines otherwise. We will need to craft your speeches with more care and, in time, you will be replaced. At that moment, we will move you here to the SCC, and you will always maintain your intelligence status in AmEarth, maybe even rising to level six. You cannot, of course, divulge what you know to anyone, not even family members. That is for their safety and yours. Can we trust you, Peter?"

There was a long pause, and Peter laid his gaze on Sergio. He seemed bottled up and a bit edgy. He noticed that Sergio was not a dark-skinned Mexican, but rather a tanned Caucasian. He looked like he had just arrived from a tropical beach.

"Of course you can trust me, Neil," Peter said, deliberately using former President's Chen's first name. "You have given me the privilege of clearance and my allegiance to AmEarth is absolute."

"Then let's agree that the best route is to keep Peter Johansen as supreme president." Chen directed his comment to the room.

"With what level of clearance?" Peter asked.

"We will keep you at level five, but whenever you need to access Essie, anyone in this room can ask her any question that you have. How is that for a compromise?"

Peter nodded in agreement. He was getting what he needed, even if it wasn't in the form he had expected.

"This way, Essie will be satisfied that the supreme president is at the level she chose. In a way, we are co-opting her wishes," Chen continued.

"Is she not hearing all this?" Peter asked.

"She is off right now." Chen said.

"We are the masters of the computer, after all," Sergio added.

"Human survival is the computer's first directive," Chen went on, as though Sergio hadn't spoken.

"Exactly, but this committee is the only fail-safe Essie, in case she veers off track," General Redford said.

"That settles it. All those in agreement, say aye," Chen ordered, still very much the most powerful man in the room.

"Aye," all twelve members said in unison.

"All those against?"

The brief silence marked the decision that began a strange new friendship at the highest level of AmEarth. Peter would use Sergio to access Essie. He was the least busy, and something about Sergio resonated strongly with him. Peter now knew that his son had been correct on all counts. He needed to speak to Scott as soon as possible, but couldn't arouse suspicion and didn't want to put his son in any danger. His position implied constant monitoring and the feeling of being watched and even oppressed by the

AmEarth system was growing stronger. The presidency was both a blessing and a curse all in one—something that only Chen before him had known.

Chen disbanded the meeting and sent everyone to their respective floors. The emergency meeting of the Supercomputer Committee was over. Neil Chen was not happy that his succession plan had backfired so quickly. Peter would begin to falter and his knowledge would make him untenable. If only he could return to his former status…if only he could lie better.

TWENTY

The health care directive to curb population growth was rational and made no allusion to alien subject matter. It was easy for the president to give truthful speeches without jeopardizing his position, so Peter decided to make a surprise visit to Columbia University with Barbara. This way, he could make her happy and visit Scott at the same time. He would speak on the education portion of the population directive, which would look great with the backdrop being his alma mater. Rosemary arranged everything and they were in the helicopter the next morning, making the short hop from Brooklyn to Harlem.

President Johansen was greeted by a crowd of thousands at the college grounds in front of the famous marble cupola structure known as the Library, even though it wasn't one. Rosemary had arranged for Scott to be on stage with him and had advised him to dress up. They sat in lawn chairs on the wooden stage that had been built for the occasion; a large canvas backdrop hung from the frieze of the building. It sported a very large graphic of the official seal of AmEarth. The pair looked remarkably similar with their dark blazers and dark ties—almost like twins. The temperature was a perfect sixty degrees. These were the days that made living on the East Coast so beautiful in the autumn. Peter touched his son's knee.

"I need to talk to you about my investigation," Peter said. This was one of the first times he had been alone with Scott in some time.

"Here? Now?" Scott said, trying to keep his expression from changing too much.

"I don't want to speak to you on a device. I came here to give this speech so that I could see you. I took your suspicions seriously."

"I told you!"

"Stop it. Don't look excited. We're being filmed, and there are a thousand lip readers out there. Look at me and listen. Don't speak."

"Okay."

Peter talked to Scott as he scratched at his nose. He looked like he had an itchy nose, but in reality, the gesture blocked his lips from all the main camera angles.

"You were right, but you need to keep what you know a secret. It's very important. And very dangerous if you don't. Nod if you understand me?"

Scott nodded.

"This is the hardest part. You can't confirm to anyone that there is no alien threat to our planet. Not even to your mom or Bri."

"You're not telling Mom?" Scott asked, surprised.

"Not sure yet. Now, Scott, who else knows about this? How are they connected to us? Cover your mouth."

"Only a professor at the high school. He knew people in New Zealand."

"So you don't see him anymore?"

"No," Scott lied, and immediately felt bad.

"What's his name?"

"What will happen to him?"

"Nothing," Peter replied honestly; it pained him to hear such distrust in his son's voice.

"Please, just keep him out of this. He's harmless," Scott pleaded.

"Fine, just tell me what you know about the artist."

Before Scott answered, Peter moved on to rubbing his eyebrows and temples, essentially covering his face.

"Ramirez-Bulatov?"

"Yes, keep your lips covered. Whisper in my ear."

Scott casually placed his hand on one side of his cheek and whispered the entire love affair of Sergio into his hand, cupping it to direct the sound to his father's ear. He threw out Weta studios, Peter Jackson, the girlfriend—everything that he knew. The more Peter heard, the more he felt like he understood Ramirez-Bulatov's attitude at the meeting the day before. At that moment, the president of the college began to speak; he would bring Peter to the podium at any moment.

"Scott—keep this to yourself. I mean it!" Peter said urgently.

"Yes sir," Scott promised.

Scott was exhilarated. He had been right, and now the president of the world knew the truth—all thanks to him. He felt overjoyed, but tried to act naturally. He felt like a kid trapped in a candy store, but he was also proud of his dad.

Peter made his way to the podium and began a rather boring speech on the virtues of education and parental responsibility. He had purposefully made the speech short. He ended by sharing his warm feelings toward his alma mater.

"So, as we stand here in this campus of higher education, which gives me such wonderful memories, I reiterate to the student body that it is not unreasonable to legislate childbirth. I don't even think it conflicts with your present plans. This directive might not prevent all of the world's problems, but it will steer us onto the path toward sustainable life. I sincerely hope that you understand the purpose of this new legislation and that it will allow you to become responsible, healthy, and happy adults. Now, I'm going to visit my son's classes and his dorm room. After all, I'm a parent before a president."

The audience clapped, but far in the back, Peter could see some detractors with signs that had crossed-out lines over the AmEarth logo, a few with Alien Lies posters, and even some Jesus posters scattered in there. However, the vast majority of the campus, like the vast majority of the world, liked Peter. Peter signaled Scott to get up from his chair and stand with him at the podium. Scott was reluctant, but Barbara, the ever-proud mother standing next to Peter, motioned for Scott to get off his butt. He couldn't say no to her. All three saluted the crowd and then the trio exited the stage.

"Barbara, go with the Secret Service to the helicopter. I'll meet you there in twenty minutes," Peter instructed her.

"But I'd like to see his dorm as well," Barbara argued.

"Barb, this is important. I'll explain later."

Barbara shrugged her shoulders and headed toward the helicopter. Peter was left alone with Scott.

"Where is your computer?" Peter whispered in Scott's ear.

"In my room," Scott replied.

"Good. Let's go."

Peter smiled at the crowd, shaking hands and signing some autographs as he moved through them. The Secret Service scrambled in a web around him and Scott, pushing the crowd away as they made it out of the stage area and onto the path that led to John Jay Hall. Peter walked at a determined pace, and Scott struggled to keep up. Then, Peter grabbed Scott affectionately by the neck and slowed to walk with him at the same pace. It was a rare gesture from his father, and Scott felt a wave of reassurance. They stayed ahead of the Secret Service detail of six men, who followed closely, in addition to about thirty other agents on roofs and in doorways, offering support to the local police. Once they entered the hall, Scott found his room and they entered, stopping at the threshold to instruct the detail waiting outside.

"No one comes in. Not even the roommate. Is that clear?" Peter told the head of the detail.

"Yes, sir," the stocky man answered.

Peter closed the door behind them. The small dorm room had two old beds, two wardrobes, two dressers, and two desks all crammed into a rather tiny space. It looked like the desks repelled the articles that should have been on them, and the smell of dirty clothes permeated the room. Nothing was where Peter would have imagined it to be.

"Okay, get it," Peter said simply.

"Get what?" Scott responded, not catching on.

"The computer. Let me see it."

Peter opened the laptop and waited. He typed in *Kepler 3763 in the search bar.* Nothing showed up.

"Where is it?" Peter demanded.

"I deleted it," Scott answered, trying to sound convincing.

"Do you have a printed copy?"

"No."

"The only copy you ever read was in here?"

"Yes."

"I'm going to have to destroy this computer."

"What? No! I have all my shit on there! I'll flunk!"

"You have ten seconds to show me the document or you can kiss this computer good-bye." Scott could see that his father was not kidding.

"Fine."

Scott typed a new search term:

01

The computer immediately showed a folder. Scott clicked the folder, and it opened to reveal a PDF also named 01. He opened it, and the Kepler document appeared.

"Okay, now move," Peter commanded.

Peter sat at the computer and dragged the file to the trash, where he then used a secure empty trash.

"All that crap about responsibility in your speech and you don't even trust your own son," Scott said, although he knew that it was a weak argument.

"Well, you lied, and you're too young to understand, anyway," Peter snapped back.

"But I wasn't going to show it to anyone."

"That's not the point. A lot of things could happen. Your roommate could find it. You might have your computer cloned or spied on by enemies of AmEarth and the first family. I don't know and I don't care. This needs to be erased from our lives."

"You hate me."

"Don't be silly, Scott. I'm doing this to protect you."

"But AmEarth can be destroyed with that evidence. Others have it."

"Scott, listen to me closely. If others use it, then they will be the only thing that will be destroyed. AmEarth will survive as long as the directives are followed."

"How do you know this?"

"I asked the supercomputer," Peter lied.

"Did you ask what would happen if everyone knew Kepler 3763 didn't sustain life?"

"Not in those words, but it did say that aliens do exist. And they probably do."

"But we're not in touch with them." Scott wasn't going to roll over on this issue that easily.

"So what? It's us against them. Period. That fact has united the world. Don't you see? If Kepler is debunked, there are other planets to take its place. AmEarth can and will say whatever it needs to survive. Always. AmEarth controls the information that reaches eight billion people. No one has ever been able to handle that power. Who will inform eight billion people, credibly, that those Kepler aliens don't exist? I doubt YouTube could handle it."

"Dad. I'm sorry for lying, but…"

"It's okay, Scott. I understand your desire for the truth. Believe me, I'm shocked myself, but we need to be on the winning side. You can't survive with ideals alone. Governing is about the spin placed on the truth to perpetuate the work needed to advance our civilization."

"I'm just disappointed."

"I know. Me too."

After a short pause, Peter continued with a more important thought.

"You can only talk to me about this, Scott. And even then, only in person and absolutely nothing on your wafer. We should have a code when we need to meet in person."

"I'll tell you I am worried about Han."

"Okay, Han it is."

They hugged, another rare moment of affection between the two men, as though this secret bonded them more than their blood.

"Come with me to the helicopter. Do you want to come home with us tonight?" Peter asked, hoping his son would agree.

"No, I'll just say good-bye to Mom. I need to study."

"Okay. And Scott, clean this mess up and do your laundry, for god's sake!"

"Yes sir!" Scott agreed and laughed.

Scott actually thought that deleting the Kepler document was a relief. Mr. Landon still had his copy, though. He could do whatever he wanted with it, but Scott had to warn him of the consequences!

Scott felt that he was now free to study and go on with his life. A great weight was lifted off his back that afternoon. The same weight shifted on to Peter’s back, but he gladly accepted it in his role as a father.

TWENTY-ONE

"Ask, 'What is the meaning of life?'" Peter ordered Sergio.

"That's not going to work. I've tried philosophical types of questions before. Essie is not going to explain the vast dynamics of human emotion and unpredictability. She is best used for statistics and number-crunching. Also, on those types of questions, it tends to answer with a question, which can go back and forth for some time," Sergio explained.

They sat at Peter's desk playing with the computer like two children. Peter had called on Sergio to access level six clearance, and also because he felt more at ease with a civilian, even if he was an artist and a fraudulent mastermind.

"Try it anyway," Peter said.

"Essie, what is the meaning of life?" Sergio said.

"Life is needed for the survival of a species. Reproduction is the method to multiply life. The meaning is intrinsic. All life is organic and reproductive from single cell organisms to complex beings. Are you asking in the religious sense?" Essie replied

"You see? A question," Sergio said condescendingly.

"Try, Are you alive?"

"Are you alive?" Sergio typed.

"No."

Peter scribbled a question as Sergio read and repeated.

"Where is Jimmy Hoffa?" Sergio asked.

"There are 437 Jimmy Hoffas in North America, 37 in Latin America and 3 in Asia. Which one do you need to locate?"

Peter wrote frantically and Sergio read as he did so.

"Where is the body of Jimmy Hoffa, deceased in 1975 and President of the Teamsters Union of the United States?" Sergio read out loud.

"There are twenty-three building foundations poured in a hundred-mile radius of the diner where Mr. Hoffa was last seen alive. There is a 97 percent probability that his body lies inside the concrete of one of these twenty-three buildings. The probability of finding his body increases as these old buildings are condemned, but the fate of the foundation is not always demolition. There is a 25 percent chance that his body will be found during demolition in the next ten years, 35 percent in the next twenty, and eventually an 89 percent chance that the body will be found by the end of this century."

"How about that? You didn't think it would know," Sergio said, snarky again.

"A ninety-seven percent chance that he is in the foundations of an existing building," Peter repeated.

"You're not going to demolish twenty-three buildings just to satisfy your curiosity? Are you?"

"I might be the president, but I'm not an idiot," Peter retorted.

"Good. Now ask something that you can really sink your teeth into."

"Okay."

"Who killed John F. Kennedy?"

Sergio smiled with a wide grin showing his large white teeth. It was a great question.

"Essie, who killed John F. Kennedy?"

"John Fitzgerald Kennedy was assassinated by two people with different motives in the same location. Lee Harvey Oswald fired two rounds from the Book Depository Building and hit President Kennedy from behind in the back lumbar region, which was probably not a fatal shot. The second shot hit Governor John Connally in the back. The third shot was fired consecutively with the second shot from a grassy knoll, hitting the president in the head from the front right side. This shot was instantly fatal. The fourth shot missed the convoy altogether, ricocheting off the pavement and nonlethally hitting an innocent bystander with a ricochet fragment. The United States House Select Committee on Assassinations was correct in its assessment that it was not a single shooter. Lee Harvey Oswald was a sharpshooter paid by those involved in organized crime with interests in casinos in Cuba. The other assassin was a foreign Vietnamese mercenary paid by the military-industrial complex with the intention of keeping the Vietnam War from ceasing." Essie replied.

"Boy, that was a long answer. Had enough?" Sergio asked.

Peter thought long and hard in silence. He wrote a last question and slid over to Sergio.

"Why did AmEarth expropriate all fossil fuels on the planet?" Sergio asked.

"Fossil fuels were fast exterminating the citizens of the Earth via global warming and pollution. Most forms of cancer were derived from petroleum byproducts. Even medicine meant to cure humans was ignorantly fabricated with cancer-producing derivatives. The alien threat provided the perfect argument for the need to regulate the use of these fuels. The apparent scarcity of these resources helped prioritize their use for the launching of rockets. The real need was to use these fuels only for aging military ships, airplanes, and rockets, while forcing humans to use battery-powered vehicles and civilian airplanes. AmEarth controls this energy resource to maintain its power and control the greenhouse gas emissions on the planet."

"Okay. Satisfied now?" Sergio said.

"Somewhat. Let me try one looking ahead, rather than back," Peter stated handing him another note.

"Really?, Peter?" Sergio said after reading the note.

"Please."

"How long will the AmEarth empire last?" Peter typed.

"The projected duration of the AmEarth system is indefinite, provided the directives are followed, and the human race remains psychologically engaged with the artificial enemy."

"In other words, we're here to stay," Sergio translated.

"It seems that way…Of course, the caveat is the artificial enemy. Hmmmm…" Peter thought out loud.

"What happens if humans find out that there are no aliens threatening them?" Peter whispered.

"Essie what would happen if all humans knew there was no alien threat?" Sergio asked.

"There is an 80 percent probability of mass defection from AmEarth to the former border system of independent republics. There would be immense pressure to dismantle worldwide directives, and the immediate short-run consequences would be disadvantageous to humanity. In the longer run, new powerful ruling classes would rise to control their regional areas again. There is a greater than 70 percent chance that the Earth would become a small grouping of powerful AmEarth-style countries controlling large blocks of geography. The initial mass defection would be anti-American and would cause many regions to fall into conflict. The outcome would lead to violence and huge human loss of life."

"Wow. I am impressed, Peter. These are things I've never thought to ask," Sergio admitted.

"Pretty awful stuff," Peter said, and then wrote again.

"Why does AmEarth need an enemy to continue?" Sergio read the note.

"Humankind is an evolved species, but it has many limitations. Psychologically, it cannot live without a higher purpose. The absence of a single religion and race requires a powerful uniting element. Survival of the species is an ideal goal. The threat to the entire globe is perfect for uniting and controlling the emotions of humans."

"Which emotions?" Sergio asked of his own volition.

"Mainly the ones caused by freedom: anxiety, loneliness, societal anomie, lack of purpose, distraction, and the need to belong with others."

"Why do some people profit more than others in the system?" Sergio asked again without a need for Peter.

"Directive Number 7. Private property shall be a core principle."

"Just like that. Programmed in," Sergio muttered.

"Would you have it any other way?" Peter asked him.

"Ha ha." Sergio laughed.

"Is communism better than capitalism?" Peter showed another paper.and Sergiio asked..

"The system you refer to as communism has never been practiced. The human species has inherent emotions that make communism impossible—an important one being greed. There will always be different emotional reactions in humans, even under the same conditions, making a communal experience diverse. Capitalism is rough and lacks regulations, making it one of the most barbaric systems of governance ever devised by man. It is impossible to judge which is best—a chimera or a monster."

"Turn it off," Peter said, his mind overflowing with too much information all at once.

"Okay," Sergio said.

They sat there in the private office of the president.

"Would you like a cup of coffee? It's probably the best coffee I've ever had," Peter said.

"Would love one," Sergio replied blankly, obviously considering his own new perspective.

Peter ordered the coffee from Rosemary.

"So you lived in New Zealand?" Peter said.

"Yes. Beautiful place," Sergio replied.

"You were in the film business at Weta, right?"

"You obviously know my story, Mr. President. Is there something you really want to know about me?"

"I just want us to be allies."

"You want to be my friend?"

"I do," Peter answered honestly.

"You know that friends forgive."

"What?"

"Friends are defined differently in your culture than in mine. Let me be clear. Where I come from, a friend never expects anything but friendship, and we pick up where we left off, no regrets or guilt trips."

"I see that as the basis of friendship, too," Peter said, unsure as to where this line of conversation was going.

"Good. Because last I checked, Anglo-Saxons like you are always trying to profit from relationships. You rarely smile unless there is some sort of profit involved."

"I can't deny that about our culture," Peter admitted with a slight blush.

Coffee arrived and was served, and their conversation stopped as though someone had pushed the pause button.

"Do you feel sorry that you'll never be famous?" Peter asked.

"Fame is not the end goal. It's not equated with being happy. Do you know how many famous people commit suicide? Or are unhappy? What makes you think I wouldn't be?"

"You know what I mean, Sergio."

"I do, but my motivations have never placed fame very highly."

"I suppose I thought that all artists wanted some type of fame."

"No, Mr. President. Many artists have no desire for it. Art is expression beyond the here and now; most of the accomplishment is derived from the actual process of creation. Anticipating riches and rewards in one's lifetime is conceited. Most artists are appreciated in earnest only after a few centuries, when we look back and say, 'tow! That guy really knew what he was doing.' At that point, a name is just a reference to follow the work, and it's the work that actually matters."

"I see. A thankless job, one might say."

"The same is true of politicians."

Sergio drank his coffee. Peter thought about Sergio's remark and realized that his own deeds were largely based on the decisions of a computer. Could there be a place for him to make his own mark? He guessed that Bri and Scott would be his legacy. Perhaps that was enough.

"Why aren't you married?" Peter asked.

"I left my heart in New Zealand. Never met one as good," Sergio said bitterly.

"Why don't you go find her?"

"You don't know?"

"Should I?"

"It's part of my AmEarth contract. I can't return to my former life. It could jeopardize the secrecy of the entire project. You know they like to keep the lid on things around here."

"I'm sorry, Sergio," Peter said compassionately.

"It could be worse."

"How?"

"I could go back and find her married with three kids and no interest in me." Sergio said it with a laugh, but he didn't look amused.

Peter smiled. "Yes; that would be worse."

"Women."

"Women indeed."

Peter was actually having a good time with Sergio, and he was not looking forward to all the traveling he had scheduled for the remainder of the month. He would love to sit here and chat with Sergio every day, and talk about things truthfully.

"Listen, Sergio, I have a proposal for you," Peter began.

"I'm all ears," Sergio said.

"I'm scheduled to visit four continents this month. I was wondering if you wanted to come? I may need your access to Essie and I enjoy your company. A friendship has to start somewhere. We'll start in New Zealand, since they just entered AmEarth and completed the unity of the globe. We will then go to the Far East and return to America from Africa and South America. Mainly in Bolivia."

Sergio felt his own blood rushing up to his brain when he heard the president say "New Zealand." He drank from his coffee and hoped that his shock was not too obvious. *Had Peter not listened to him? He was forbidden from traveling to New Zealand...*

"I could come," Sergio offered innocently.

"Do you have any work pending?"

"Nope."

"None?"

"Nope."

"What do you do all day?" Peter asked.

"Do you see this tan? I didn't just wake up like this. I have a sailboat, and I'm keen to learn how to sail it properly."

"Then come with me, Sergio. I'm not looking forward to so much travel and you could help me with my speeches."

"Chen used to ask Essie for help in writing speeches."

"No wonder he sounded like a machine half the time," Peter joked, feeling good about making Sergio the offer of traveling with him.

"How true, but I'm not really a man of words. I'm more an ideas man."

"Well, I happen to be a man of words, and I know that ideas can be helpful. I also need some extra help."

"What do you mean, 'extra help'?"

"Turn Essie back on."

Sergio turned the computer back on.

"Ask about the technology for lie detection. How does it work?" Peter said.

"What? Why?" Sergio asked but Peter did not reply and just edged him to ask with his gaze.

"Essie, how does the lie detection software work?" Sergio asked.

"Lie detection is based on blood flow fluctuations between truthful answers and lies. Humans cannot prevent this change, as the brain shows greater activity when lying, which requires more blood in the cerebral cortex. The visual scan of the retina provides this with a precision that is 99.999 percent accurate within the first minute of a scan and 100 percent accurate within five minutes."

"OK, Turn her off," Peter said.

"What's going on?" Sergio answered, confused but switching Essie off.

"Remember what you said about Anglo-Saxons? That we need to trade profit for friendship?"

"Yes."

"Well, maybe you're right. I need you, and you need me."

"I need you for what?"

"You do want to go to New Zealand, right?"

Sergio stiffened. Apparently the president hadn't missed that overlap.

"What do you need?"

"I need my eyes."

"What?"

"I need a pair of contact lenses that look exactly like my eyes when I am relaxed and comfortable. Can you do that?"

"I can, yes."

"I know. I'm familiar with your alien eyes, and you are truly a wonderful artist. But can you make me human eyes, unflinching and undetectable to the camera software?"

"Absolutely."

Sergio immediately understood where Peter was going with his request.

"This is because you know the truth…." Sergio mused to himself.

"Yes. I don't want the computer to know that I know. I must be able to fool all lie-detectors."

"That's what brought Chen down. It made him too stiff."

"Exactly. How long will it take you to make the contacts?"

"Let me photograph your eyes, Absent any problems I think I can have them to you in a couple of weeks. I'll need the exact size of your eye so they can be comfortable. Let me see…"

Sergio took out his wafer and activated the camera app. He photographed Peter's eyes from mere centimeters away. Then he grabbed a piece of paper and cut it into small circles with Peter's scissors. He placed one directly on Peter's eye.

"Don't move. I need your tears to soften the paper. Don't blink," Sergio said, the director of his own mini-movie session.

"Easier said than done," Peter told him as he fought back the urge to blink.

In a few moments, the paper was wet and Sergio folded it to make a tight fit on the surface of the eye, just like a contact lens. He took a pencil and made two gentle dots on the paper on Peter's eye. Peter trusted Sergio and remained frozen in place. This was uncomfortably intimate, but necessary. Sergio removed the paper lens and picked up his things, carefully putting the mold for the new contacts into a small box for safekeeping.

Sergio nodded.

"A week. Probably even five good days," he said.

The lenses became an unspoken pact between them. Peter arranged for Sergio to travel as a speechwriter, and Sergio was happy to have a relationship with someone in AmEarth who wasn't a military type and actually appreciated his craft. In the American tradition, this friendship began by trade, but would grow through experience and trust.

For Sergio Ramirez-Bulatov, visiting New Zealand was a dream come true. This was a golden opportunity to skirt the travel ban that had been imposed more than a decade ago. He could think of nothing but his former love, and many repressed emotions began to surface as he left Peter's office and walked toward the elevators. Peter evoked executive privilege to bypass Sergio's ban and no one thought to question his override. Being the president did have some perks.

TWENTY-TWO

Peter was in his Shadow White House bedroom looking at pictures of Scott as a young boy. In the pictures, he and Scott were playing with swords, and he remembered Scott's love for *The Lord of the Rings*. He rang Scott's wafer in a haze of nostalgia.

"Hi. It's me," Peter said.

"Hey, Dad. What's up? Do you want to see Han?" Scott asked, expecting this to be a coded conversation.

"Nope. I'm calling so you can play hooky with me."

"What? Explain."

"I'm going to a very special place, and I think it would be great for you to take a week off school and join me. Can you?"

"Dad, these courses are really hard. I don't know if I can—or should."

"I understand, but this is seriously a great place to visit. I'll give you a clue: we can hang out in Middle Earth…"

"That is extremely nerdy of you, Dad. But shit…New Zealand! Wow," Scott said, the excitement in his voice unmistakable.

"We would take the FF. The flight's only four hours," Peter said, sweetening the offer.

"I'll talk to my teachers. I definitely want to go."

***

Scott arrived at the presidential hangar at La Guardia airport, where Air Force FF was parked. It was a small-bodied, elegant, needle-type aircraft. The small wingspan at the rear of the fuselage indicated that it was a plane made to surpass the speed of sound. He was greeted by an aide who took his suitcase and showed him onto the plane. Inside the main cabin, the headroom was barely six feet in height, and Scott instinctively ducked slightly to the left. The seats were grouped two and one, so there was a bit more headroom over the aisle seat in the middle of the fuselage. The experience of traveling in the FF was amazing, akin to flying in a fighter jet. Inside, he saw a single man who had arrived before him; Sergio Ramirez-Bulatov sat facing the cockpit from the last row. He held a frosty glass and sipped on his freshly poured beer from time to time.

"Hi," Scott shyly said, intimidated by Sergio's demeanor of power and wealth combined with coolness.

"You must be Scott," Sergio said.

"Yes. And you are?" Scott asked, although he knew who this man was.

"Sergio."

"Nice to meet you, Mr. Bulatov."

"So you've heard of me?"

"My dad told me a bit about you."

“I’m interested to hear how he described me. What did he tell you?”

“That you would be coming with us and helping him write speeches.”

“That’s all?”

“Yes, but I’ve heard a few other rumors about you,” Scott confessed with a twinkle in his eye. Sergio’s face twitched slightly and Scott could tell that he was getting under his skin.

“What sort of rumors?”

At that moment, Peter walked onto the plane and Scott ignored Sergio’s last question.

“Dad!”

Peter greeted the captain and moved back toward the rear of the plane. Behind him were half a dozen other staff members. Through the window, Sergio saw someone carrying Peter’s bags from the limousine to the rear of the plane. He was on edge, but also excited about the trip back to New Zealand. In his mind, he pictured Robbie just as he had left her, midtwenties and beautiful. He hoped to see her, but he was wildly nervous. He had sent a few emails to her last address, but had received no response. She had never been on social media, at least not with her maiden name. Sergio had attempted to reach her using an alias, and this also proved to be a problem; he couldn’t use his real name, as it might endanger her, so they never managed to reconnect.

Peter sat facing Scott and Sergio in the middle seat. The two seats at his right were quickly filled with staff members. The seat next to Peter was taken by a striking female staffer in her early thirties. The remaining staff filled the other six-seat bay closer to the cockpit. Twelve was a small number for a

TWENTY-FIVE

In the SOI café, overlooking Wellington Bay, Sergio Ramirez-Bulatov sat contemplating the body of water through its huge glass windows. The recent victory for him and Peter had given him precious time and he was more relaxed than ever before. Sailboats shuffled right and left across the bay as he waited for Robbie and Marianne. He didn't need to follow Peter any further on his trip and had no real desire to continue the speech tour. The contact lenses worked marvelously and as long as Peter wore them before leaving for any speaking engagements, he would be fine. Sergio took out his wafer and spoke into it.

"Call Rosita."

Soon, the wafer showed a picture of Rosita, his secretary, on the line.

"Hello, Mr. Ramirez?" Rosita replied in her accented English.

"*Si, Rosa. Soy yo. Quiero que me haga un favor,*" Sergio said in perfect Spanish.

presidential trip. The Air Force FF2, a matching supersonic plane, was also packed with staff. Twenty-four passengers would arrive in Wellington in only four hours. Other less important staff and press representatives had left the day before.

"I trust that you two have met," Peter said.
"We have," Sergio confirmed, somewhat coldly.

The captain appeared in the aisle and addressed Peter.

"Ready for takeoff, sir," he said.
"We're all ready to go," Peter told him.
"We need to move the seats for takeoff, sir."
"Go ahead."

The captain stood up straight and announced to the remaining passengers;

"Everyone on seats facing backward, please stand."

All six passengers facing the rear of the plane stood, and the captain signaled the copilot, who pressed a button that rotated the seats 180 degrees.

"It would be very uncomfortable during our acceleration to face the rear. We will turn them around when we reach optimal altitude," the captain explained.
"Captain?" Scott said.
"Yes, son?"
"What is optimal altitude?"
"About fifty to fifty-five thousand feet."
"That high, eh? Wow."
"Well, there's almost no turbulence at that height."

"Good to hear."

The captain moved up to the cockpit as the plane continued moving toward the takeoff strip. Scott leaned toward Sergio's large round window and looked up.

"I wonder if we'll be able to see it," he said.

"You mean the honeycomb?" Sergio questioned.

"Yes."

"You won't be able to—not from fifty thousand feet, at least. The honeycomb is out beyond the stratosphere," Peter answered, turning around in his seat, as Scott was now behind him.

"If it's there at all," Scott mumbled.

Scott's subversive remark was immediately drowned out by the roar of the engines kicking in, pushing everyone to the backs of their seats. Peter looked at Sergio, his gaze like that of a father asking an uncle for help with his unruly kid, and then immediately moved his head back to use the seat's headrest as support for his neck. The g-forces that the plane created were extremely strong; he could see that rotating the seats was a good decision.

"Listen kid, I want you to pay full attention to me," Sergio whispered into Scott's ear.

"Okay," Scott nodded and avoided turning his head.

He had heard that tone from his father before, but coming from Sergio, it felt ten times more serious.

"You *cannot* be critical of AmEarth in public. This is not a commercial flight. Everything here is wired, and presidential staff members hearing your doubts can harm your father," Sergio warned him.

"I'm sorry. It won't happen again," Scott replied.

"I'm in your camp, Scott. I also distrust authority and power. I come from a place where abuse of power is not only constant and expected, but pervasive. I have learned to separate the lies and deception that were crafted to get AmEarth into power from the actual governing of its system. You should, too."

"I am, kind of, joining the two issues. Someone in the family that also has the right questions."

"Mexico and Russia. That's where I'm from, and let me tell you, institutionalized corruption was rampant, but today they both have a unified rule of law and a clean political system. AmEarth has imposed laws and governing bodies that follow the will of the people. Life has improved dramatically for the people there. Dramatically!"

"Even if they are governed from thousands of miles away? By foreigners?"

"AmEarth is huge, yes, but the world is wired and instant. Mexico and Russia are like states of AmEarth, and share laws, have ministers and vote on local and worldwide elections. They still have a local prime minister that holds their local customs and traditions so they don't feel overwhelmed by being part of AmEarth. It is a new dawn for these places and totally corrupt free. Also we are more integrated and more than ever a single species, so there are no foreigners and no discrimination. Think of the advances in justice with the introduction of powerful computers that help with trials and verdicts. The invention and implementation of the AmEarth anti-perjury software has changed the world. Now that they can detect lying on the witness stand, perjury is a thing of the past."

Bulatov talked with his hands in small gestures and emotionally engaged Scott.

"My Russian family—that is, from my mother's side—was an affluent family that lost everything. They had beautiful land—a large estate near Minsk—in a fertile valley. When my grandfather died, my mother was immediately sued by a debt collector for a debt that she knew nothing about. My mother swears that her father had never gone into debt, but the forged documents went all the way up to the superior court. The judges dismissed my mother's claims because they were in bed with the fraudsters. As soon as my mother lost her land, the new train routes were announced and ran exactly through her estate, making the land much more valuable. My mom was left penniless and moved to Moscow, where she met my dad while he was on vacation. It took them years to get her a travel permit to Europe, but as soon as she crossed the border, she went to Mexico with my dad."

"It seems like a happy ending after all."

"Don't be silly. My mother was affected all her life. She was constantly depressed and sad and often bitter that her stature had been robbed from her. It made for a strange environment in my home. She was the person who introduced me to painting and music. She needed to be in constant connection with a higher sense of existence—one even higher than the position she lost. Even so, her life was not an easy one."

"I'm sorry."

"Don't be. Just remember, putting a stop to lies and deception in the courts is a great improvement to society," Sergio stated with finality.

"I get it..."
"Your father can tell you more."

The plane had reached its desired "safe" altitude. Peter got up and pushed the button that returned his seat to face Scott. The woman next to Peter did not turn her seat around. Sergio immediately stood up and spoke to her.

"Aren't you going to join us?"

"I'm going to try to sleep. I don't feel like traveling backward. Thanks, but no thanks. Is that okay with you, sir?" she asked Peter.

"No problem," Peter replied and raised a partition that gave her more privacy.

"Your loss," Sergio teased her.

"New Zealand, here we come," Peter announced with a smile.

"Sergio was telling me about Russia and the old system of justice. Really interesting stuff," Scott told his dad.

"AmEarth's unification of the world has helped to free and uplift billions of people. Essential human rights have been guaranteed to peoples who lived in oppression for generations—centuries, even. I have recently been briefed on how necessary a central world government is for the survival of mankind and our planet."

"By any means?" Scott asked.

"Certainly not, but AmEarth has mainly been peaceful. All of the European countries joined AmEarth as a block and were immensely powerful, so they did it without significant violence. I think that the unification of the planet has been the single most valuable result that the alien threat has yielded."

"Maybe that was the—" Scott stopped himself, remembering the cautions from his father and Sergio. Everyone was listening.

"If mankind had not united in time, there would have been major threats to the population. It would have been damaging and hurtful, resulting in widespread chaos and famine, as well as major outbreaks of diseases," Sergio added.

"I know that it sounds kooky, but think of it like this: If Earth is a living organism, and it could possibly die due to our misbehavior, then we should place its survival as our top priority. In the old days, we would not accept guilt for any man-made global threat because we didn't trust that people far away would do their part to fix the problem."

Peter was going into lecture mode. Scott could feel it. The four-hour trip became a short master class on the benefits of centralization. Scott thought of various questions, but held back from firing them. It was hard to talk openly with so many onlookers watching them. He bit his lip more than a few times, but kept nodding in agreement. When you catch a government lying, it is hard to swallow anything they say after that, even if the sum total is "good." Four hours of hearing about the great deeds of AmEarth had made Scott numb to the benefits. He really just wanted to look for its flaws.

The captain came to speak with them again, and the turning of the seats ritual was reenacted for landing. Sergio and Scott looked out of the window at New Zealand on their right. It was a mostly green and lush landscape with pure white snow covering the peaks of its mountains. It was as beautiful an island as Scott had imagined. Within minutes, they had safely landed at Wellington International Airport amid huge A380s that made the FFs look like toys.

Before disembarking, Peter, Scott, and Sergio were given bulletproof vests. Sergio and Peter didn't even flinch as they donned theirs, but Scott was a bit taken aback.

"Dad, after all the talk of how good AmEarth is, why do we need these?" Scott asked.

"New Zealand has just entered AmEarth, but most of its people have not. These are common-sense precautions, Scott. In a few years, you'll be able to come here without any fear. It'll be just as easy as traveling in Europe is now, but for today, we'd rather be careful," Peter explained.

Peter was slightly annoyed by Scott's attitude, but it seemed normal for a teenager to question and rebel. Peter was sure that Scott would outgrow this constant need to question, although his own curiosity had been integral to his rise within AmEarth. *Wasn't it enough that he had listened? What else did he want?*

When the doors opened, a blaring heat they had not expected swiftly entered the cabin. Sergio smiled like a young child in a toy store and made satisfied sounds that left no doubt as to his approval of the heat and humidity. When they left the plane, something completely unexpected happened to Scott. Teenage girls were in the crowd, screaming at the top of their lungs; they held handwritten signs with *Scott* written all over them. He had become a global star as his images, shown during the campaign and the Columbia University event, circled the globe. Peter, Scott, and Sergio walked down a long red carpet that led to the reception committee, which included Prime Minister Robert Smith.

"I guess they like you, son," Peter spoke out of the corner of his mouth.

"A politician is born," Sergio added.

"You're both crazy. This will pass," Scott said, trying to hide his grin and blushing cheeks.

Prime Minister Smith shook hands with Peter and Sergio, as well as Scott.

"It seems you are quite the item with our Kiwi youth," Robert said as he shook Scott's hand.

The Secret Service detail stood inches away from the trio. Their attitude was all business and many AmEarth soldiers could be seen around the perimeter. At about one hundred paces, a short chain-link fence held the onlookers back. There were also bleachers behind it that held a few hundred other visitors. In the background, thousands more stood at the fence line. Sergio walked toward a spot at the fence, looking at nothing but a single woman who stood there staring straight at him. The security forces moved to stop him from wandering off, and Scott sensed his wish to depart, so he decided to go with Sergio, leaving Peter to chat with the PM and his entourage.

"Dad?" Scott called.

"Yes?" Peter said.

"Can Sergio and I go talk to the crowd?"

Peter saw that Sergio and his son were being held back by security forces, so he nodded his head, giving Sergio and Scott permission to go and greet those behind the fence. The security detail kept close by and they reached the fence quickly. Scott was cheered and girls moved to touch him as if he were a Windsor. Scott shook hands and greeted as many girls as his eyes could take in.

In the chaos of people's cheers for Scott, Sergio stood motionless and largely ignored. Through the fence, he was holding Robbie's hands, their fingers interlaced. Their foreheads touched through the cold metal and tears flowed from their eyes, streaming with happiness and sadness, but mostly love.

“You’re okay?” Robbie asked.

“Now I am,” Sergio answered breathlessly. “I never thought I’d see you again!”

“Are you married? Do you have children?” Robbie looked up at him pleadingly.

“No and no. Are you?”

“I’m divorced…”

Sergio was approached by a Secret Service agent from behind.

“Sir, we need you to stand back. For your safety,” the guard stated sternly. He noticed that something was happening as soon as he saw their faces.

“I’m sorry to interrupt, sir. Do you need me to clear her?”

“Yes, can you? Please. Clear her.”

The guard asked the people nearby to move back from the fence and motioned for Robbie to come toward him.

“Ma’am, are you alone?” the guard asked her as he looked her up and down.

“Yes, I came alone.”

The guard nodded and pushed up on the fence hinges to unlock two sections and pull her through. Then, he closed the sections and proceeded to search her with a wand device. No beeping was heard.

“You’re cleared, ma’am.”

Scott looked at what was happening and knew that the woman must be Robbie. He saw the moment when the guard cleared her and Sergio embraced her like she might disappear at any second. They had been apart for so long and seemed unable to separate. All along, AmEarth authorities had prevented this reunion, which felt like an injustice and a true tragedy.

"You received my message! I didn't know if that old email address was still active. I'm so happy to see you. So you live alone? How are you? God, you're just as beautiful as ever." Sergio kissed her as he spoke.

"So many questions. I didn't respond to your email…I'm sorry…later I'll explain that. I don't live alone. I have a daughter."

"Really? I'd love to meet her."

Robbie smiled.

"Why are you here? In New Zealand, I mean?"

"I'm traveling with Peter Johansen, welcoming New Zealand to AmEarth. I'll explain why it took so many years for me to return, but not right now."

"Okay. How long will you be here?"

"I don't know yet. For now, this moment is enough. So, a daughter. She must be beautiful. How old is she?"

"Twenty-two."

Sergio couldn't stop his jaw from dropping. Twenty-three years had passed since he had last seen Robbie. But a daughter who was twenty-two…Could it be?

"Twenty-two? Is she…?" Sergio wasn't able to finish the question.

"Yes, Sergio. She's yours. She looks just like you. Her name is Marianne," Robbie confessed with a huge smile.

Sergio was speechless, and the following moment felt like an eternity. Behind him, Peter walked toward them, followed by security. He lightly touched Sergio's shoulder. Sergio was unresponsive to the touch; his mind was a million miles and years away.

"Are you going to introduce me?" Peter asked quietly in his ear.

Sergio looked at him dumbly, in shock. The feeling of blood rushing to his head made him drunk with happiness. Sergio cleared his throat and found his voice.

"Peter, this is Robbie Taylor. My friend from a long time ago," Sergio explained. Scott had heard the entire conversation about Sergio's daughter, but Peter was still out of the loop.

"Nice to meet you, Robbie," Peter said as he shook her hand.

"Nice to meet you, Mr. President," Robbie answered, star-struck.

"Dad, Sergio and Robbie have a daughter!" Scott said, unable to keep the revelation to himself.

"Really? A daughter?" Peter asked, shock and happiness on his face.

"I just found out," Sergio fumbled with his words, but the huge smile on his face told the story.

"When Sergio left New Zealand, I didn't know that I was pregnant, and then he disappeared. I've been looking for him, but it was like the earth had swallowed him whole," Robbie informed the trio of men.

“He’s been busy working for AmEarth in New York,” Peter told her.

“I know. But back then, I had no idea where he went. He was so opposed to that sort of work,” Robbie said.

“Why don’t we all go to the ambassador’s residence and settle in? Tomorrow I have an important speech to make, and I think that we all need to focus,” Peter said, trying to change the subject and move on.

“I’d like to meet her,” Sergio said, ignoring the president’s words.

“Absolutely. How about tonight?” Robbie suggested.

“Is she here in Wellington?”

“Yes.”

“Do you live here?”

“No. I have my parents’ old flat, though, so we use it when we come into town. We live in Westport, on the other island. Just a small fishing village.”

“You’re not at Weta?”

“No, I sold it when my dad died.”

“I’m sorry…I think,” Sergio said with a smirk.

“He really did hate you,” Robbie said and laughed.

“And your mom?”

“She passed away last year. She was too sad to live alone. Died of a broken heart.”

“I’m sorry, Robbie.”

The group began walking toward the main airport building. The prime minister joined them as they moved to the limousines that would take them to the house of the AmEarth ambassador, formerly the US ambassador’s residence. New Zealand felt like a tiny America, complete with small-scale buildings in its downtown area. It was like being in a small city of an industrial country with people mostly of English descent in buildings that belonged to some point in the past. The contrast was that these people were highly intelligent and lived *mentally* in the future. Some people did turn out to see the motorcade and Peter was keenly aware of the bulletproof glass that protected them.

Sergio couldn't stop touching Robbie, holding both her hands and staring longingly at her. Scott thought that it was almost creepy, but couldn't judge too much, as he knew they had been separated for longer than he'd been alive. The residence was a sprawling home in the best neighborhood of Wellington and sat behind tall walls; cameras were everywhere. The garden was manicured with a beautiful green lawn and flowerbeds all around it. The home was modern in a Frank Lloyd Wright imitation style that had been popular in the 1960s and dated back to that era. The use of steel and stone was quite beautiful, and made the flat roof of the living room appear to be floating over the home. Glass covered two sides and a stone wall composed the third, but the stone wall did not meet the roof because there were glass panels high above the wall, creating the optical illusion of a flying roof. Scott was totally oblivious to the architectural details, but Peter was not.

"I grew up in a house from this era, Scott," Peter told his son.

"Bringing back any memories?"

"I'll say. Good ones."

That evening, Sergio left with Robbie to meet his daughter for the first time. Peter sent armed bodyguards to keep Sergio in one piece and he didn't return to the ambassador's residence until late that night.

TWENTY-THREE

Neil Chen Tyson had been furious at Peter's behavior at the last Supercomputer Committee meeting and still could not believe how short-lived the new "ignorant president" scheme had been. Peter would lie and the world would discover the alien hoax even faster than before. Chen was determined to stop this as soon as possible. He traveled from his home in upstate New York to the AmEarth headquarters and ordered an emergency meeting of the committee. The quorum was seven members and if unanimous, a resolution could pass. The computer room was empty when he switched the machinery on. Lights turned on inside the huge glass table that housed the computer keyboards that the members used, and two large monitors lit up with the familiar date on screen.

'10/5/2045 — Good evening, President Chen,' Essie said.

"Call the committee members. I would like a quorum for an emergency meeting." Chen responded.

In various homes and apartments in the New York and Washington areas, the wafers summoned a quorum of members. The monitors flashed members' names as they agreed to join in the meeting. Chen saw the names light up, and about five minutes later he had five members joining him on the screen: General John Redford, General Roberts, Director of NASA Larry Kanter, Economic Minister Susan Petrov, and Secretary of Foreign Affairs Jonathan Richardson.

Then there was a pause. No quorum yet. Chen waited the agreed twenty minutes and was about to call off the meeting in frustration when a final name began to flash.

Director of Extraterrestrial Affairs Sergio Ramirez-Bulatov

A quorum at last.

The connections were made, and all six members joined virtually. Some just communicated via an avatar phone call, while others were represented by a video call. Chen disabled Essie before starting the meeting and all members could see this on their screen. It was well understood that Essie needed to be kept out of the Committee's decisions if their where to keep her in their control.

"Welcome, members. We barely have a quorum, but I called this emergency meeting because I am very worried that our new president is going to drop the ball. He knows about our fabricated past, and this problem needs to be addressed. I move to inform Essie that President Peter Johansen was the wrong choice; that he is aware of the truth behind AmEarth and will not be able to fulfill his duties appropriately. We will then her decide Peter's future."

Jonathan Richardson of Foreign Affairs immediately voiced his concern.

"We just finished an election cycle, Neil. It was a lot of work and quite an expense to boot. Do you really think this is warranted?"

"I'm really not willing to open the discussion. You all know me, and when I am certain of something, I'm usually right. I want Peter to go," Chen stated.

"What does the resolution say?" Ramirez-Bulatov asked.

"Sergio, this is perhaps the first time you've chosen to engage in any way with this committee. I actually expected you not to show, as usual," Chen snapped at the dissident voice.

"*Et alors…*" Sergio replied.

"The resolution simply states that Peter was the wrong choice because he is an inexperienced president and will not be able to successfully lie to the people. He has compromised the intent of the last directive, and the computer should be informed." Chen rattled off his answer as though it should be common sense.

"I would like to read the resolution before it is entered. Can you send us copies?" Sergio said.

"But you've never…" Chen began with a note of suspicion in his voice.

"I would like to read it as well," General Redford added.

"That's fine. I have the document here. Sending it now," Chen replied.

General Redford objected a few moments later once he had the file in front of him.

"This is twenty pages long! I cannot and will not make a decision on this in an emergency time frame. I will read this and we can revise it tomorrow."

"But we need this done tonight. Peter is about to go on air in New Zealand, and there are provisos in the resolution to stop him from doing so," Chen shot back desperately.

"Neil, if Peter is caught lying tomorrow, then so be it, but you will not have my vote on this tonight," General Redford replied.

"Nor mine," Sergio added, and then signed out of the conference call.

"But gentlemen!"

They were already gone.

"Hmmm, well, I guess we will need more time. Thank you all," Chen said before signing off himself.

With that, the remaining four members signed off and disappeared. Neil Chen sat alone in the Supercomputer Committee room, looking slightly defeated, but determined. A fight is what Peter would get, and as soon as his speech in New Zealand ended, he would be able to determine the true efficacy of this new president.

TWENTY-FOUR

That October morning in New Zealand was marked by unusual weather. The summer had arrived faster than in previous years, and the night air was barely chilly. As soon as the first rays of sunlight emerged, even the slight morning dew was immediately evaporated by the heat. Modern air-conditioning had made life tolerable, but the swings in temperature on the remote island constantly kept the inhabitants on edge. The AmEarth embassy compound had state-of-the-art equipment to maintain a luscious garden, despite these climate challenges.

Behind the glass walls of the dining room, a few baby kangaroos spied on the group of humans arriving gradually to the buffet table. Breakfast was laid out in silver settings with plates of scrambled eggs, sausages, bacon, assorted pastries, French toast, and pancakes. Sergio had to be pried from his bed, as he was not only jet-lagged, but also exhausted by the emotional meeting the previous evening and the ridiculous Supercomputer Committee telephone call. Sergio needed to convey the events of the meeting to Peter, but he needed to do so privately.

During the limousine drive to Wellington's city center, where Peter would deliver his speech, Scott remembered that Sergio had gone to meet his daughter the night before.

"How's your daughter?" Scott asked.

"Yes, of course. What is she like?" Peter echoed, eager to take his mind off the speech looming before him.

"This is her," Sergio said.

Sergio swiped a picture onto his wafer and pressed the play button. A short video of his daughter played on the limousine monitor. She was a beautiful girl with red flowing hair and a magical smile. She looked at the camera shyly, as if she were being forced to allow the filming because it was her father asking for it. Behind her was the dining room/living room of Robbie's flat in downtown Wellington, which looked luxurious.

"What's her name?" Scott asked.

"Marianne," Sergio replied proudly.

The short video ended, and by that time they had arrived at the city center. The mood outside was both festive and sour at the same time. The streets had police line fencing and many citizens were flocking rows deep along the streets, hoping to get a glance at the president of the world. It was evident that half of New Zealand was relieved to finally join AmEarth, while the other half was still bitterly independent and resentful of the invasion, although it had been a peaceful one. The members of New Zealand most affected and outraged by the AmEarth annexation were astronomers, but that was a minuscule segment of the population.

The city plaza was filled with people; the bodies stretched as far back as the bridge that led to the ocean. Large screens provided video and audio of the live event in the plaza, throughout the side streets, and across the globe. This would be Peter's first major speech since the Columbia University speech on reproduction; having it come from New Zealand made it particularly special, so it would be widely disseminated. Neil Chen Tyson and the Supercomputer Committee were monitoring this speech with more care than any other in their history. Peter had skirted alien issues in other speeches and had therefore appeared truthful, but this time, the alien threat was front and center on the topic block. Before getting out of the limousine, Peter dismissed everyone, including Scott, and stayed behind with Sergio.

"You look like shit," Peter told him.

"What do you expect? I think I only slept for an hour!" Sergio replied. He brought out the kit with the contact lenses from his pocket and handed it to Peter.

"Make sure no one is watching," Peter said.

"You're clear. Do it now."

"Okay."

"If they make you cry, make sure you're saying something emotional."

"Shut up!"

Sergio chuckled, but immediately contained himself and changed the subject to something more serious.

"Peter, not to add any pressure, but Chen called an emergency meeting of the committee last night in a bid to replace you before your speech. Interestingly, before I could object, Redford threw a wrench into it. He said that he would not vote immediately. I guess he didn't think that it was an emergency," Sergio explained.

Peter had placed the lenses in his eyes and was squinting while looking down, trying to summon up tears to moisten the lenses. They covered about a third of his eye and felt uncomfortable, but manageable.

"Did you vote?" Peter asked, slightly distracted.

"It never reached a vote, but I'm sure that Chen will keep at it."

"I can't deal with that right now," Peter said,

Sergio shrugged in agreement.

Handlers were tapping at the glass windows of the limo, implying that they needed Peter. He left the limousine and squinted into the sun. He could see normally and in a few seconds, he forgot that he even had the contact lenses on. Peter walked to the podium that held the teleprompter and microphone; the dreaded camera feeds were leering at him from every angle. Different groups around the world would pull these feed images into their programs to detect any lies. The warm summer air of the southern hemisphere still felt strange to him, but he welcomed it after the bitter weather in New York. He waited to be introduced by the prime minister.

"I want you all to know that I have personally met Peter Johansen and I must say that he is a grounded, intelligent, and compassionate human being with a beautiful family and a good heart. Ladies and gentlemen, I give you the supreme president of AmEarth, Mr. Peter Johansen," Robert announced grandly.

"Thank you, Prime Minister Smith and all the people of New Zealand—or should I say, Kiwis!" Peter began.

Some cheering was heard, followed by some light booing.

"I am officially here to welcome New Zealand to the community of AmEarth. I know that this is a controversial decision to some of you. New Zealand is not the first country to go through a transition like this—in fact you are the last. Without you, AmEarth has not been whole and completely safe. If anything, the duty of a civilized government is to provide safety to its citizens, which is why AmEarth has been so keen on having New Zealand join us. Finally, we can confidently tell the world that we are safer today than we have ever been in the past."

Clapping erupted from the crowd, and Peter quieted them after a moment with a raised hand.

"AmEarth will not endeavor to change your culture, your values, or your way of life."

More clapping was heard, and he was pleased to hear less and less booing with every statement.

"Change will only be felt in some aspects of your life, but we believe that this will be a positive change. For instance, you will automatically join the World Center for Disease Control and its registry, allowing you to receive valuable medicine and proven techniques to fend off illnesses. With your inclusion in the WCDC, many of the remaining diseases will be eradicated from the planet."

Peter paused, but the clapping didn't start, so he quickly moved forward.

"AmEarth will employ all military personnel and able-bodied men and women who need work to complete the World Protection Project, commonly known as the WPP. That is the honeycomb structure that AmEarth has been building in the exosphere. We intend to finish the honeycomb protection grid around the Earth as soon as possible. This will not disrupt civil society and life will continue here in this pristine and beautiful part of the world, just as it always has, but you will have the added benefit of full employment. Other former countries plagued by unemployment and underachievement are now prospering societies within the AmEarth global community. All new employees of the WPP begin a mandatory training that lasts from twelve to twenty-four months, depending on the current education levels of the individuals. The employment is immediate, so in any given year, AmEarth is educating millions of people and improving their livelihood, even when they leave the WPP for civilian life. This core AmEarth education is mostly science-based, but also has history and humanities in its program. It is curated by top educators from around the world and also prepares our young men and women for basic AmEarth concepts, such as respect for all races, respect for life, and respect for our environment."

He paused, and the applause was even stronger. Full employment was one of the most popular perks of AmEarth.

"Your elected prime minister has accepted the position of world minister of parks and wildlife, with its headquarters in New York, but he will remain here until you elect his successor. You will always have democracy and your elected leaders, as well as the same court system and legislative branch. New Zealand will also have a representative voice in the central government and a legislator of your choice will join the legislative branch of AmEarth in New York."

He paused for effect, but a heckler's voice carried loudly through the silence.

"Why did you take over the observatories?"

Peter hesitated, undecided whether to respond or continue with his script. He decided to wing it.

"The gentleman has asked me why AmEarth took over the observatories in New Zealand. It is perfectly logical that if our threat is coming from space, we should control all observation and access points to space. In the past, observatories had no military value and we appreciated them as sources of scientific knowledge and discovery. Today, however, they are our first points of defense against a threat that could decimate our species."

Clapping ensued, making Peter feel good about his spontaneous oratory skills. He had put the heckler in his place without coming off as arrogant. He continued his speech.

"AmEarth has valued the New Zealand dollar at a rate of 337 to one Orb. All of your currency will be exchanged at this rate in the banking system as of tomorrow, and for the next three months, your paper and coin currency can be redeemed at your nearest bank. Therefore, I urge you all to exchange your notes and coins before they become null and void. If you have family members who do not bank and save in their mattresses, I also encourage them to understand that things are changing. However, make no mistake, there has never been a complaint from people who have joined the Orb monetary system. The Orb has a savings rate of six percent and inflation is pegged at two percent per annum worldwide. Everyone can now save without the fear of inflation or the devaluation of currency. Savings are an integral need for our society, and through them, we can have an appropriate credit system to ensure the funding of projects and businesses. These political and economic advantages should not be taken lightly, as they represent the epitome of human economic achievement."

A smaller round of clapping ensued, but Peter had expected the financial details to be less exciting.

"From now on, all alien threats are the responsibility of the entire human race and we are finally closing the gaps. Together. This is the necessary union of our species, as we have a common enemy and purpose. Our life as a species will prosper as we join together in common causes. You will all be better off tomorrow than ever before in your past. Not only has the alien threat united us as a species, but it has also made us better and more efficient. We can now unite to protect our precious resources, keeping them viable and renewable so that we can be the best species in the universe."

Some heckling was audible.

"There are hundreds or thousands if not millions of alien life forms in the universe; this is a statistical and scientific fact. We cannot know their intentions or technologies until contact is made. To date, there has only been contact with Kepler 3763, home to an alien species that for years we believed to be friendly. Now, we know that they are a threat, but there may well be other hostile aliens in the universe with even more advanced technologies. It is not only fear that motivates AmEarth, but also survival and smart thinking. We know the types of weapons they have deployed and the recent success of the WPP. Now, it is a race to close all gaps in the honeycomb to prevent the worst-case scenario from occurring. We need to lead the universe, so if we don't move forward, we will regret it."

"We must also remember that our unified human race has managed to reverse the trends of global warming and overpopulation. Diseases and epidemics have been eradicated through central planning. New trends point to humans living longer and better throughout their lives, which is good for all mankind."

Another round of applause interrupted his speech.

"Medicine has improved for all, not just for a few, and humanity has recognized the importance of every single human life in both legal and social terms. Humans are no longer discriminated against, and there are no more boundaries separating countries to create unfair differences between us. The rule of a single law in the world is proving to be the most effective tool that mankind has to ensure our well-being and happiness. As we speak, new directives are being written and vetted by ministers from all over the world, like the reproductive responsibility directive I recently announced, which legislates the duties of reproduction as a subject of great importance. We are in a long-term trend for the better."

Clapping ensued once again.

"Let's celebrate the potential of every single human on this planet and give them what they need to live a successful and productive life. Welcome to AmEarth! Now, it is your turn to welcome AmEarth into your life."

Peter finished to resounding applause and he waved broadly as he exited the stage. That is where he found Sergio on his wafer. He motioned subtly that they should talk. Sergio covered the wafer microphone and whispered to Peter.

"They just called another meeting of the committee. I need to attend to see what Chen is up to."

"Go ahead." The pair walked to a waiting limousine, and Peter sat down, keeping quiet while Bulatov joined the meeting.

In New York, ex-president Chen Tyson sat in the Supercomputer Committee room in the AmEarth Tower. General Redford and Director Kanter were there with him, as well as enough other members to constitute a quorum, regardless of whether Sergio participated. In one PiP screen Sergio appeared, looking sleepy and disheveled, although this was hardly noticeable to the attendees, as he always looked slightly unkempt.

"To all those joining us, we are still waiting on the lie-detection score from President Johansen's speech, which just ended. Please bear with us," Chen announced to the members.

They waited patiently and quietly for Essie to deliver the results.

"Number of lies: 0" Essie said.

"I can't believe it!" General Redford sputtered.

"That's impossible!" Director Kanter said.

"Either he is the best liar on Earth or he's not human. His performance was flawless," Chen said softly, almost to himself.

"I'm going to verify this," General Redford said as he grabbed his wafer to call someone.

"Yes, this is Redford. Let me speak to her. Mary, did you hear the speech? And…Really? That's what we're seeing here as well. Okay. Thanks." Redford hung up.

"Well?" Chen said.

"Same result. Zero lies."

"But that's impossible." Chen said and turned Essie off.

"We know that he's lying. He even asked the computer about the temperature on Kepler 3763. We all saw it. This is some kind of trick," Chen muttered angrily.

"The software would not fail completely. If there is a trick, it's not from the computers; it's from him. Only a deep emotional disconnect can fool the computers, and even then, there would be some false positives. I have never seen a zero score. It is statistically impossible," Director Kanter insisted.

"He is a liar of psychopathic proportions! I called this meeting to discuss the succession, as I expected Peter to fail miserably. Essie was expected to react negatively Peter after this speech. But this…I never imagined." Chen was practically speechless.

"It might be good," Redford suggested.

"How? He knows," Chen snapped.

"So did you, and you became ineffective. Computers could read you like a book. Now we have a president who can be effective. Who cares if he knows? The computers apparently think that he doesn't, and as long as that's the case, I can live with that," Redford stated.

"He is right, you know. This is a particularly sweet solution, because we don't have to put on an act in front of him the whole time," Director Kanter added.

"But my resolution would inform Essie of what the situation really is," Chen ventured.

"You also wanted to strip him of all his dignity. Your resolution is like an impeachment, as if Peter was a traitor whom you then pardon. It would turn him into nothing," Redford argued.

"He is nothing. I made him," Chen shot back.

"You are wrong in voicing these opinions. Peter has been loyal and efficient. Look at how well he handled the crowd in New Zealand. If anything, he's exceptional. You haven't been able to deliver a speech like that in years." Director Kanter said.

"What are you trying to say? That I'm just jealous? You insult me, Larry!" Chen's face was crimson.

"Please, gentlemen," Redford said loudly. "Control your emotions. Peter is effective, so I do not see a need to inform Essie. We have a president whom the people like and trust. He is also an excellent liar, so let's celebrate, rather than shoot AmEarth in the foot unnecessarily. We need a good communicator for the sake of AmEarth!"

"All those in favor of keeping Peter in his position, say aye," Chen declared suddenly, feeling that he had lost this battle, but perhaps not the war.

"Aye!" Every member present, whether virtual or in person, consented. This included Sergio from the other side of the planet.

"So your resolution is off the table, Chen," Redford announced.

"I understand. It is withdraw." Chen said, defeated.

Neil Chen was furious that this young nobody had somehow figured out a way to fool the computer. Chen had been removed from his cherished position by the very supercomputer that he had helped to create years ago. Neil Chen's reign could have been the start of a dynasty but instead it was now in the hands of a completely ordinary man. He disliked his shift out of the limelight and into the secrecy of the Supercomputer Committee. He itched to find out how Peter had done it, if only to satisfy his own curiosity.

***

Sergio looked up at Peter as he turned off his wafer and smiled widely. Peter had become the world's most powerful man thanks to Ramirez-Bulatov's special effects handiwork in crafting him the perfect set of contact lenses. He owed more to New Zealand than he imagined, as it had been at Weta Studios that Sergio had learned his craft.

"The contacts worked," Sergio announced happily. "Essie scored you a zero for lies and Chen withdrew his resolution to remove you. You have the support of the Supercomputer Committee!"

"This calls for a celebration!" Peter said.

"I don't know if Chen will stop. He sounded furious!" Sergio cautioned.

"Let's worry about him later. I want to take out the lenses and go for a drink!"

What Peter hadn't considered was that this computerized lie analysis did not occur solely at the high level of AmEarth, but also in many communities around the world. Different organizations had the software to detect lies; some were journalistic, some legal, and some were certain wealthy individuals and corporations. Across the globe, the zero score for lying shocked experts. Among the holders of this software were rebel forces that also looked for clues in speeches from the government. In fact, there was one particular rebel group only an island-hop away from New Zealand, near Mount John University Observatory.

Deep in a remote ravine at the end of a narrow country road, this rebel group had camped out at an old farm belonging to the well-known astrophysicist, Oliver Cook. At that location, wafer communications were impossible because the nearest transmission towers were miles away. The only communication was through a satellite dish that gave them access to the Internet. They knew that former President Chen had constantly been lying, especially when talking about aliens or their technology.

Oliver Cook, who had been released by AmEarth after the take-over of the observatory as they had no evidence to hold him, now sat in his country home with Pat Jackson. They speechlessly watched as their computer flashed a zero score over Peter's frozen image. The speech had played on a large monitor in the Arts-and-Crafts-style living room of the ranch house. Pat played and rewound the highlights regarding the aliens and was baffled once again by the computer's response. To the side of the TV, on a bookcase, were pictures of various people, among them Robbie and Marianne.

"Yes?"

"*Quiero que me mandes el "Queen" a Nueva Zelandia, a Wellington. A la brevedad.*"

With that single phone call, Sergio had ordered his sailboat and crew to be sailed halfway around the world to New Zealand from Long Island. The longer the boat took to arrive, the better, as spending time with his girls had become his first priority. His life had literally changed overnight. He called Peter next.

"Sergio, where are you? We need to go. The winds are increasing, and they say gusts here could prevent departure. The pilots want to leave." Peter spoke urgently.

"That's why I'm calling."

"Where are you?"

"I'm in a cafe, waiting for Robbie and Marianne. I can't go with you, Peter."

"Finish your reunion and come to the airstrip."

"No, Mr. President. I already sent for my boat. You can go on without me."

"What about the rest of the tour? I need you, Sergio. The lenses and the speeches!"

"Peter, all you need to do is put them in on speech days. You tolerated them perfectly. Just take them off later so that people don't figure it out. Remember, at night, pupils get bigger, so be careful."

"Sergio, you're nuts. When will you be back?"

"I think we'll arrive back in New York at about the same time as you. Try to understand what I'm going through here. Please. You have a daughter, after all."

"I guess that's true," Peter admitted.

"You'll be fine. Just keep your eyes open for Chen's next move."

"I'll do that. Enjoy your time with them."

Sergio hung up. At that moment Marianne, Robbie, and Scott entered the cafe and immediately headed toward Sergio. Scott sped up to reach him first and spoke quietly to him.

"I hope you don't mind that I tagged along when I saw them in the hotel," Scott said.

"Your dad is leaving right now. Does he know you're here?" Sergio said.

"No."

"Well, you need to call him right now. He'll be looking for you," Sergio insisted as he pulled out a chair for Robbie, who had arrived at the table.

"I'm not scheduled to go with him. I have a separate flight back to New York, so he said that I could stay for a few more days," Scott explained.

"Hey you," Robbie said.

"Hey yourself," Sergio replied with a smile.

"Hello…Dad," Marianne spoke, still hesitating with the new word in her mouth.

"Hi, sweetie." Sergio turned to Scott. "When are you going back?"

"Day after tomorrow," Scott answered.

"Cool."

The afternoon meal was pleasant, although Scott couldn't figure out why Marianne was being so cold to him. He tried to be funny and smart, but she treated him like he had the measles. The only subject that somewhat sparked her interest was his father, much to his dismay. He was determined to be his own man and wanted to connect with people because of who he was, not because of his father. However, her cold shoulder was relentless.

"Tell me, Scott, how did your father end up being supreme president?" Marianne asked.

“Well, I think Sergio knows more about that than I do. Why don’t you explain to Marianne how my dad got to where he is?”

“The answer is simple. He was facially recognized by the masses, and he was qualified to do the job. The supercomputer provided his name after assessing thousands of senior-ranking officials with hundreds of parameters, one of which was popularity. Frankly, your father was well thought of by a lot people. He reported on foreign affairs for AmEarth and the powers that be decided that he was a good communicator. He polled well. You know that politics is all about perception. That’s why I can’t be president. Some of us are too good-looking, so we poll badly.”

Scott laughed.

“He is handsome, though,” Marianne said.

“Yes, he is,” Robbie agreed.

“Were you considered, Dad?” Marianne asked.

“What? Of course not…I told you, I’m much too handsome for that job,” Sergio joked.

“All kidding aside though, you’re a senior-ranking official, right?” Marianne asked.

“I’m in a different category, though. I’m not a public figure, and my work is top secret.” Sergio lowered his voice on that final phrase.

Scott felt supremely insecure, but Marianne thought his father was handsome, which gave him a bit of confidence, as they did look very much alike. All his life he had been badgered by aunts and uncles, teachers, and friends about this similarity, but it was finally a good thing. An emotion he had always felt for Cate had surfaced, but this time it was directed toward Marianne, despite barely knowing her. It seemed to grow stronger and more painful by the hour, like increasingly hard punches to the gut.

The “second honeymoon” of Sergio and Robbie was fast becoming overwhelmingly romantic for both Marianne and Scott. He did not know how to approach Marianne to ask her to spend some time alone with him. Finally, he mustered up the courage and asked her.

“Marianne, do you want to go for a drive or something? I’d hate to go back to America without seeing the sights.”

“I don’t know,” Marianne said warily.

“Come on, I don’t know anyone in this whole country. Please?”

Marianne got up. “Only if you explain some things to me about AmEarth.”

“What do you want to know?” Scott said, standing up from the table, curious about what she would ask him. Perhaps she would ask things he might know about that weren’t on the public record.

“Mom? We’re going for a drive, okay?” Marianne asked.

“Sure, honey,” Robbie said and looked back at Sergio as they returned to gazing at one another.

“I thought they would never leave,” Sergio whispered and kissed Robbie long and hard.

As they walked to the entrance of the restaurant, Scott realized that his security personnel were waiting for him outside. He stopped Marianne.

“Marianne. I can’t just leave and get in your car,” Scott said.

“What? Why?” Marianne asked, confused.

“We’ll be followed. And I’m tired of the whole security detail thing. I want to leave, but I don’t want us to be followed.”

“Okay…how about I just leave alone, get in the car and drive away? You go back inside and leave from the side door. Then walk along the water. There’s a small sidewalk that hugs the water, so just avoid being seen between the restaurant and the next building. Go down to the corner of the sidewalk, and I’ll be there waiting by the townhouses.”

“Perfect.”

Scott walked to the rear of the restaurant near the toilets and found the exit to the little sidewalk Marianne had mentioned. He turned left and followed it to the first gap between the wooden buildings. He peered back and saw the Secret Service agents eyeing Marianne as she started her antique VW convertible. It was clear that she was alone, so they didn’t notice Scott run the twenty-foot distance to the cover of the adjacent building. From there, he walked on the sidewalk beside the water to the road where Marianne was waiting. She had gotten there only a minute or so before him. He jumped in without opening the door, and they sped off.

“Whew…I love this,” Scott announced, grinning.

“Freedom is new to you?” Marianne said.

“You have no idea.”

“Try me.”

“Imagine that one day you’re no longer alone. Ever. Besides the bathroom—I think,” he chuckled.

“Seems overwhelming.”

“It is. Whooooweeee!” Scott screamed as he stood up on the shotgun seat of the clunker.

Marianne drove fast around Oriental Parade Road, which hugged the waterline and rapidly merged into Cable Road. She looked at her watch, as though she was in a hurry.

"Where are we going?" Scott questioned, although he hardly cared about the answer.

"Picton. If we make it," she replied.

"What's Picton?"

"Freedom."

"Make it? What do you mean, 'if we make it'?"

"The ferry leaves in five minutes."

"Where?"

"There."

Marianne pointed to a large blue and white ship that had an entrance port for vehicles at its rear. She sped directly onto the ramp and made it with a full two minutes to spare. Their car was in the last row of cars on the Bluebridge Ferry.

"Let me see your wafer," Marianne asked Scott.

"Why?" Scott asked, intrigued, but pleased that things seemed to be going better.

"Do you trust me?"

"I'm here, aren't I?"

"Then give me your wafer." Marianne flashed that gorgeous smile of hers.

Scott handed his wafer to her, and she got out of the car gently, watching that he did the same. The ferry disconnected from the port, and the road to access the ferry was blocked by the safety barrier. No other cars had arrived. A little less than fifteen minutes had passed since they had left the SOI cafe. The Secret Service agents were probably still outside the cafe waiting for Scott and Sergio.

As the ferry slowly started to move, Marianne looked at the wafer, pretending to be interested as she walked along the railing. With her fingernail, she deftly opened the sealed plastic cap that made the device water-resistant and immediately dropped it into Wellington Bay.

"You wanted to be free. Here is your chance," Marianne said proudly.

"Are you crazy? I need that!" Scott practically shouted.

"Come on, you've never lost one before?"

"Actually, no."

"Well, now you can see what that part of life feels like."

Scott was furious, but Marianne was too beautiful for him to hold onto that emotion. He was playing hooky and things felt weirdly right.

"Okay, so how long is this boat ride?" Scott asked.

"Only three-and-a-half hours," Marianne said.

"What! Are you nuts? Where are we going?"

"The south island. Where I live."

The ferry moved quite quickly, and the movement soon became noticeable, causing them to hold on to the railings.

"Let's go up to the front. The air is cleaner, and I won't get seasick up there," Marianne said.

"Okay." Scott followed her up the stairs to the front terrace, where there was a bar serving huge pints of beer.

"Let's sit over here." Marianne pointed to a pair of deck chairs on the outdoor part of the ferry.

The view was stunning. Scott felt like New Zealand had opened its arms to him.

"So tell me, Scott, do you believe in the alien threat?" Marianne asked.

"No," Scott said.

"But your father does. Doesn't he?"

Scott was silent for a moment, but he was pretty thrilled with this little adventure with a beautiful woman, and didn't want to ruin it before it even started.

"I don't know if I should say this to you, but I'm not sure if he does, either. You obviously don't, but you haven't told me why."

"You're kidding, right?"

"No, I'm just curious. Explain."

"My dad is the artist who created the aliens. How could I believe they are real?"

"Did Sergio tell you that?"

"No. But I know."

"How?"

"It's obvious to us. You're a horrible poker player, by the way. That grin…really!" Marianne said.

"So I gave it away?" Scott broke down and laughed to himself.

"Ages ago."

"Do you know a man named Pat Jackson? He's friends with an astronomer," Scott asked.

"You know Pat Jackson?" Marianne seemed very surprised at this sudden name-drop.

"No, and yes. Sort of…I know someone who knows him and I was partly involved in the safekeeping of a document about Kepler 3763. It's kind of a long story."

"What? Does your father know about this? Did Pat give it to you?" Marianne became deadly serious and her questions rattled off fast and hot. Scott was surprised at her sudden interest.

"Oh…no, no. I gave it back to Mr. Landon a long time ago."

"Scott, you have to tell me what's going on…I have so many questions." Her voice had taken on a somewhat sultry, pleading tone, and it sounded wonderful to Scott's ears.

Scott stared at the sea as it hugged the two shorelines ahead and smirked. She was engaged with him…finally.

"What do you want to know?" Scott said.

"Well, if AmEarth's alien threat is a hoax, then how can you stand to hear lies and deception around you all the time? Don't you hate your father? And the government?" Marianne's voice was rising, and some other people on the ferry started to notice.

"Relax! Don't get all worked up."

"Are you nuts?"

"People are staring, Marianne. Please, let me explain."

She stopped speaking for a moment and took a deep breath. In her mind, all she could think about was getting Scott to Oliver Cook's house, but this conversation was distracting her.

"This whole thing is huge," Scott began calmly, "so it's hard to understand. I barely do."

"I'm calm, okay. But just tell me one thing. How can you live with yourself?" Marianne asked harshly.

"I know what you're thinking. I used to be that way, too, until I realized that the AmEarth conquest is inevitable and possibly necessary. Do you really think a solitary group of intellectuals can really turn back the tide?"

“It’s worth a try.” Marianne practically spat the words at him.

“It’s too late. I’m sorry. This whole thing is bigger than you can imagine. I thought that I could change things, but if the upper levels of the government know that it’s a hoax, then you can imagine how fiercely they’ll fight to stop any dissent.”

“But it’s evil…”

“I’m not so sure it is,” Scott replied.

“Of course not. You’re American.”

“I don’t think that’s fair. There is a greater good behind uniting humans for a common purpose, isn’t there?”

Marianne felt a flash of remorse. She couldn’t blame Scott for the existence of AmEarth, and she didn’t really dislike him. She had actually begun to like him a bit; there was a wild, rebellious side to him with which she identified. After all, he had come with her on the ferry, and he hadn’t really freaked out about the phone for long. At any minute, the Secret Service would be scrambling to find them, but he didn’t seem all that worried. Scott’s eyes were a bit bloodshot and Marianne wondered what was wrong.

“I guess. Maybe…” she replied finally. “Listen, Scott, I’m sorry. I know that this isn’t your fault. Are you okay?” Marianne asked compassionately.

“What do you mean?” Scott asked.

“Your eyes are bloodshot, and you look a bit sick.”

“It’s just the jet lag. I’m so sleepy that I can barely stand.”

“Well, take a seat. I think we should have a beer.”

Marianne went to the bar, ordered two pints of cold Kiwi beer and returned to the table. Scott downed his beer like water and leaned back, quickly falling into what became a three-hour slumber. He was awakened by the angelic face of Marianne and her red hair; the light glancing through it looked like a sunset. He felt spaced-out but happy, and behind her head, he saw the actual sun setting behind the tree-covered hills of Picton Bay. He stood up and looked around at the beautiful bay overflowing with yachts. It was probably the prettiest bay he had ever seen, with crystal-clear water stretching into countless inlets. The mountains and hills surrounding the pristine water were covered in luscious emerald vegetation. The ferry was nearly empty, as the boat had already docked.

"Time to go, sleepyhead," Marianne said.

"Okay, right," he answered groggily.

In the belly of the huge ferry, the cars were all gone except for Marianne's car, way in the back. They got in and drove off as though they were starting a race. Marianne didn't look back and headed straight for the highway. Picton was gone, and although Scott would've liked to see more of it, the opportunity passed and they sped down Highway 1 on the East Shore, heading for the unknown night.

TWENTY-SIX

(October 2045)

That same evening, without any idea of Scott's whereabouts, Peter was flying in the FF to Canberra to deliver his next speech and make the Aussies more comfortable with the New Zealand transition. He hoped that the heckling had come to an end, but he was pleased with his handling of the incident in Wellington. In Canberra, he would meet leaders and businessmen to discuss the different objectives that the annexation of neighboring New Zealand presented. The copilot came into the main cabin an hour into the flight.

"Sir, there is an important call for you on the cockpit phone." The copilot handed Peter a headset.

"Thanks," Peter responded and placed the phone against his head. Then, he looked up at the copilot, who quickly realized that the president would not commence his conversation until he'd left.

"Oh, sorry, Mr. President."

Once the copilot had gone, Peter spoke.

"This is President Johansen," Peter said sternly into the device.

"Sir, it's Rogers with the security detail here in Wellington"

"What is it?"

"It's your son, sir. He has eluded his detail."

"Really? So where is he?"

"He went to the south island with the Bulatov girl."

Inside, Peter was secretly impressed, but this wasn't the time for praising his son's cocksmanship.

"So what are you doing about it?"

"His wafer went off-line but we still have a lock on his location with his inner chip. Do you want us to retrieve him?"

"Absolutely not. Let him be. Just keep him monitored."

"Full monitor or just GPS?"

"Full monitor. Over and out."

"Yes sir. I'll let the WSS know."

That last command meant that a satellite would be moved and placed directly above his son's location. Scott had been only eight when Peter had had the tracking GPS chip installed during a routine tonsillectomy. The chip was functional for a minimum of twenty years and still worked on his son. This was still a popular practice with parents today and doing it without their children's knowledge did not violate any privacy laws, provided they informed their kids when they reached adulthood. Scott knew about the chip, but satellite oversight was not something that he often thought about. Peter had also had a chip installed by AmEarth back when he was cleared to level three.

From the satellite, images of Scott's movements were gathered as if he were in grave danger. All of this information was recorded and gathered back in New York City by the Secret Service branch dedicated to the safety of top government officials around the world. This government branch was called the WSS, which stood for World Secret Service, and many conspiracy theorists thought that this was the agency responsible for most of the oppression and killing throughout the world. They did keep tabs on people around the globe at different levels, including trigger alerts of all types, but they were not the agency responsible for the many terrible and orchestrated things still occurring in the world.

The agency that was responsible was hidden away in the former Pentagon building. Washington had become a city museum, with no governmental purpose, and all of its buildings were now open to the public, including the White House, the houses of Congress, and the Pentagon. People from all over the world visited these sights and everyone knew that nothing important had come from that city for many years. The stealth WSA's covert operations used the center of the Pentagon as its offices, a top-secret installation hiding inside a tourist attraction. The building was so huge that the tours never got close to those areas, and all of the World Security Administration staff commuted through tunnels and a seven-level system of entry and exit that ensured that no change to normal vehicle volume could be sensed on any nearby roads.

The WSA routinely moved satellites in the thermosphere at high speeds to monitor its security objectives, which in many cases ended up functioning as locking beacons for drone strikes. The satellites were placed over the enemy and the drones arrived as if by magic to eliminate the threat. All of the military satellites circling the Earth were the property of AmEarth and were controlled by a handful of powerful agencies. The information was shared on a need-to-know basis, and the WSA was the hub where all of the satellite locations were held. A few hours after the WSS began to move satellites to follow Scott, a red flag was triggered at the WSA.

***

Marianne's car sped at sixty-five miles an hour; anything above that started to feel dangerous. Marianne had been driving for two hours when they stopped to pick up batteries. The power station catered only to electric vehicles and had batteries of several standard types for replacement. The station had twenty or thirty small manual deer cranes that look like mini-forklifts with two antennas resembling antlers; hence their name. One side of each antler held freshly charged batteries. and the machines were operated by the customers. Marianne placed her wafer next to the unit and it lit up, allowing her to use the rear joystick. She gently drove the crane close to her car. The crane had a small red-and-blue-striped battery. She opened the rear trunk and with the empty "antler," pulled its cable, and snapped it onto the battery hook in her car. Then she pushed the switch on the cable itself, and the crane began to retract the cable, allowing Marianne to remove the heavy battery without any effort, other than ensuring that the battery would not hit the car. It gently floated out of the car and Marianne held it so that it would not rock. Then she pushed the button on the other battery and pulled the new battery gently down into place. The whole operation took only a few minutes.

"Let me drive. You should rest," Scott said.
"I'm not tired," Marianne answered defensively.
"Don't you trust me?"
"All right, fine."

Marianne chucked the keys at Scott, and they switched sides of the car. Halfway around, they had to pass through the narrow space between the deer crane and the back of the car. They clumsily moved close to one another, and Scott purposefully made contact with her.

"Excuse me," Scott said, with as much charm as he could manage.
"Hey…Easy there, mister," Marianne replied with a smile.

This minimal amount of intimacy revealed a certain magnetism between them, something that neither had expected. Scott sat down behind the wheel and began to drive the strange old car.

"What's that pedal on the left?" Scott asked.
"That's the old clutch. Just ignore it," Marianne said.
"Okay."

Scott drove for the next two hours on Highway 1 until Marianne directed him to take the exit north along Highway 7. About half an hour later, they switched again, and Marianne continued on smaller and smaller roads with taller and taller trees. Scott felt immersed in the depth of the forest surrounding them as night fell and it became ominously dark. Marianne turned onto a remote dirt road that would lead them to the camp. The drive was approaching five hours and both of them were tired, but Marianne was also wired in anticipation of what was to come. Scott kept looking at Marianne as she drove masterfully along the bumpy road.

"You sure know your way around here," Scott said.

"What?"

"Nothing."

Their conversation was minimal as the wind blowing through the convertible made it hard to talk. The radio played all of her favorite music, which happened to coincide with some music that Scott liked. The blasting radio kept them awake and Scott felt admittedly exhilarated without the security detail. Somewhere in the back of his mind, he felt bad that his father wouldn't be able to speak to him through the wafer, but he was with Sergio's daughter, and they could reach her wafer if they really needed him.

They drove until they left the trees behind and entered a valley, where the clear sky opened up, revealing millions of stars. Scott looked up in awe at the pure quality of the night sky. There was no city or manmade lighting system that interfered with the view.

"Wow," Scott said breathlessly.

"You said it," Marianne agreed as she also drank in the sight.

A few hundred yards ahead, they could see a small light. The home of Oliver Cook was at the end of the country road and was completely dark, except for the dim light escaping from the windows. Scott followed Marianne into the house, thinking that it would be morning before he actually saw where he was.

However, inside the home, in the large living room, a group of people were talking loudly. Their discussions sounded as if a political meeting was going on. There were so many arguments and voices floating around that Scott and Marianne's arrival went largely unnoticed. People looked no different from normal students at any university and they were dressed casually; despite that, Scott sensed that he was in another world. They sat down in the living room in spaces made by people scooting over to create room, which separated Scott from Marianne.

"These bastards have rigged the president. It's unbelievable," an anonymous voice said.

"If he can lie without anyone knowing, then what's next? People will believe the AmEarth lie machine," another suggested.

"What if he's not lying?" someone offered.

Scott laughed at this, at which point Oliver noticed him.

"Are you…? Marianne can I talk to you for a minute?" It had not been a request.

"Sure," Marianne said, and stood up.

Other members of this meeting started to look at Scott and mumbling began. Marianne approached Oliver, and he whispered in her ear. Scott stared intently, feeling increasingly uncomfortable.

"Is that the president's son?"

"Yes…" Marianne uttered in a nearly inaudible whisper.

"Why the fuck is he here?"

"I met my Dad. He introduced us."

"Are you out of your mind?"

"I thought this might be a good thing." Oliver's expression showed her that she had been wrong.

Oliver got up and ordered everyone to be quiet. Silence fell quickly over the group.

"It seems that Marianne has brought a distinguished guest into our midst. I imagine that he will be followed soon by AmEarth security personnel," Oliver announced with disgust.

"No! We dumped his wafer. He's with me," Marianne said loudly, trying to calm the growing rumbles of dissent.

"Then they'll track your wafer, Marianne. They probably know that you're together."

"Yes, and they know that I'm showing him the countryside. He is not expected back in New York for two days. He's on vacation. No one is following us. We left his security detail on the other island."

More aggressive mumbling began among the people present; it would soon grow into chaos if Oliver didn't take control.

"We will have to refuse hospitality to you and your guest. Sorry. I need you to move on and I need you to do it quickly. This location is the only safe haven that our movement has. Bringing the son of the president here was probably the stupidest thing you could have done."

More people were speaking now, and Scott heard, "son of the president" and "Johansen" throughout the assembled crowd. He could sense hatred mixed with reverence, a mixture that could turn ugly if anyone misspoke.

"He laughed when someone suggested that his father wasn't lying," Pat chimed in.

"Yes, he did," someone seconded.

"Explain yourself," Oliver said to Scott, irritated that this was becoming a discussion, but willing to entertain the question.

"I...I just know that my Dad was lying. I just know," Scott said.

"How do you know?" Pat demanded.

Scott knew that this could get ugly if he didn't give them something to work with.

"I was with Professor Landon when you sent the Kepler 3763 document. I'm the one who told my father about the lies. He believed the alien threat until I proved that it was a lie. So...he knows," Scott confessed, hoping it would help his case.

"Unfortunately, that also means your father knows that you're here and who we are," Oliver reasoned.

"No. He doesn't."

"Did you tell him who we are? And where we are?" Pat demanded angrily.

"I swear I didn't. My dad doesn't even know Ted Landon."

"I don't know how we can believe him," Oliver concluded.

"My dad is in Australia and he doesn't know I'm here. I don't even know where here is," Scott practically shouted.

"It's true, Oliver! Honest!" Marianne insisted.

"Well, tell me something I don't know, Scott. How did your father lie without being detected?" Oliver asked seriously.

"That I don't know, but I do know that he was worried about the lie detection systems and he was certain that there would be a new election soon. I overheard that Chen was forced to resign because his lies were being detected."

"That much we know. It's how your father lies that is worrisome. It will be much harder to prove our case if we cannot prove that he's lying," Oliver explained. The room had begun to calm down.

"I'm certain that having Scott here will be trouble. He should leave. Now!" Pat said with finality.

"I agree. Marianne, you've both gotta go," Oliver said.

"But—"

"No, Marianne. Leave. Now. Go to Christchurch or somewhere else. I don't care, but do it now."

"Let's get out of here," Scott whispered quietly in her ear.

"Fine," Marianne assented.

There was a feeling that the best move would be for them to leave immediately. Some of the men there did not seem as stable as Pat and Oliver, so who knew how they would react? Marianne moved swiftly, but without panic, back to her car. Scott followed in the same manner and didn't look back. One glance could spark anything.

***

Meanwhile, Peter was lying comfortably on a king-size bed in the AmEarth embassy in Australia, finally getting some rest. He was scheduled to speak tomorrow and was happy with how things were going when his wafer lit up in red. The special security tone chimed.

"Yes?" Peter answered.

"Sir. This is Rogers again. It's about Scott," Rogers stated succinctly.

"Go ahead, Rogers."

"It seems that our satellite followed him to a hotspot being monitored by the WSA."

"The WSA? Are you sure?"

"Yes, they are monitoring a rebel camp deep in the mountains of the South Island. Our satellite was so close that it was deemed best to jump to their signal. They were immediately made aware of whom we were tracking and General Redford was informed. I have been asked to patch you in to him. Is that okay with you, sir?"

"Tell him to call me directly on this line. And tell him to call me on a single secure line. You understand?"

"Yes, sir. A single secure line. Over and out."

"Good-bye."

Peter hung up and immediately realized that leaving Sergio and Scott behind had been a mistake. Before he could clear his thoughts about what to do, his phone lit up again.

"Hello?" Peter answered.

"Mr. President, John Redford here. We have a situation,"

"I understand, John. I honestly don't know why Scott is where he is. I do know that it involves a very pretty young girl. We should try to extract him naturally before any operation is contemplated. What was your mission in the area?"

"Our operation was to clean up any dissent in New Zealand as quickly as possible. We want to establish the new territory as quickly and cleanly as possible."

"I hope you understand that Scott's presence there changes your scope. I cannot have my son in the middle of any hot operation. Do you understand?"

"Yes sir. We do have other means to quell dissent. More humane methods…"

"General, I do not approve of any operation while my son is near that camp. He is with Sergio Ramirez-Bulatov's daughter. Did you know this?"

"No."

"This is more complicated than you know."

"I cannot stop the operation. We have intel that needs to be addressed. What I can do is wait until Scott leaves the rebel camp and then use a minimal force operation to eliminate the threat."

"John, I need you to be one hundred percent sure that the girl is out of the camp as well. Do you have any way of tracking her?"

"We do not."

"Call me back in five minutes, and I will give you her wafer number so that you can at least GPS her. She cannot be hurt, do you understand? She is a Ramirez-Bulatov and must be protected."

"Even if she's a rebel?"

"She's not and neither is my son. Period. That is an executive order, John. This is a family matter. There has been no treason here. That girl is probably related to some scientist or something and that may have put her in harm's way!" Peter was almost shouting.

"Okay. Get me the number. I'll wait for your call. You have my word that nothing will happen to those two."

"Thanks. Oh, and John?"

"Yes sir."

"Thank you for your support in the last Supercomputer Committee meeting. I'll call you back."

Peter dialed Sergio and hoped that he would answer quickly. Fortunately, he did.

"Sergio, it seems that my son's wafer is out of batteries or something. Can you give me Marianne's number, please? I know that they're together," Peter said.

"Sure, Peter. Is something wrong?" Sergio asked, a note of concern in his voice.

"No, nothing at all, I just want to give him a message from his Mom. That's all."

"Sure. Her number is 8585-0808-1961."

"Thanks."

"Are you okay?"

"Yeah, doing fine. Have to run. Say hello to Robbie. Bye." Peter hung up and immediately dialed John Redford.

"John?" Peter said.

"Mr. President."

"The number is 8585-0808-1961. Got it?"

"Yes. I'll take care of this."

"This is in your hands. Keep me appraised and be careful."

"Will do. We will use minimal force, sir."

"But only when they are well out of range."

"Yes, don't worry, sir."

"Thanks. Good-bye."

***

General Redford was in his office at the AmEarth headquarters and upon hanging up, he headed for the elevator bank and descended to the War Room where all the screens monitoring the world's hotspots showed on the satellite live feeds. As he entered, about half of the personnel got up and saluted. He ignored them and focused on the screen with New Zealand in its scope. He spoke briefly to Colonel Williams, who was handling the operation. Onscreen, Oliver Cook's house and its surroundings were visible, with heat detection showing the various bodies in the home, as well as several in the surrounding areas. Cars and trucks were also visible all around the home.

A red pinging light could be seen in the middle of the living room. Colonel Williams spoke to a technical assistant who had plugged in Marianne's wafer number. On screen, a second red ping appeared right next to Scott's.

"Fucking lovebirds," Redford muttered.

"I'm sorry, sir?" Williams said.

"Nothing, nothing…Listen people! We're changing Operation Blind Mice to a minimal force op. Get a sound eraser ready for launch and a magnetic field on the main exit to the compound. We will need a cleanup crew and there are to be no weapons fired. Williams, once the two people we are pinging leave the compound, the operation is a go. Understood?"

"Yes sir," Williams said.

With that, various operatives began calling the different air force carriers stationed near the New Zealand islands and asked them to prepare the equipment needed for the type of operation General Redford had described. Onscreen, the two pings in the center of the many heat-sensed individuals began to move, and as if orchestrated by General Redford, the two red pinging dots began to make their way alone out of the building and into a vehicle. Then, the red pinging dots moved rapidly away from the compound.

"This is working out better than I thought. Are we ready?" Redford asked.

"The jet can be ready to deploy in seven minutes, sir," Williams replied.

"What is the radius of the sound eraser?" Redford said.

"Five miles."

"Keep tracking them. When they reach five miles from the camp, the operation is live."

"Yes sir."

Marianne's car traveled away from the camp, with Scott driving a tired Marianne toward Highway 7. It was slow going in the rough terrain at night, so their five-mile radius was still a few minutes out.

"Let me know how the operation goes," Redford ordered as he left the room.

The operation began smoothly a few minutes later, and all of the personnel followed their instructions. However, no one noticed that soon after the car had passed the five-mile boundary, it took a U-turn and headed back toward the camp. Marianne had forgotten her backpack in the haste of their departure and needed her things. She said that she would go in alone and grab it quickly, so as not to raise any more anger.

A supersonic jet plane arrived over the site and launched three missile-like units, each of which was remotely operated via camera to strike pinpointed targets. One fell on the rear of Oliver Cook's home, making a loud thud as it wedged itself into the earth with incredible force. The bomb-shaped device did not explode, but instead began emitting a piercing noise that could deafen any human ear. Animals and insects immediately fled, and humans had little recourse but to do so as well. A few seconds later, two other devices of a similar nature landed on either side of the road leading away from the home and created an invisible magnetic field between them. The two pieces also set up a radioactive field between them that made an imprint on any object crossing it. This was a simple radioactive isotope that tagged any crossing object with tiny electrons that had a short half-life and posed no real danger to humans or animals.

Inside the house, no conversation could penetrate the noise coming from the "sound eraser," although a few men tried to quell the sound by throwing quilts over it. However, they didn't diminish the sound at all and the longer a person remained near the noise, the sooner a deep pain developed in the temples and eardrums. Everyone held their hands to their ears and a few grabbed important information and laptops as they fled from the noise. They all leaped into their vehicles and drove away, passing through the magnetic field, which erased their computer drives and showered them with invisible low-grade radiation.

Marianne and Scott heard the noise, and it gradually became unbearable. They stopped about halfway to the house when they met the cars leaving the house. The first car had about eight people crammed inside it and they all seemed shocked and in pain, holding their hands over their ears.

"What happened?" Marianne asked.

The driver pointed to his ears in a gesture that meant he couldn't hear her.

"Turn around and get away…Get away from here! There's been an attack," the man screamed, as he couldn't hear his own sound level.

"Okay! Turn around, Scott. This is scary," Marianne said.

Scott immediately swung the vehicle in the opposite direction.

Behind them they saw more and more cars coming their way. The pair drove without stopping until they reached an open parking lot near the road where the other cars where stopping. The noise here was like a low ringing sound in their ears, but it was bearable. There they waited with the others, hoping that Oliver or Pat would arrive and know what to do. More cars stopped, full of deafened, terrified passengers. Then, Marianne spotted Oliver and Pat in Oliver's vintage Mercedes Benz. As she approached them, she could see that Oliver was turning his laptop on. Scott stayed in Marianne's car, trying not to draw any attention to himself.

"Oliver," Marianne spoke through the window.

Oliver couldn't hear her and was staring at his computer, waiting for it to start up. She saw him flinch in desperation. The computer screen was blank. There was no start screen or system loading. It had been wiped clean of all its contents. Pat looked over and shared the moment of desperation and hurt. He saw Marianne in the window and swung his head around to see Scott about a hundred yards away, sitting in her car at the other end of the parking lot. He opened his door and stormed out, pushing Marianne to the side and heading straight for Scott, hungry to unleash his anger.

Scott saw this happening, but he kept his eyes on Marianne the whole time. He pushed the accelerator, which immediately bucked the car straight toward the oncoming Pat. Pat hadn't expected that, so he stopped and stood his ground, raising his arms in front of the car, as if he could stop it with his will alone. Scott swerved at the last instant, passing Pat by only a few inches, and drove to Marianne's side.

"Get in," Scott said.

Marianne jumped in the back seat, and Scott took off for the highway, leaving Pat standing in the middle of the parking lot, furious. Oliver had just reached Pat's side by the time Scott looked in the rearview mirror. He was unclear what their intentions would be, so he stomped on the accelerator and fled. Marianne moved up to the front seat, visibly shocked by Pat's behavior.

"I thought he was going to kill you!"

"I know. I had to get us out of there," Scott agreed, shaking with adrenaline.

"But why? You could have just left me behind."

"Are you crazy? I couldn't do that."

"Why not?"

"Have you ever fallen in love at first sight?"

"What?" Marianne screamed.

Scott regretted saying that immediately, realizing that this was neither the time nor the place for stupid sappy shit.

"Haven't you thought that they might blame the attack on you, not just me?"

"What does that have to do with love?"

"I don't know, Marianne. I don't know what I'm saying. This is all a bit much."

Scott turned his head to see if they were being followed. Scott was red in the face, flushed with excitement and embarrassment, but the emotions of the situation were so strong that this faded fast. Marianne looked flustered, but she smiled.

"I needed to get you away from them!" Scott said.

"Did we…? I mean, did we cause that?" Marianne demanded, suspicious of him again.

"I had nothing to do with this. Nothing."

Meanwhile, an AmEarth helicopter flying over the camp dropped a single marine. This trained operative wore a special helmet that shielded his ears from the "sound eraser" via specialized reverse frequencies. He dropped rapidly and opened a black parachute about 7,000 feet from the ground. He navigated his fall to land on the driveway of the Cook home. With a special key, he disabled all three cone-shaped mechanisms. The noise stopped, and the operation theater was ready for the real work. A team of nine other marines arrived a few minutes later in exactly the same way and proceeded to collect all printed matter in the home, as well as all digital files. They took all the materials, including books and films, photos and posters. With special hand-held magnetic resonance viewers, they quickly saw through walls and found all of the secret compartments within the home.

They placed all of the found materials in containers lowered by a cable from winches on various helicopters, which were making rounds to the aircraft carrier. As they began the mop-up part of the operation, the agents used a magnet/microwave gun to ensure that any tiny computer drive would be irreparably damaged if it were left behind in any nook or cranny of the entire home. The helicopters lowered more cables and marines hooked up the three bomb-like devices and removed them from the camp. One short hour later, the Cook home was left devoid of any information in any format, other than the art on the walls. No human life was taken, but all of their electronic and written records were gone, from novels and real estate deeds to email accounts and family pictures. Gone.

Peter was informed of the operation and the proximity of Scott to the camp, so he ordered an immediate extraction. That command dispatched a group of helicopters, which soon intercepted Marianne's car as it traveled down Highway 7 toward Highway 1. The car was closely followed by Oliver and Pat, as well as other rebel-filled vehicles, but they were stopped by a very effective helicopter roadblock. Scott and Marianne were greeted at gunpoint by marines who ran toward the stopped vehicle in the middle of the road.

"I think we'll be fine," Scott said, before the marines were within earshot.

"You, sure. You're the president's son. I'm not that lucky," Marianne said.

"I'll protect you, and so will your dad. You have no idea how powerful he is."

"I sure hope so…"

"Just keep your mouth shut. Not a peep about anything. Especially not about the alien threat. That's treason. Okay?"

"Got it."

Scott was relieved. He was exhausted from all the driving and the wild emotions; particularly from being followed by a pack of furious rebels. The helicopter took off safely with Scott and Marianne, their bodies pushed against one another in the cramped seats. He grabbed her hand just as the helicopter took off, and she didn't pull away.

The marines stopped all the cars moving north and south on Highway 7, and allowed vehicles without the radiation signature to move forward. The AmEarth marines began a routine ID operation. In minutes they erected a tentlike structure with many fabric cubicles and a remote robot drilled anchors into the earth inside these cubicles. Pat and Oliver, along with all the intercepted rebels, were kept in this makeshift tent-jail. There was fabric material between their "cells," and all of the men were handcuffed to the metal ring exposed on the surface of the floor. Communication would have been possible, had they all not still had a horrendous ringing in their ears that prevented any discernible speech. They were all given water that contained a special solution that put them to sleep within fifteen minutes. AmEarth personnel used this sleep aid to insert miniature microchip devices into the livers of the rebels. This organ had no internal nerve endings, so it caused no residual pain; the only evidence of the insertion was a small cut that was quickly cauterized, so its final appearance was that of a small scratch.

From that day on, all of the rebels from the camp were tracked. Red lights on the World Security Administration computers lit up if any of them met. Any meeting by this group could be monitored for content or "crashed" by AmEarth, essentially neutralizing whatever threat it represented.

TWENTY-SEVEN

Peter sat in the living room of the luxurious embassy in Canberra, speaking on the phone with General Redford.

"Chen is on his way to Canberra. ETA six p.m.," General Redford informed him.

"Thanks for the heads-up," Peter said.

"Mr. President, you should know that Chen will not be there to help you. He's there to investigate you. He wants to know how you did it."

Peter looked out at the lovely manicured garden of the embassy and spied a baby kangaroo jumping across it with great agility and beauty. It jumped all the way to the flowerbed near the property wall and just as gracefully jumped backward. The embassy was similar to that in Wellington, and had obviously been built by the same architect, but this one was grander.

"I know, John. I expected some kind of move, but not this. Does he think that I'm going to share my speech technique?"

"What is your speech technique?"

"Why, are you interested in the presidency too?" Peter joked, feeling that he was beginning to trust Redford.

"Absolutely not!" General Redford laughed.

"Then I'll keep my trade secret to myself, but tell me something…"

"What?"

"I need to know, are you with me?" Peter asked.

"Mr. President, you are my commander-in-chief."

"Thanks, John. That's all I needed to know."

"Good-bye, Mr. President. Keep up the good work."

"Thank you. Good-bye."

Peter looked at his watch. It was 5:45. Chen would be there soon. He spent the remaining time making a few calls to his security personnel. Only a few hours earlier Sergio had arrived at the embassy, mad as hell at the travel disruption Peter had caused. Peter ordered Sergio and Robbie to Canberra, and they had been literally pulled off the sailboat as it sailed between the islands of New Zealand. A helicopter had dropped them on to the *AES Reagan*, from where an F27 fighter jet immediately flew them to Canberra. Sergio left Robbie in the bedroom they had been assigned and looked for Peter to give him a strongly worded piece of his mind.

"What is the meaning of this?" Sergio entered, furious with the president.

"Sergio, I have a problem that has just presented itself. Please, bear with me here," Peter answered.

"Are you mad? Airlifting me out of my own yacht and forcing me to come to this terrible city!"

"Will you wait a minute, Sergio? It has to do with Marianne and Scott."

"Why? What's happened to her? Is she okay?"

"Get ahold of yourself. She's fine, but listen. Chen is going to be here any minute. He can't know that you are here. Do you understand? I don't want him to figure out how we've trumped the lie-detecting software. All you need to know is that you and I are a team now. We'll have more power than Chen ever did, but we need to keep him back. Where's Robbie?"

"She's in the room they gave us."

"Stay there and don't come out until I personally come and get you. Now go! Chen will be here any minute."

"What are you going to do?"

Peter dialed his wafer and looked at Sergio with a cold stare that said everything he needed to say. Sergio understood his meaning and walked briskly to his room. No more than five minutes later, ex-president Chen entered the living room, looking defiant. Peter knew that Neil had a long-winded rant prepared for him; a twenty-hour flight in a normal jet plane had given him a long time to prepare a speech.

"Peter, at last I find you! Nice place…enjoying yourself?" Chen asked innocently.

Peter looked up, ignoring his comment completely. He had his wafer phone to his ear, although no one was on the other end. With one finger, he signaled Neil Chen to be quiet and sit down. It was a polite gesture, but dismissive at the same time. Then Peter coolly turned his back to Chen and began agreeing into the phone and murmuring assent.

"Mhm. Yes. Mhm. Mhm. Yes. Got it…aha, okay, I'll do that."

Ex-president Chen was becoming furious, but managed to contain his emotions. Peter moved the phone down and made another call. This made Chen even more furious, but he was helpless. Here was his computer-chosen, ignorant replacement, who was supposed to fully believe in the alien threat, making a fool of him!

"Rogers? Now…thanks," Peter spoke into the phone.

Peter continued looking at the baby kangaroos and ignoring Chen. He was no longer speaking on his wafer.

"Peter…" Ex-president Chen broke the silence, clearly irritated.

Peter turned around.

"Yes, Neil. I'm sorry. What can I do for you?"

"You know damn well why I'm here."

"And you came all this way hoping that I would tell you?" Peter inquired, obviously implying that he wouldn't do this.

"I need to know, damn it. You at least owe me that," Chen demanded.

"I'm sorry, Neil, but that's simply not going to happen."

"Peter, you have to. I made you! From *nothing*! I need to know!"

"I'll never tell you, Neil." Peter reverted to using his first name, which blatantly ground on the man's nerves.

"Peter, this is horrible! Why are you treating me like this? After all I've done for you!"

"Keeping people from knowing the truth is your specialty, Neil. Now you can know what that feels like. At least a little bit. Rogers!"

Rogers arrived, followed by two Secret Service MPs, who gently took ex-president Chen's frail arms in their hands. They led him toward the hall and the front door.

"Peter—I just arrived. I'm hungry! You can't treat me like this! I was the supreme president!" Chen moaned pathetically.

"Wait a moment," Peter said to the security detail.

He walked directly up to Chen and looked him in the eyes.

"My dear Chen, I'm not only sending you back to New York, but you will be met there by AmEarth personnel. I have ordered you to be confined to house arrest. Any further attempts to undermine my presidency will be treated as treason. You are still a member of the committee, but you can only attend virtually, unless I allow you to be there in person. I repeat, any further attempts to undermine my presidency will be treated as treason. I have read all the transcripts of the committee meetings, as is my right as the president. Don't try to present any further information to the computer that could jeopardize my position. It will be the last mistake you make. They have food on the airplane," Peter finished coldly.

"This is how you treat a former president? I'm shocked!" Chen pretended to be outraged.

"All you want is to regain the position. Did you think for one second that I would be so foolish as to return this honor back to you? Did you really think that I would be your puppet?"

"I didn't, Peter. I swear it."

Peter turned around and ignored Chen's pleading. He walked to the large staircase leading up to the bedrooms above as the guards forcibly moved Neil Chen toward the front door.

"I've just been on a plane for twenty hours!" Chen shouted as a last-ditch attempt to gain some mercy.

Peter didn't even react; he barely heard him. Above, Sergio had been spying through a crack in his door and had heard most of the exchange. He stepped into sight as soon as the front door slammed.

"Well played," Sergio said.

"Well, this should be interesting," Peter replied, already wondering if this was the right play.

"What happened to my daughter?" Sergio demanded, ready to move on to the next crisis.

TWENTY-EIGHT

Marianne and Scott descended from the helicopter onto the deck of the *AES Reagan*, a huge aircraft carrier, and were quickly surrounded by military personnel who began to separate the two of them.

"Wait, do you know who I am?" Scott protested loudly.

The officers knew who they were, but acted professionally, explaining that for the next few hours, they needed to cooperate.

"But we need to stay together," Scott argued.

"We have orders, Mr. Johansen. Everything is under control. You both need to be debriefed separately," an officer explained.

"When can we see each other?"

"I do not have that information, sir."

"Who does? I want to see your superior." Scott tried to use whatever authority he had.

Throughout this exchange, they were being moved indoors through separate corridors. In no time, Scott realized that Marianne was gone and he felt something akin to pain; it was anguish to be separated. This feeling was a physical and emotional nightmare that he had never felt before. He had fallen hard and fast for Marianne and wanted to protect her at all costs. It felt as if every step he took away from her was increasing his pain and concern for her. He felt as though he suddenly needed her to breathe, to think, to feel, to live.

Marianne was led to a room with a medical table and a group of doctors waiting to evaluate her. A female doctor moved toward her.

"Marianne, please do not be alarmed. We're going to put you through a series of tests to see if you are carrying any devices in your body that might be of harm to yourself or to others. Do you understand?" the doctor said.

"Yes. But what tests? Where is Scott?" Marianne asked in a panic.

"Scott is fine and he will be debriefed separately. Do you understand?"

"Yes."

"Please take all your clothes off and put this gown on."

The female doctor pointed her toward a changing area behind a metal accordion screen. Marianne went back there and felt uncertain as she disrobed and put on the medical gown, which was open in the back. A massive wave of insecurity and powerlessness crept through her and she realized that she desperately needed Scott to reassure her just in that moment. He and only he could help her get away from these people.

“Marianne, please come and lie down here,” a male doctor directed her.

Marianne felt that she had no real say in any of this, so she did as she was told. She lay down on a hard metal bed covered in a white sheet. On the wall, she saw that a porthole revealed the ominous slice of dark blue ocean beneath a light blue sky. A few scattered clouds in the distance seemed to be the only remarkable feature in her suddenly stark and cold reality. As she leaned back on the bed, she noticed the huge wand-like device on wheels that was meant to scroll over her body. It was eerily low and close to her skin. Directly above her on the ceiling were three black half-dome devices. These cameras would track her eyes and detect her lies, although she didn’t know this.

“We will scan your body with this machine. It will be totally painless, and you can move if you like. Just do not raise your legs or arms or sit up. We are not only checking for broken bones or trauma, but also foreign elements in your system. Okay?”

“Okay,” Marianne agreed, knowing that she had no choice in the matter.

The machine made an awful noise. She noticed that there were three doctors and two nurses in the room. The male doctor who spoke to her was running the scanner and two others looked intently into a monitor. The female doctor kept her eyes on Marianne and was preparing to draw blood. The other doctor was a male in his sixties, who looked like a wise old man. He approached her slowly.

"My dear, I'm Dr. Walls and am here in a psychiatric capability. I only need to ask you a few questions. Please answer them truthfully. Okay?" the psychiatrist said calmly.

"I will only answer questions if you answer some as well. One for one," Marianne negotiated.

"Fine. Are you a member of the rebel forces fighting AmEarth in New Zealand?"

"No. Where is Scott Johansen?"

"He is on board."

"I already know that."

"He is being debriefed."

"What does that mean?"

"My turn. Are you in contact with the rebels?"

"No. What is Scott being debriefed about?"

"We want to see if he is a threat to AmEarth," the doctor replied, annoyed, but then he proceeded with his own question. "Are you a threat to AmEarth?"

"I hardly think so," Marianne said.

"Where is your mother?" Dr. Walls asked.

"She is with my father."

"Where?"

Marianne forgot the *quid pro quo* and began to answer.

"I don't know. Last time I saw them, we were in a café in Wellington. I haven't spoken to them since. Can I call my mother?"

"No. But can you tell me where the rebel forces keep their weapons."

"Weapons! Are you kidding me? The rebel forces fight with truth, not weapons."

"I see. So you don't know anything about the weapons. What about their plans?"

"No. Do you know who my father is?"

"Yes, my dear, but that does not protect you here. This is a military vessel, and we are fighting a war. I'm probably your best bet as a friend here. Do you understand? Please, just cooperate with our questions or you could face dire consequences."

She felt panic set in. This seemed like an impossible situation compared to her previously simple life, and the people around her truly scared her. Her arm was being pricked, and she could see the blood flowing into a variety of small tubes. Scott was nowhere to be found, and she felt completely alone. Suddenly, she felt the opposite of a blood flow; instead, it felt like something warm was entering her system. *Am I being drugged?* she thought, even as a calm settled over her mind.

"Wait a few minutes and then continue," the female doctor told the psychiatrist.

Scott was not being debriefed in the same manner. He was given a cabin with a bathroom, a complete set of clean clothing in his exact size, and a paper with the direct number of General Redford written on it. Before taking a shower, he called Redford, using the wafer with which he had been provided.

"General Redford," Scott began.

"Scott, are you okay?" John said, and Scott appreciated that his voice sounded genuine.

"Yes. They took Marianne to another location. They separated us and I don't know if she is okay."

"She's fine, son. She's in good hands. You, on the other hand, will be leaving tonight."

"I'm not leaving her here."

"Marianne is going to meet her father in Australia. Your father wants you to go back to school. That is final."

"I'm not going anywhere without her."

"That is simply not up to you to decide."

"Can I see her before I leave tonight? Please?"

"You cannot."

"What! Why?"

"She is being debriefed. They are assessing her level of threat."

"What are they doing to her? I demand to see her."

"You cannot demand anything, Scott. I am simply telling you what is about to happen."

Scott cut the connection to General Redford and threw the wafer across the room. He walked to the door, only to find a marine on guard outside.

"I need to leave," Scott demanded.

"I have orders to keep you in your quarters until further notice," the guard stated emotionlessly.

"Please move. I need to go see someone."

"Sir, go back into your room."

"That's how this is going to be, huh?"

"Yes sir."

Scott didn't feel like picking a fight with a marine, so he reentered his room and checked to see if he could get out through the window. He opened the window and peered out. It was a good hundred feet down to the water. A fall from this height would be deadly. He was stumped—and apparently trapped. He decided to take a bath and clear his head while he figured out what he could do.

***

Meanwhile, Marianne was feeling the full effects of the drug. It was like swimming in a huge pool of viscous, warm, and breathable water. She felt like a fish moving slowly, like a whale, and was very happy with that state of affairs. She could hear voices and tried to understand these people; perhaps people whom she could help.

"Marianne, this is Dr. Walls. Do you remember me?" Dr. Walls asked her gently.

"Yes. Hello. Are you okay?" Marianne asked.

"I am fine, yes, just fine. We want to know if you can help us with something. Can you?"

"Of course."

"Do you remember where Dr. Cook keeps his weapons?"

"Weapons? Dr. Cook is an astronomer. He has knives in the kitchen, if that's what you mean."

"Do you know how many people are in the rebel force?"

"In the rebel force?"

"Yes, in the groups that meet at Dr. Cook's house."

"I don't know, exactly."

"About how many people do you recall seeing there?"

"About thirty or forty people. Maybe fewer."

"Are you aware of their plans?"

"Yes."

"What are the plans?"

"To tell the world the truth."

"The truth about what?"

"About the alien hoax."

"And how do they intend to do this?"

"On the Internet. In the media."

"What do you think happens to people who do this kind of thing?"

"They commit treason against AmEarth."

"So you are aware of the consequences for this offense?"

"Before AmEarth took New Zealand, we didn't have these consequences, so they were meeting to discuss what to do now that AmEarth controls the law of the land."

"I see. And what did you plan to do?"

"I don't know. Some said that we needed to go to a different island and make that a sovereign state, but others said that was impossible. Others wanted to send messages online from different locations, moving every day, so they couldn't be caught. It was disorganized, and people were afraid. Then I brought Scott there, and they panicked and told me to leave. Then the high-pitched sound began, and everyone fled. I think that I brought on the attack by accident. I'm guilty of harming my friends." Marianne whimpered and began to cry.

"No, no…Marianne. Listen closely. You saved them. They were all going to be taken prisoners and treated as traitors, but because you brought Scott there, they were all saved. The sound bomb was a humane method to disperse them. Your friends are all fine."

"Really. Do you mean it?"

"Yes, don't be alarmed. All is well. Relax."

"I'm very sleepy."

"Why don't you go to sleep then? Just relax."

TWENTY-NINE

Peter and Sergio were still in the middle of their exchange at the former US embassy, now the AmEarth embassy, in Canberra.

"Marianne is okay and so is Scott. Let me talk to you downstairs," Peter spoke gently and motioned for Robbie to stay out of things by pointing to the room and then placing his finger on his lips. Like two kids, he and Sergio tiptoed down to the living room, where Peter poured a pair of whiskies on the rocks. A servant arrived, but Peter gestured for him to leave.

"And close the door behind you," Peter said quietly to the servant.

Then he began to explain what had happened.

"Marianne and Scott went to the South Island after sneaking away from Scott's Secret Service detail. They also ditched his wafer, but not hers, so we tracked them with her wafer and his microchip."

"But they went sightseeing. Scott wanted to see New Zealand, and she offered to guide him…it was harmless," Sergio said, confused.

"I don't know why, but they went straight to the rebel holdout in the mountains, a place that belongs to an astronomer named Oliver Cook."

"What?"

"We have learned that Marianne and Robbie are friends with Professor Cook, and that he is the leader of the strongest opposition group to AmEarth here in New Zealand. They know that the alien race was designed by you."

"I know…Robbie told me, but she didn't mention being a part of any rebel group."

"In their defense, most of New Zealand felt the same as they did. Even the prime minister shared thoughts to that effect. It seems that you're famous after all," Peter remarked ironically.

"My fifteen minutes of fame are only known to the guerrilla population? Great," Sergio joked. "Where are the kids now?"

"I was following them with a security satellite, and its path crossed with a military satellite that was already preparing an operation to neutralize the rebels."

"An attack! So what happened?"

"Relax…I ordered the operation to be nonlethal. I did not want anything to go wrong while Scott and your daughter were nearby. I gave the order to continue when—and only when—Scott and Marianne had left the area."

"Thank you."

"We extracted them safely on the outskirts of the rebel camp."

"Where are they now?"

"On the *AES Reagan*."

"But we were there just a few hours ago. Why didn't you tell me?"

"Too complicated. I didn't know when we would be there or what time they would be arriving," Peter's words rang untrue even to his own ears.

"You could have told her. Are you trying to scare her?" Sergio's voice filled with a father's rage.

"Not at all, Sergio. I promise. I think that the entire experience was enough of a scare, but we will need to be on the same page when we talk to them, which is why I need you here."

"I don't know what to say…"

"Take Robbie and Marianne back with you to America. Only through you can they be safe, and I don't mean from AmEarth, but from the same rebels that we apprehended and released. At this point, they might see Marianne and Robbie as the cause of the attack. The rebels can't know why they brought Scott there, and coincidence is not going to cut it as an explanation. She is in danger anywhere in New Zealand. The rebels were micro-chipped, and they will be monitored for the rest of their lives, but any of them not at the camp during the raid might retaliate. Even a chipped rebel could move too fast for AmEarth forces to intercede."

"She'll hate me for this," Sergio said, clearly troubled.

"It was not your doing. AmEarth personnel have already told Marianne that she saved the rebels. Nonlethal force was used, and the rebels scattered. You can also tell her that she actually saved her friends' lives, if that is any comfort to her…In any event, we need to know what to do with Marianne."

"Maybe she would like to go to New York. I have no idea. I barely know her."

"Well, she can't stay here. If she associates with the rebels, she could face treason charges. You should explain this to her in the clearest way possible. Please, be candid, and remind her that AmEarth is estimated to last for centuries. Don't you remember Essie's projection?"

"One thousand years…Will she believe Essie? It's like faith. Believing Essie is like believing in a new religion."

"Let's not overdramatize it, Sergio! For heaven's sake…religion! It's all numbers and probabilities—nothing like a religion. If anything is a religion, it's those March-Sevenites who stand outside the alien museums preaching that we should let the aliens in, as though the aliens are our salvation."

"What if Essie is wrong?"

Peter ignored the question.

"Do you want to encourage your daughter into a fight that Essie says is a lost cause? Has she been wrong in the past?"

They both paused and let that statement sink in.

"Even if there is huge opposition, AmEarth is likely to survive for ten centuries or—as a high estimate—indefinitely. So please, make sure that she understands," Peter finished.

"I'll do my best."

Sergio and Peter drank from their tumblers in silence and sat looking at the garden and the baby kangaroos in the Canberra ambassador's residence. It was surreal. Behind them was a large painting of a huge desert with Australian cowboys galloping on horseback. The yellow tones of the huge canvas spilled onto the glass walls that faced the garden and made the kangaroos look even stranger and wilder.

"Let's get the hell out of here," Sergio said.

"Absolutely." Peter laughed.

Peter waited while the whiskey kicked in then spoke again.

"Sergio. I think that I'll need one more pair of contacts from you."

"What? You lost them?" Sergio panicked.

"No."

"Then why do you need more? Do you have any idea how hard it is to make those? I used a special electron microscope to inlay the various veins in your retina. It's grueling!"

"And I appreciate it! Obviously. Our entire position is dependent on these. And no, I haven't lost them, but I need a pair for someone else."

"Who else?"

"Do you know how you and Robbie are able to share everything? Even the hoax?"

"Yes…" Sergio agreed, guessing where this was going.

"Well, I need to have that with my wife. I can't live without her knowing the truth. It's killing me."

"But what if she reacts in the wrong way?"

"She won't. In fact, she might just kill me for not confessing earlier. She truly lives in fear, but Scott can help me there."

"Scott?"

"I never told you this, but it was Scott who actually figured out the hoax. He's the one who opened my eyes. The truth is, I haven't been lying to her for as long as she will assume. I believed the alien threat, hook, line, and sinker…"

"So she needs contacts…why?" Sergio asked.

"She's doing all sorts of charity and AmEarth work, so she is constantly in the public eye. All they need is two or three feeds, and they will be able to tell that she's lying—once she knows, of course. I can't have her afraid to speak whenever she is out in public."

"But the whole world is afraid."

"She's my family. I can't keep her living in fear while I know. You understand, don't you?"

"I do. I certainly do…"

"It was okay when we both believed in the same reality, but this is killing me."

They sat there, silently pondering this dilemma. Evidently, if a couple shared the same fears and were in the same boat, then it was somehow all right. However, if that equation was lopsided, then it was morally objectionable. Peter needed to comfort Barbara, and Scott already knew. Brianna, on the other hand, would be a different matter entirely. Maybe she would understand when she got into college in a few years.

Barbara needed those contacts, as she was officiating many of the alien museum openings around the world. Sergio's company would make these lower quality imitations of the higher quality pieces placed at the Smithsonian Museum._Rockets, computer chips, and sculptural statues made in factories were designed to convince the population of their existence. After all, "seeing is believing." New openings were scheduled in Costa Rica, Bolivia, and New Zealand; inevitably, she was interviewed at many of these events. Her score in the lying scale was always in the single digits, and he wanted it to remain that way.

"I'm going to call her right now." Peter said.

"Carpe diem, my friend." Sergio said standing up and leaving Peter to it.

"Honey?" Peter said into his phone.

"Yes?"

"Where are you?"

"I'm at the Hotel in La Paz, exhausted."

"Are you alone?"

"Yes! You are scaring me, what is the matter?" She stammered.

"Nothing bad, relax. I just need to know no one is listening to us."

"I am alone Peter. Is there a threat? What is it?"

"That is exactly why I am calling you. I need you to know something I found out recently. It is very important you know that what I about to tell you is the truth. It is also very important that you not tell a single soul about this." Peter was talking slowly and thinking he should do this in person and not by phone.

"Is this anything to do with the Aliens?" She asked.

"Yes."

"What is it Peter?"

"There has never been any contact with any alien species by man. Ever."

"Are you mad?!"

"Barb, listen to me. I found out all the truth about AmEarth. Its an elaborate hoax to unite and rule the Earth before it self-destructed. It is really important that you know we are not in any danger, but humankind needs an enemy to unite and be motivated so AmEarth was designed to control the population through fear."

"But, but isn't that disgusting?"

"Perhaps, but maybe less so than creating a real fear of mutual elimination through nuclear weapons. That is a real fear."

"Fear is fear. I have been paralyzed by fear and now it is all a lie?"

Peter knew this was a delicate moment, he needed all the help he could get.

"Honey, I believed in AmEarth and Chen and all the lies, but it was Scott that opened my eyes. He found the evidence about Kepl…"

"Scott! What has he to do with this? Don't get him involved in this!"

"Barb, Barb, listen. Scott got me involved, not the other way around. He had a teacher that had connections in New Zealand and knew about the Kepler planet not being able to sustain life, also they knew about the human that created the alien life forms..."

"Peter, if this is true then AmEarth is doomed. As soon as people find out the whole system will collapse."

"It won't, they can't? AmEarth now controls all the telescopes on earth. They also have total military power to quell any dissent. It is not something that can be stopped even by the truth."

"That is scarier than the aliens."

"Not if the government is benevolent."

"When has a dictatorship been benevolent? I can't think of a time when power wasn't abused."

"I am having contact lenses made for you."

"What? What in heaven's name are you talking about?!!"

Peter explained the entire situation for hours. Barbara became calm and regained her trust in Peter finally acknowledging that the hoax was a brilliant plot to dominate the Earth. She agreed to stay quiet and cancel all her speeches until her lenses where crafted by Sergio. Bri would have to live in fear a few more years and then they would ease her into the new reality the miniscule ruling elite shared.

***

Peter now had developed a new fear. The fear of having the contact lens trick discovered. To prevent this, he decided that he would have a ritual before every new speech or event with public questions. This ritual would give him and Barbara the time to insert the contacts and would also remind them to do it. Strangely, he felt like many other emperors must have done in the past when they became superstitious and crafted silly ceremonies. A new solemn ceremony would make their lives foolproof, and they needed foolproof measures if the Johansen presidency was to continue. Peter called Sergio in his room.

"Hey, come back down." Peter said.
"How did she take it? Sergio answered.
"OK, I guess. Come."

Sergio re-entered the living room and sat right next to where he had left his drink. The ice had melted and he drank scotch-flavored water. Peter walked up to him and poured more scotch into his glass from an elegant glass decanter.

"I was thinking…" Peter started.
"Oh really?"
"Stop it. I was thinking that your knowledge can't die with you, should that ever happen. AmEarth needs to operate well, and a president who does not know about the hoax is a constant danger as he gets closer to the inner truth. After all, there are various agencies that know about the reality. The computer is right in wanting the president to be truthful to the public on the whole, but now that this is corrected, I think that we have a formidable solution. There will be no need for a constant succession."

"So, what are you saying? You want me to teach you how to make the lenses?"

"Not me! I can't draw, and I don't want to take you out of the equation. You're reading this wrong."

"Then what is it you're actually saying?"

"I want you to teach Robbie and Marianne. They will be your successors and the ones who will provide my successor with these lenses."

"And your successor will be…?"

"Could be Scott. Who knows?"

"A new monarchy! Do you have any idea how much humanity has suffered from monarchies?"

"Or it could be Barbara. What if I die? After that, it could be Scott or Brianna. Heck, I don't know, but this system is just so strange to work within. There is no precedent."

"Obviously!"

"AmEarth and its structure requires top-down rule. This system is benign as long as the parameters of Essie are basically structured to benefit the majority of the population. The president has no say on these settings, and the committee ensures that it is kept that way. You're a voting member of the committee, and that is where true power lies. Think of this: I'm happy with the salary I have, and if I remain president, then I really have no expenses, so I will be set for retirement. All we need to do is ensure the responsibilities of the presidency are limited as they are today. This way, the office is only a communication service. The president is, after all, a public servant that should be incorruptible and beholden to no private interests. We need to keep this a trade secret, and this seems like the best way."

"I can teach my girls, although I don't know if they'll be interested."

"I know that there are many options, but if we play this right, we could be ensuring that our families are taken care of for generations. Isn't that what a parent truly wants? To provide for his family?"

"I'm beginning to see why history repeats itself," Sergio said ominously.

"Mh mm…" Peter agreed.

Both men were content, but Peter was beginning to feel the ruthlessness that power offers. He was not prepared for it, and it started as just a thought, but suddenly it grew.

"One last thing…" Peter began.

"What is it?"

"Chen."

"I thought you sent him back into house arrest. What are you thinking?"

"I just don't think he is going to go quietly. His nature is to fight, and he will do anything that he can to undermine this presidency. We need to hit him hard enough to neutralize him for good."

"What do you have in mind?" Sergio was wary, seeing a dangerous glint in the president's eye.

"I want Essie to remove the noncompetition clauses on his industry."

"That will hurt him, but he's already ridiculously wealthy. He could still use the money he has to hurt you," Sergio argued.

"I'm afraid you're missing a vital aspect of human nature. Chen is like all businessmen; he wants a safe bet and hates to speculate with his own money. He will be hurt, just like a child whose favorite toy has been taken away. He won't part from the fortune he has left, not if the golden goose is killed."

"All right. And you want me to…?"

"Present a noncompetition resolution before he lands. You have twenty hours to do it."

"But he'll be notified. He'll object."

"Not if his plane coincidentally needs its wireless communications repaired."

"You sent him on a plane without any wireless communications?"

"There are none in the cabin."

"That's brilliant, but there's one problem. The quorum needs to vote against Chen's economic power, and that will look like direct payback. They'll see right through it."

"I know, which is why I have a plan. It will still look like payback, but they'll vote in our favor."

"How?"

Peter motioned to Sergio, and they moved from the large living room with the glass garden-facing wall to a library that shared the same view. Peter had a computer there and opened a document he had been working on. Sergio read the resolution that Peter had written.

"This might work," Sergio muttered under his breath after reading it.

"I need you to take this and rework it on your journey. You can pick up Marianne at the *AES Reagan* and sail back to the States. Don't forget that before Chen lands, you need to call the meeting. Chen will be absent, and hopefully you can pass the resolution as is. Then, when Chen arrives, I will inform him of the developments personally. I'll enjoy that."

Peter clicked a few times on the laptop and sent the document to Sergio's email. Sergio was pleased to see that not only were ex-president Chen's industries being stripped of their noncompetition clauses, but Peter had also removed them from all industries that had unfair advantages in place. Now that AmEarth was global, it no longer needed to protect the founding families that had helped it reach its current place.

THIRTY

October in New York can be beautiful and sunny, and if the wind hadn't been blowing cold Canadian air down through the streets, it would have seemed like just another summer's day. Scott was sitting in a cafeteria terrace at Columbia University; behind him was the huge Library building that no longer housed books. Digital books had freed up all of that beautiful space, and the building had been "optimized." He sipped a black coffee as he read a copy of *The Idiot* on his enlarged wafer. The novel was a part of his world literature core class, but the prince had sparked his interest, mainly because he was beginning to feel like one. He looked for parallels, but couldn't properly identify with the sickly prince. The only positive quality he enjoyed was his blunt tongue. Behind Scott, two Secret Service men sat sipping their coffee milkshakes through green straws. At that moment, a stunningly beautiful student approached Scott. The two men stood up and immediately scanned her with a metal detector device.

"Hi," she said, seemingly unbothered by the scan.

"Hi," Scott replied.

"Are you Scott Johansen?"

"Yes."

"I was wondering if you wanted to come to a party tonight. Everyone is supposed to be there. I'm Lisa, by the way."

"Lisa, nice to meet you. Where's the party at?"

"Delta."

"Are you a Delta?"

"Yes."

"Great. I'll think about it. Thanks for the invite."

"Bye now."

Lisa left, smiling, and rejoined a group of girls who had obviously dared her to invite him. Their actions and voices betrayed their excitement as they walked down Broadway. Scott lowered his eyes to his book, intent on finishing the chapter he was reading. He was troubled by Prince Myshkin's constant procrastination, which had lost him the possibility of conquering the lovely Aglaya in the Dostoyevsky story. He was actually mad that so much thinking went on in the prince's head, which thwarted his actions. Scott thought of Marianne and how he could not afford to lose her to inaction like Myshkin. He took out his wafer and called his dad.

"Scott, what is it?" Peter answered.

"I need to speak to her, Dad," Scott demanded, cutting right to the chase.

"You can't call me every ten minutes about the same thing, son. I'm busy."

"Dad, this is the last time I'm going to call you. You're not helping me, but she needs me. Where is she?"

"She's in the middle of the ocean, son, traveling with her father on the slow boat to America."

"Dad, do you think that for one minute I believe that you can't communicate with Sergio? Please, Dad, just give me a minute with her. She needs to know that I know where she is, and that I care."

"Scott, you need to put some distance between yourself and this girl. I can't guarantee that she will even want to live in America. What if she decides that she wants to return to New Zealand? I can't change her mind."

"Dad, what would you prefer?"

"I wouldn't mind either way."

"You know that I can always tell when you're lying. You want her here. I know it."

"So what if I do?"

"So let me call her! I can convince her that coming here will be a good choice."

Peter remembered his recent conundrum with Barbara, and how important it had been to him that she knew about the alien hoax. His admission had been quite traumatic for her, but she had reacted better than he had expected, especially when she learned that Peter had only recently found out the truth. Peter felt much better with Barbara on his side and considered the possibility that Marianne could end up being Scott's other half. He opted for empathy and finally gave in.

"Okay, Scott. I'll text you the link to Sergio's boat. You can do a video chat there. You'll be able to see the location of the boat, and then calculate the time difference so you don't call them in the middle of the night. Understood?"

"Yes, Dad. Thanks!"

Scott got up and went to the cafeteria to pay. Above the counter, between menus of coffee beverages and sandwiches, was a large TV screen. Scott noticed that the images were showing a familiar scene. A threat had been detected, and the AmEarth logo appeared. It was similar to the old Emergency Broadcast signal, but it was a video. On this video, a threat had been detected and an alien rocket ship appeared. The AmEarth honeycomb was activated, and the matching pentagram corner beamed a laser focused on the incoming rocket. Then there was a soundless explosion followed by calm, peaceful images of space toggling between different views, like a home security camera bank.

Scott was so used to these videos that they had no effect on him. In the cafeteria, some kids were actually engaged and cheered when the alien rocket was blown to pieces.

"Yeah!" a handful of kids yelled.

Scott felt the urge to participate, despite the strange weight that his knowledge of the truth had on his mind.

"Long live AmEarth, long live Earth," Scott cheered along with them.

"Long live Earth," they chanted back.

A few other students approached Scott and patted him on the back. Others shook his hand and they were suddenly a small community united in the success of the military campaign against the Keplerians.

Scott noticed that he had done something that actually made the social network in the cafeteria better. He called his father back and walked away from the group, waving to students on his way out.

"Dad?" Scott said.

"Scott, what now? I told you I'm busy," Peter answered with a sigh.

"This is nothing to do with Marianne. I think I realized something important about AmEarth."

"What, son?"

"It needs to be renamed."

"What the…What are you talking about?"

"Dad, I was just in a cafeteria when a PSA of another rocket being destroyed came up. Some students cheered and some didn't. Then I began to cheer, and I said something that made everyone seem to take notice and wake up. They came over and shook my hand and cheered with me. Do you know what I said?"

"No, what?"

"Earth."

"What?"

"I didn't call it AmEarth…just Earth."

There was a silence from the other end of the phone.

"That is interesting," Peter spoke slowly, as if thinking deeply.

"You get it, right? After New Zealand fell…"

"Yes, I understand. I'll see if that is something we should do. Thanks, Scott. You really are a born leader."

"You think so?"

"Of course, Scott. I'm proud of you."

"Thanks, Dad."

The Secret Service detail paid for the drinks and left Scott behind. Scott went back to his dorm, intent on calling Marianne.

***

Marianne, Robbie, and Sergio were having breakfast on the huge sailing vessel *Queen.* They were sitting in the outdoor teak dining room as they calmly sailed across the Pacific Ocean. The places were each set with fine china bearing the *Queen* logo and silverware of exquisite design. The handles on the silverware also had a unique design on the lower drop that matched the boat's logo. It was a flower, created by Sergio, which looked as though fire had engulfed a tulip. Sergio had explained to them earlier that red tulips reminded him of Robbie's red hair and that the boat had been named after the Holland Queen tulip that he had used to craft the logo. Everything was a tribute to Robbie; he had never stopped loving her. It was a beautiful day, and they were engaged in heavy conversation, carefully ensuring that the crew was not listening.

"Dad, how did you become this wealthy? Does AmEarth really pay that well?" Marianne asked.

"You know that it's impolite to talk about money," Robbie chastised her daughter.

"Yeah, but come on…I think I should know."

"Of course you can. It's not a secret," Sergio interjected. "I, well…we own the factories that make all the "replicas" of the alien life forms and technology. As you know, almost every museum and school on the planet buys these trinkets and sculptures. In other words, it's a very large market. New Zealand was the only place that didn't sell our family's wares! However, it is quite an enterprise."

"And a monopoly," Robbie added.

"A monopoly?" Marianne asked.

"Yes, AmEarth controls every aspect of the production and sales of the alien material. In turn, we profit from every item that moves. It's a great business," Sergio explained, gesturing at the ship around him.

"Wow," Marianne exclaimed.

"Who knows, Marianne…Perhaps you'll want to run the family business someday," Sergio suggested.

Marianne felt conflicted.

"Dad, I just spent my entire adult life, short as it may be, trying to expose the lies of AmEarth and the fake Keplerian threat. It feels a bit strange to inherit the factory that distributes the lies!" Marianne said cautiously.

"Life is unpredictable. What can I tell you? You may need to be more practical and look at the world in a different light. Look at the positives, not the negatives."

"I also don't have much of a mind for business," Marianne said.

"It's not a business that requires expertise in business. Remember, it's a monopoly. You can't lose money, and there is no risk. On top of that, you have a constant stream of demand so the place basically runs itself. Most of the designs are already in place; that is the body of work that I am leaving to you. It is our family legacy, although no one is ever to know that I designed it. You own it."

"What if they take away the contracts and construct other factories? I just don't know."

"I don't think that is anything you'll have to worry about. The last thing AmEarth needs is a Ramirez-Bulatov exposing them."

Marianne sat thinking about everything around her. She was being continually showered with contradictions, so she changed the conversation.

"Dad, how did you decide on what to make the aliens look like? Where did you get the idea?" Marianne asked.

Sergio double-checked that no one was anywhere within earshot.

"First of all, I thought long and hard about this. Every alien in every movie had to be trumped by what I made. It was very important that I came up with something new, so that it would be believable," Sergio explained.

"And that you certainly did," Robbie piped up.

"Yes, they're so disgusting. So, so…" Marianne trailed off.

"Intelligent?" Sergio finished her sentence.

"That's not exactly what I was thinking," Marianne said.

"I know," Sergio replied, grinning at her. "But you see, every alien is usually limbed like humans. And limbs are very important, so we needed them, but why in pairs? And why different ones like hands and legs, and why two eyes? Most aliens are humanoid, which is highly unlikely to be the case. A different life form has more chances to evolve better in conditions other than our own. It is actually quite unlikely that aliens would ever be able to contain a human inside—this was all done for theatrics and movies; you needed a human to wear the alien costume and animate it, so they all had legs and hands and a head like us. However, if you really think about the separation of the cell…six instead of two, or four or eight…I looked for a totally new species, but also one that could create rocket ships and function highly. They needed a large brain and fingers. I thought of three fingers as the minimum for holding tools—a thumb and two fingers. Five is actually quite strange if you think about it. These two fingers don't do much." Sergio pointed to his little finger and the one next to it.

"So three, being odd, needs to relate to an even number—six or twelve. I decided that twelve identical limbs could surround the body, making it ideal for running. It can run on four limbs and when these tire, it tilts to another set of four and continues on. Very efficient. The result was the creature we've been seeing for the past few years all over the world. This design had never been seen before. And the six eyes really pushed it over the edge!"

"Ugh. I just think it's…disgusting. Why does it have no mouth? How can it communicate?"

"Oh, but it does have a mouth and ears. However, they are small and the mouth is not used for eating. Its eating system is like plankton, consuming nutrients directly from water through the skin. It's really quite efficient, and has no problems of production for sustenance like us. Therefore, all of its efforts as a species are related to arts and crafts, building, and entertainment. There are no restaurants, no starvation, and no poverty. They all simply swim and eat at the same time. Then, they can come out and get to work."

"Can we change the subject? This is really not conducive to eating," Robbie commented, looking slightly green, either from the boat or the topic.

"Sure. I want to talk to you about something rather intriguing. I want to teach you a craft," Sergio said.

"What?" Marianne inquired.

"I would like you to learn about some specific techniques and tools that I have perfected to make eyes."

"Eyes? What's so special about alien eyes?"

"Not the eyes of the aliens."

"What?" Robbie and Marianne answered in unison.

“What I am about to tell you cannot leave this family. Ever. Our livelihood and our safety are both in serious jeopardy if this ever gets out.” He looked around suspiciously again, but no one seemed to be paying them any attention.

“I swear, Dad, I would never betray you or Mom! I swear.” Marianne didn’t hesitate.

“I’ve created perfect human eye replicas in contact lenses for the supreme president of AmEarth. It’s a technique that uses an electron microscope. I invented it,” Sergio said.

“Why did you do that? Scott’s dad needed them?” Marianne questioned, trying to put the pieces together.

“So that he could lie.”

“This is all a bit mind-boggling. A few days ago, I was determined to expose the lies of AmEarth, and now you want to entrust me with exactly the opposite task! You want me to learn how to make the very device that allows the president to lie?” Marianne’s voice was getting heated.

“Relax, darling,” Robbie said.

“Mom! Are you okay with this?”

“Mary, listen to me. The AmEarth conquest of the world is complete. Sergio said that the supercomputer has determined that AmEarth will likely rule the Earth for centuries…maybe forever. You can’t beat them, and your kids can’t beat them. A dozen generations of our family will live under AmEarth. Period. Now, we’ve joined them, and thanks to your father, we can join at the top level. The top. Look around; isn’t this nice?”

“Yes. But…”

“No buts. Eat your breakfast and then go have a think. Think hard. Remember, we can’t begin a revolution where we’re going.”

"All I'm saying is that it seems unfair that the whole world is scared of the aliens. And they don't even exist," Marianne stated simply.

"Darling, it's just not that simple. Humans were on a path to destruction, and countries found enemies where there weren't any. America had to keep the weapons factories producing, and sometimes they started wars just to perpetuate that system, so they made enemies, both inside and outside their borders. Isn't it infinitely better that the enemy is "supposedly" twenty-three point five light years away? There were always enemies and fears of mutual destruction, but now we have one fear that has united the whole world, eliminated racial favoritism, halted overpopulation, decreased pollution, reversed global warming…The list of the good far outweighs our fear of the enemy, which has always been a part of our lives," Sergio declared proudly.

A crewmember arrived, and they all fell silent.

"There is a call for Ms. Marianne. It is from Scott Johansen on the onboard computer screen," he announced.

"Thank you, Steve. Marianne will take it in her cabin," Sergio replied.

Marianne rushed away and ran down the hall to her cabin at the front of the sailboat. She opened her laptop computer and saw Scott's face looking at her within seconds.

"Scott!"

"Marianne," Scott's voice was filled with relief.

"How are you? Where are you?" she said.

"I'm back in the States. In my dorm. How's Sergio's yacht?"

"Amazing, but you should have seen what they did to me before my dad picked me up! I was questioned and treated like a rebel! They even drugged me!"

"What? On the Reagan? I tried to stop it, I swear. I called my dad and…"

"Don't worry, they stopped after I told them everything. I actually think they were disappointed."

"What do you mean?"

"They thought the rebels had weapons and were dangerous, but I just told them the truth."

"So what did they do? They could have charged you with treason!"

"Well, they didn't. I think that between your dad and mine, they decided to let me go. Now I'm in the custody of my father, who I barely know…"

"Your dad is great, Marianne. I wish my dad was more like him."

"He's cool, but do you have any idea what he wants me to do?"

"What?"

"He wants me to learn how to make all the alien stuff, and work with him in his shop."

"Are you into that kind of thing? Do you want to go into art directing like him?"

"Scott, it's not art directing. If anything, it's art *mis*directing. I'll be helping to keep the lie going, exactly the opposite of what I was doing in New Zealand."

"I know. I kind of feel the same way. I know it's all a lie, but…"

"I know, everyone is telling me the same thing—AmEarth is not all that bad and will be around for centuries. Who can fight against that?"

"That's not what I was going to say."

"Oh, sorry."

They paused and simply looked at each other for a few seconds, trying to read the other's expression.

"Look at it this way…if you sell your soul to the devil, he will come and take it from you in seven years, right? So, here we are selling our souls to the system, but we will live like kings until we die. It's not bad, really. Considering that the other option is to rebel, be found guilty of treason, and gggggghhhht…" Scott made a gesture of being hanged by pulling his t-shirt upward and tilting his neck to the side.

Marianne laughed, and it warmed Scott to hear it through the microphone.

"That's true, but I see that my options are narrowing everywhere I go."

"Why don't you give it a go? I think Columbia University might be interested in a new student with your qualifications."

"What are you saying? You're going to pull strings to get me into the best college in America?" Marianne asked in disbelief.

"No, it's just *one* of the best. Not really *the* best, but I don't have to. It was just an offer. After all, you're an intelligent foreign student and they also look for that. But if all else fails…well, my dad can pull some strings."

"I don't know…" Marianne spoke softly.

"I miss you." Scott's words sprang from his mouth before he could stop them.

"Do you? You barely know me."

"I know, but I like you."

"I like you, too."

"Then come and try this new life, even if it's the polar opposite of the life you just left."

"I'll let you know. This is all a bit too much to digest right now. My dad just told me about the contact lenses."

"The what?"

Marianne realized in that instant that Scott didn't know.

"Oh, nothing," she lied.

Marianne felt guilty at having lied to Scott and thought that it might have been the wrong thing to do. If there was anyone with whom she was going to discuss the alien hoax and this new reality, it was going to be Scott.

"Contact lenses…That is how he does it!"

"Yes."

They both paused looking at each other briefly.

"My dad made them with an electron microscope. They have tiny veins that the computer can't detect as fake."

"Wow. Now we even know that. What don't we know?"

"Oh I don't know, why we are here?, where we are going?, do we have a purpose?"

"Ha. I know. I was being presumptuous. Do you know when you'll get here?"

"I don't know exactly…. I also don't know if I want to do it." Marianne was serious.

"Do you have a choice?"

"I like to think that I do. Don't we always?"

"Sure, we have free will. However, the key question is, on which side of history do you want to be?"

"I'm leaning toward the winning side," Marianne admitted sheepishly.

"Ha, ha. I guess I do too."

"I think we're still a week out from New York."

"I can't wait to see you in person."

"Me too."

"Okay. Goodnight, I guess."

"Yeah."

They continued saying slow, drawn-out "good-byes" and "good nights" for a few more minutes without hanging up the line. He didn't want to click off, and nor did she, but once she began drifting off to sleep, they finally cut the connection.

THIRTY-ONE

Ex-President Chen sat in his luxurious home office under house arrest. The paneling had been brought over from a seventeenth century castle in France. Books with cracked, ancient bindings surrounded him and a huge painting by Claude Lorrain hung over the marble fireplace. The room's high ceilings and double French doors had a palatial scale that made him look, as he now was, insignificant.

Neil Chen was still furious at the president for confining him to a ridiculous house arrest. What was he thinking? Chen spent most of his time at home anyway; his staff tended to all his needs and cooked and cleaned. He lived like a king with his beautiful third wife. Nothing had actually changed, except that he couldn't go to New York for dinner. This was the first weekend he spent entirely in his home in decades.

That coming Monday Peter had allowed him to go to the Supercomputer Committee meeting. Chen was still reeling from what he called the airplane incident. Now they would see him in person and hear all about the indecency of Peter Joansen! He'd left his palatial home in his Mercedes Benz, which was driven by his personal driver, and was followed by the Secret Service. His usual drive down the Saw Mill River Parkway was scenic enough, but none of those golden trees and fall landscapes could diminish his anticipation of seeing Peter face-to-face again.

At the Supercomputer Committee meeting, the usual members were in attendance, including Sergio and Peter. Chen arrived and sat as usual at the head of the table. Some participants were projected in on computer screens from their foreign locations. The meeting began with a summary of the past resolutions prepared by Sergio, expressly for Neil Chen's benefit. The familiar light that announced Essie was present as well was lit. A loudspeaker presentation narrated by her began.

"Before we begin this meeting, members have requested a summary of resolutions from the prior meeting of October seventeenth' 2045. A quorum was obtained and the resolutions 25861, 25862, and 25863 were passed unanimously," Essie announced.

Ex-president Chen turned white as a sheet. That date hit him like a punch in the stomach and he could barely contain his emotions. He had been on that damn plane on the seventeenth!

"Resolution 25861. The removal of anticompetition clauses in the commodity industries. No longer will the world economy be able to sustain the growth and concentration of wealth in the following industries with monopolistic protection: semiconductors, fishery farming, pork, cotton, wireless technologies…" Essie rattled off dozens of monopolistic clauses that would be removed.

Chen stood up. Everyone ignored him and focused on Essie's speech. Peter, however, locked eyes with Neil. He wanted the ex-president to know that he was behind this. They kept gazing at each other, not speaking, until Essie finished. Chen sat down again, cooled off, and thought about what to do. He then pushed the button that turned off Essie.

"I'm not happy about this. This is a direct attack on me and my family," Chen began boldly.

"Essie agreed that monopolistic clauses needed to be removed to ensure peace on the planet. It was needed," Sergio said.

"Who the hell do you think you are?" Chen replied in a nasty tone.

"Just hold off one moment, Neil. You're speaking to the most important member of this committee," Peter interjected.

"You're mad," Chen said.

"Last time I checked, the work that Sergio does is irreplaceable and unique. Everyone in this room can be replaced, except him. Can any of you create a unique species of aliens? What if we need more evidence? Will we use your sketches, Neil?" Peter shot back.

"No one is irreplaceable," Chen muttered.

"Well, what's done is done. I also have a new resolution to propose to Essie today," Peter announced.

"I also have a resolution," Chen shot back.

"Fine. Let's put them in and see what she thinks. Acceptable?" Peter invited Chen to insert his drive.

They both inserted the small drives into the table and downloaded their resolutions as Essie's light went back on. Chen was ill-prepared. He had no counter-resolution for the damage done to his industry. He was proposing a resolution to remove Peter because his lying scale score was far too good and was probably a glitch that could fail at any time. Essie was quick with its response.

"Former President Neil Chen Tyson, your resolution is not tenable. Peter Johansen is the acting supreme president, and his speech score was flawless. There is no need to replace an effective president." Essie spoke in her matter of fact tone.

"President Johansen, your resolution is being considered. The database is performing a quick scan of the potential for your concept for a name change to AmEarth. Preliminarily, it is good. In the next three minutes, I will have a definitive answer," Essie said.

Chen stood up again.

"What is this about? You think you can change the name of AmEarth now? Are you mad? What are you possibly going to call it? Johansenville?" Chen screamed, losing his fragile sheen of calm.

Peter didn't answer. He let Neil's emotions run their course. He had already told everyone on the Supercomputer Committee about the name change proposal before Chen came in. They had all agreed that it was a brilliant idea and had no issue with it. Chen looked around in desperation to see if anyone would help to stop this moment.

"Just Earth," General Redford softly said.

"Is anyone going to do something about this man?" Chen waved his hand at Peter, losing what little credibility he still had.

"Earth," Redford said again.

"He is hell-bent on destroying me! What did you say, John?" Chen asked.

"Earth."

"Earth what?"

"Earth is the new name."

Chen sat down, pained, panicked, and sweating.

"Bring him some water," Redford said.

A member poured a glass of water for Chen, who drank it slowly. It felt like his last gulp on AmEarth…Earth. It was brilliant. How could this idiot have come up with that? Chen considered that perhaps he hadn't played this situation right from the beginning. Essie interrupted his thoughts.

"The resolution by Peter Johansen is approved. AmEarth will succeed with greater strength if the name is changed. Earth shall be the new name for the global government."

The meeting continued without any further comments or shouts from the broken ex-president. He just sat there until the meeting ended. When it was all done, he could barely get up to go home. He was exhausted. All he wanted was to go back to his mansion and rest.

Peter and Sergio left together and took the elevator to the Shadow White House for dinner with their wives and kids. It was the eve of Thanksgiving and they had prepared a turkey dinner with all the trimmings as a sort of private Thanksgiving party, a tradition they would continue for many years.

"Whew, that was something," Sergio said, feeling the cold air from the elevator fan cool the sweat on the back of his shirt.

"Yes. I think we have put Chen in the rearview mirror," Peter said.

"I hope so."

There was a short pause.

"Sergio?" Peter began again.

"What's up?" Sergio said.

"The one thing we need to make sure is that we keep the lenses as guarded a secret as the formula for Coke. It needs to be foolproof."

"I have news for you. Nothing is foolproof…But we can try."

"Only all of this depends on it…"

Peter said this slowly as the elevator doors opened and finished the sentence while moving his hands showing the Shadow White House foyer as if it where a showcase in *The Price is Right*.

The foyer had beautiful high ceilings and mahogany staircases. A butler waited on them and followed them around until Peter dismissed him. They went to the Oval Office and sat in comfortable sofas perpendicular to the fireplace, exhausted from the battle with Chen. Now, they were content and just sat there, quietly resting. To their side, behind the presidential desk, were the familiar round windows through which Manhattan was visible. From that high up, it was an amazing view, shimmering in sunset's golden tones.

THIRTY-TWO

Scott met Marianne for lunch that day at the same Italian restaurant near campus where they dined almost every night. It was an inexpensive but delicious spot that catered to students with a somewhat larger budget than those living on campus and forced to eat cafeteria food. Their relationship was flourishing, and they would both be traveling to the Shadow White House for their family's special Thanksgiving. Marianne was enjoying school, and was particularly excited about her political science classes and her teachers. She found Columbia exhilarating and challenging, and she appreciated that Scott was there to help her adjust.

"I wanted to see you before we went to the thanksgiving dinner tonight," Scott said over lunch.

"What is it?" Marianne said, curious and a bit nervous.

"Nothing, I just wanted to see you alone. Like this."

Scott was in love and hoped that she was feeling something similar, or at least had the potential to. The fear of her rejection consumed him, so he decided to risk it all. He looked her in the eyes and moved in closer until their lips finally touched, something he'd been wanting for weeks. Marianne didn't resist; she had been waiting for him. They kissed gently, testing each other, but that was soon replaced by greater passion. When Scott sensed her soft tongue touching his, he realized that he had been right; Marianne was all he ever wanted. The feeling was mutual; the union felt right. After about ten minutes of sitting in the restaurant, kissing, he stopped and looked at her.

"Do you want to come to my place? We have a few hours to kill before we need to be there, anyway."

"Sure," Marianne happily agreed.

They walked the streets of the Upper West Side until they reached Scott's building. They held hands the whole time, but spoke very little. They looked just like the lovebirds they were and they hardly noticed the world around them. In his studio, she found the standard mess of a single guy, but didn't even acknowledge it. Before she could say anything, they were locked together again, rapidly stripping off clothes and running hands over skin. It was a mission that they both rushed to complete, and they were not disappointed.

They needed to dress again and in better clothes for the dinner that night. Scott was ecstatic and he sang as he showered in happiness. Through the small high window in his bathroom he could see a sliver of the West Side Highway and the Hudson behind it, and parked across the street was a dark car with his Secret Service detail. In a rush, his emotions changed as a thought entered his head; Assistant Professor Ted Landon! He still had the Kepler document, which could take all of this away. What were the odds that anyone would ever take Landon seriously? He continued whistling, reflecting happily on the entire structure of Earth. Everything should have made sense now that he was with Marianne but somehow his knowledge of the truth scared him. He felt a strong desire to come clean, to scream to the world that he knew the truth. If only humans could live in peace together and protect their planet together without war and greed and without made up aliens!.

Scott and Marianne were driven to the Shadow White House for the Thanksgiving dinner. Scott raised the glass partition of the limousine to get privacy.

"Love?" Scott said.

"Yes?" Marianne asked.

"I know I am the son of the President and you are the daughter of Sergio and all, but I think I need to tell you something…"

"I think I know what you are going to say."

"No. I don't think you do."

"What is it then."

"I just want you to know if I ever do something stupid, something that jeopardized our position in AmEarth, well you should know I love you."

"You are scaring me. You mean to say if you ever rebel and tell the truth, right?"

"I might."

"You know something?" She asked.

"What?" Scott asked.

"There is like a huge conscience boulder on my shoulders. Like I can't breath or something. Guilt, you know…"

"Yes. That is exactly what I feel. It is like feeling criminal all the time. I don't think I can do it."

"What are we going to do?"

"Let's wait. I think our parents would hate us if we start something now. I think we need to lay low for a while, you know?"

"I agree… we would kill them."

"Yep."

Then Scott moved closer and kissed her like it was the first time in his life. They kissed like never before. It was finally a union. Moments later they quietly entered the party and joined Sergio, Robbie, Peter, Barbara, and Brianna at a table. This small group of people had been pushed by circumstance into a very special place in Earth's history. That evening, the talk surrounded school, homework, and Brianna's new experiences at high school, but little or no politics. After dinner, the children and the wives talked in the living room, and Peter invited Sergio to the library for a drink.

"You know, Sergio, I was thinking," Peter started as he had so many times in the past.

"Not again…" Sergio joked.

"Yes, again. If Scott decides, for whatever reason, that he doesn't want to be president, it could also fall to Marianne."

"What?"

"Hear me out. I was just thinking that we can be flexible. We don't need to be so limited. There must be many options."

"Brianna?" Sergio suggested.

"Yes, but maybe you should have some more kids."

"Now you've really lost it! I plan to keep my life with Robbie as fun and exciting as I can."

"What can be more exciting than children?"

"But we're too old. You know that."

"Sergio, you're only forty. It's the new thirty, right?"

"Are you really suggesting this?"

"No, I'm merely telling you that it is a possibility…" Peter's voice trailed off mysteriously.

"Do you know something that I don't?"

Peter couldn't help but smile. He had been alerted by the health minister, Dr. Rosencrans, of this development. It was clear that anyone near the president would be unable to hide anything from him, not even health information. In fact, Peter had requested that all people close to him receive this special treatment from Secret Service security to health and wellness maintenance. From Peter's face, Sergio read clearly that he knew something.

"Sergio, she might not know yet, or she might even be considering alternative options. You must be very cautious about how you approach this, but I have an idea," Peter said.

"What?" Sergio asked.

"I will have a message sent to her wafer with the results of her blood test. You can enter the room as she's reading it and ask her then. See what happens. However, whatever you do, don't let her know that you know. Act well, my friend."

Peter sent a message to Dr. Rosencrans and put the plan in motion. Sergio went to the doorway between the two rooms and waited. Robbie received the text and Sergio moved toward her. Peter got up, his scotch in his hand, and went to the door, from where he could watch one of the most intimate reactions shared between humans. Robbie looked up after reading it and immediately called Sergio. Peter could see him bend to her mouth, where she whispered something and pulled back, quietly waiting for his response. His face split in two and he hugged her so hard that she was pulled off her feet. Marianne sat on the couch across the room and clearly noticed that something was happening with her parents. Robbie looked over at her daughter, who was holding Scott's hand, staring incredulously at her parents.

"You're going to be a sister!" Robbie revealed suddenly, unable to contain her excitement. She was shaken, but overjoyed. Marianne returned the broad smile and squeezed Scott's hand a bit tighter.

"What are the odds of that…?" Scott added and squeezed right back.

Peter looked on from the entrance to the library and behind him his computer terminal was on. The room became hued in red, and Peter noticed the color on the white trim of the door. He looked back to see the screen covered in red directives…

To be continued….

ABOUT THE AUTHOR

A.A. Dober lives and writes in Southern California.

His debut novel is called:
Ultimatus, a gaming corporation.

AmEarth is his second novel.

He has published a third novel:
Fly Diamonds

www.ingramcontent.com/pod-product-compliance
Lightning Source LLC
Chambersburg PA
CBHW030421310726
48979CB00009B/1557/J

* 9 7 8 0 9 9 6 5 4 9 1 1 0 *